WINTER'S REASON

Talon Winter Legal Thriller #3

STEPHEN PENNER

ISBN 13: 9780578552507
ISBN 10: 0578552507

Winter's Reason

This is a work of fiction. Any similarity with real persons or events is purely coincidental. Persons, events, and locations are either the product of the author's imagination or used factiously.

Joy Lorton, Editor.
Cover design by Nathan Wampler Book Covers.

WINTER'S
REASON

A person is guilty of murder in the first degree when…

(c) He or she commits or attempts to commit the crime of robbery, and in the course of such crime, he or she, or another participant, causes the death of any person, other than one of the participants in the crime.

Revised Code of Washington
9A.32.030(1)(c)

CHAPTER 1

"The worst part of being a criminal defense attorney is the clients." A pause. "And the prosecutors." Another pause. "And the cops. Oh, and constantly hustling to make rent." After a few more seconds, "Did I mention the judges?"

Talon Winter, criminal defense attorney, looked down at the office receptionist, Hannah Trimble, who was busy typing away at her computer. Talon was leaning on the raised counter that was the front of Hannah's workspace. It was where they placed business cards for the half-dozen or so lawyers who shared the office space. It was also where new clients would come first when they entered the office "Are you even listening to me?" Talon asked.

"Are you even talking to me?" Hannah returned without looking up from her screen. "It sounds like you're just talking to yourself."

Talon frowned, but not because Hannah was wrong.

"Anyway," Hannah finally looked up, then past Talon toward the front door, "it's none of those. It's the clients' families."

Talon turned just in time to see the door burst open and a small crowd of people burst into the lobby.

"Talon Winter!" one of them yelled out. She was a middle-aged woman with long red hair and a printed floral skirt. "We need to see Talon Winter!"

The rest of her entourage confirmed the demand with a gaggle of nods and affirmative grunts, along with a murmured repeating of the name. "Talon Winter. Yes, Talon Winter."

Talon pushed herself off the counter and stood up tall, her own long black hair draping across the back of her matching black business suit. "I'm Talon Winter."

The red-haired woman grabbed Talon by both arms and smiled. "Of course you are," she half-laughed as she appraised Talon. "We found you. You're here, just waiting for us. Thank you, Lord."

The woman's grip was tight. The grip of a mother, perfected over years of grabbing runaway children and ending toddler tantrums. A scan of the other faces in the lobby confirmed they were a family. Children of various ages, an adult couple about the same age as the red-haired woman, and in the middle of them all, an elderly woman with gray hair in a braid and wrinkled face, worrying behind thick glasses.

Talon raised her arms just enough to signal to the woman to release her grip. She did, and Talon pulled at her sleeves to straighten her suitcoat. "What can I do for you?"

A simple enough question. And while its answer was likely to be complex—they were looking for a lawyer after all—the response Talon received was beyond complex. It was an incoherent cacophony of facts, questions, worry, and fear.

"It's Luke!"

"They arrested him!"

"He didn't do anything!"

"It was the other guy!"

"He did it!"

"Luke was just in the car!"

"He didn't know what they were doing!"

"He didn't know what was going to happen!"

"He didn't mean to do it!"

"They won't listen!"

"He's in jail!"

"He's just a kid!"

"He would never do anything like that!"

"He didn't know!"

"He didn't do it!"

"You have to help us!"

"You have to help him!"

Talon put her hands up at the crowd. "Stop! Stop it," she instructed. "One at a time."

She pointed at the woman who had grabbed her by the arms. "You," she designated. "Just you talk. What happened? Who's Luke?"

The woman's face fell, her eyes suddenly wet. "Luke is my son."

"And he got arrested?" Talon asked.

"Yes."

"When?" Talon continued her questioning. It was what she did for a living, after all.

"Last night," the woman answered. "But we didn't find out until this morning."

"Where was he?"

"Like, what jail did he call from?" The woman shook her head slightly. "The Pierce County Jail downtown."

"No," Talon shook her own head, but sharply, once. "Where was he arrested?"

"At the check-mart over on Thirty-Eighth," the man from the crowd answered.

"By the Tacoma Mall," another voice shouted out.

"One person," Talon repeated firmly. She turned back to Luke's mother. "What happened?"

The rest of the family stayed quiet, giving the mother the chance to answer, but she shook her head again. "I don't know what happened," she admitted, sadness overwhelming her words. "I just know they arrested my boy. And I know he didn't do anything wrong."

Talon frowned slightly. In part out of sympathy, but mostly because she knew it was going to be harder to extract information from someone who was crying.

"Okay, okay." Talon was starting to put two and two together, even if Luke's mom was in denial. It sounded as if Luke had been the wheel man for a robbery, 'just' waiting in the car while his accomplice went inside. "So," she surmised, "your son was arrested for robbery?"

"No, not robbery." Luke's mom grabbed Talon's arm again, her eyes wide and brimming with tears. "They arrested him for murder."

CHAPTER 2

"Murder?" Talon's eyebrows shot up.

"Yes," Luke's mother confirmed. "Murder. But he didn't do anything. It all happened while he was waiting in the car."

Talon nodded to herself and appraised the situation in the lobby. It had gotten quieter, but she knew that was temporary.

"This isn't going to work with everyone chiming in," she decided. "I'm going to talk with just two of you." She pointed at Luke's mother. "You obviously. And..."

She scanned the crowd. There was the man who had spoken up about it happening at the check-mart, but Talon wasn't a huge fan of men who spoke up. She pointed at the woman next to him. She was about the same age as the mom. Maybe an aunt, Talon guessed. "And you. Come with me to my office. The rest of you wait here."

Mutters of disappointment and acceptance rippled across the lobby as Mom and Probably Aunt stepped forward.

"Can we get some coffee?" Talon asked Hannah.

"Probably," Hannah replied without any effort to get up. "I think there's some left in the pot in the kitchen."

Talon forced a smile. "That's great, Hannah. Thanks." Then she signaled for her visitors to follow her. They went directly to her office—do not pass kitchen, do not collect old coffee.

"Please, sit down." Talon pointed to the two guest chairs across the desk from her own leather desk chair. "Let's figure out what's happening, and more importantly, how I can help you."

The two women looked at each other, then back to Talon and nodded as they all took their seats.

"Let's start with the basics," Talon continued. "What are your names and how are you related to Luke?"

"I'm Mary Zlotnik," the first woman said. "I'm Luke's mother."

"And I'm Anna Franklin," answered the second woman. "I'm Luke's aunt and Mary's sister-in-law."

"She's married to my brother," Mary explained unnecessarily. "He's in the lobby with the rest of the family."

Talon nodded, pleased with her instincts. "Okay," she acknowledged the information. "So, your son's name is Luke Zlotnik, then?"

"Yes." Mary offered a pained nod. "Lucas James Zlotnik. He's my oldest."

"Great," Talon answered. She didn't need to know about the other kids. "And he's been arrested for murder?"

"Yes," Mary answered again, but with a catch in her throat.

"You're sure it was for murder?" Talon pressed. That bit was important. "Not robbery, not assault, not rendering criminal assistance?"

Mary looked to Anna for confirmation. "It was murder, right?"

"Right," Anna said. "Murder. That's what it said on the jail's booking roster. We went to post his bail, but the jail said we couldn't bail him out because he was in for murder."

"In *on suspicion of* murder," Talon corrected. He'd only be in *for* murder if she didn't do her job. The job she hadn't actually been hired to do yet. "So, the jail told you he was booked for murder?"

"Yeah," Aunt Anna answered. "And Luke said that, too, when he called us."

"Okay, so you've spoken to him." That was good.

"Yes," Mary said. "That's how we know he didn't do anything."

Talon smiled at the naiveté of that sentiment. "Tell me what he said," she instructed. "All of it. Slowly."

Mary took a deep breath. "He said," she began, "he took his friend Miguel to the check-cashing place over on Thirty-Eighth Street, by the mall. I don't really know Miguel very well. I know most of Luke's friends, but he's still a teenager. He doesn't tell his mom everything."

"Wait," Talon interrupted. "How old is he?" The penalties for juveniles were a lot less. Months instead of years. It was a whole different ball game.

"Eighteen," Mary answered.

Talon frowned. *Never mind.* "Okay," she said. "Keep going. What happened with this friend you didn't know, Miguel?"

"He ended up dead," Mary answered

Talon winced. "Luke's friend is the murder victim?" She had expected a security guard, maybe a store manager. Not a friend. Under Washington's felony murder law, an accomplice couldn't be charged with murder for the death of a fellow accomplice. It had to be someone who wasn't a 'participant' in the crime.

"Yes," Mary confirmed. "And a police officer."

"A cop?" Talon's eyebrows shot up again. "He killed a *cop*?"

Now *that* was a whole different ball game. They could definitely charge Luke with the death of a cop who responded to the crime.

"He didn't kill anyone," Mary protested. "He was in the car."

"That might not matter," Talon knew. "Let me see if I understand. Luke and his friend went to the check-mart, right? His friend went inside to rob it. Maybe Luke knew about it, maybe he didn't, but either way, he stayed in the car while Miguel went inside. Then the cops showed up and there was a shootout. When the smoke cleared, Luke's friend was dead, but so was a cop. And now Luke is charged with murder. Is that about right?"

Mary looked at Anna for further details, but none were forthcoming. "Yeah, I think that's about right," Mary agreed. "I don't really know. Luke didn't seem to understand what was going on either."

But Talon did. She looked at the clock on her wall. 12:54. New arraignments started every day at 1:00, and her office was five minutes from the courthouse.

"Ms. Zlotnik, your son is going to be in court in approximately six minutes." Talon stood up. "If I'm going to represent him, I need to leave for the courthouse right now."

"But," Mary hesitated, standing up as well, "we don't even know if we can afford you. We, we heard about you. That cold case murder you did. We heard you're a really good lawyer. And Luke, if they're saying he killed a cop, he's going to need a really good lawyer."

"He's going to need the best," Anna put in.

"You're right," Talon nodded, "he is. And I am. And he needs me right now. We'll talk money after court."

The worst part of being a criminal defense attorney was the clients. And the clients' families. And hustling to make rent.

But none of that mattered to Talon when she got to do the best part. The best part was dropping Lady Justice's scales, raising her sword, and charging into battle.

CHAPTER 3

Sex and drugs to the left. Rock and roll to the right.

So many people got arrested each night in Tacoma and its environs that the Pierce County Superior Court had to run two arraignment courtrooms every afternoon—and that was just for the felonies. The court grouped cases together by crime type, since the bail amounts and other conditions of release tended to be similar for similar cases. Sex crimes and drug charges were heard in courtroom one. Sex and drugs. Assaults and property crimes were heard in courtroom two. Rock and roll.

Talon got the nickname for courtroom one. But the 'rock and roll' was kind of a stretch.

"Rock," another lawyer had explained to her when she'd started doing criminal cases, "like 'rock 'em, sock 'em.' Assaults, right? And when you 'roll' somebody, that means you steal from them, right?"

She'd shaken her head then, and she shook it again as she approached the twin arraignment courtrooms on the second floor of Tacoma's County-City Building. At least she knew her new murder case would be heard in courtroom two. But as she turned the corner, she realized she didn't need a silly nickname for the courtroom to tell her where the arraignment for the cop-killer was being held.

The gallery was standing room only, with people spilling out into the hallway, including a half dozen fully uniformed police officers, their expressions ranging from solemn to pissed off. Talon knew there were likely even more cops inside the courtroom, all there to watch the arraignment, to show solidarity with their fallen comrade—and to intimidate the judge into setting an impossibly high bail on Talon's soon-to-be client.

Out on the street, a badge and a gun put you in charge. But inside the courthouse, there was a different uniform for the people who called the shots. Instead of navy jumpsuits and leather gun belts, it was navy business suits and leather briefcases. Talon cut through the crowd of cops and other spectators, slicing past them with her briefcase extended and her eyes narrowed.

"Move aside," she instructed. "Defense attorney coming through."

It had the desired effect. Effects. First, the crowd parted, and she was able to reach the secure door in the wall of bulletproof glass that separated the public gallery from the front of the courtroom. The in-custody defendants would be escorted from holding cells into the secure front courtroom to appear before the judge who would decide how much money they would need to be allowed to get out of jail and lead a normal life pending the trial on the crimes they were supposedly presumed innocent of having committed.

The second effect was to piss off the cops. Cops were always the enemy in Talon's cases, but this was special. They weren't just witnesses and enforcers; they were the aggrieved party, the victims. Hell, some of them in the gallery were probably witnesses to the incident. Normally, witnesses were supposed to avoid the preliminary proceedings on their cases. It was a rule designed to protect their testimony from contamination, and to protect that presumption of innocence the defendant was supposed to have. But cops didn't care about that. The rules didn't apply to them. Hell, that was the best part of being a cop.

Those thoughts and more raced through Talon's mind as the judicial assistant buzzed open the secure door and she left the world of cops and/or criminals behind her to enter the world of lawyers and/or criminals. And on that border, playing the role of neutral archivist, two news cameras pressed their lenses against the bulletproof glass to record what was about to happen.

The clock on the wall already read 1:01. The judge would be taking the bench any second and the courtroom reverberated with the anxiety of a dozen lawyers, none of whom were quite ready for the calendar to start. That was the nature of criminal practice. There was just too much, too fast. Right then, at that very moment, someone somewhere in the county was committing a crime. Probably several somebodies committing several crimes. All the lawyers could do was to keep the system going, like controlling a river trying to jump the banks. Or a giant mechanical wheel of death crushing everything and everyone in its path.

Well, not everyone.

Not Talon Winter.

And not Cecilia Thompson, the prosecutor already assigned to the Zlotnik case, according to the docket tacked to the wall. One of the very best in the prosecutor's office. Damn it.

Talon knew Cecilia Thompson. And despite herself, she liked her. Double damn it.

"Talon." Cecilia noted her entrance even in the frenetic courtroom. They were like that. Two of a kind, on opposite sides of the battlefield, each aware of being in the other's presence. Talon was tall, with long dark hair and a black suit with the skirt at the knee. Cecilia wore the same suit, but in navy, and her own shoulder-length hair was the same straight silk, only blonde. Her Swedish-American blue eyes were at the exact same height as Talon's dark brown Native American ones. "Tell me you're not here on the Zlotnik case," Cecilia said.

Talon grinned. "I was just thinking the same thing," she replied. "You're too good for a case like this."

Cecilia returned the smile. "A case like this needs a good lawyer."

"I didn't mean too good of a lawyer," Talon expounded. "I meant, too good of a person. If what the family tells me is true."

"Oh, I'm sure it's true," Cecilia conceded. Her smile broadened. "But come now. I don't need a defense attorney lecturing me on how to be a good person."

Talon's own smile grew. So that was how it was going to be. *Good*, she thought. Smiles in the front, knives in the back. May the best woman win.

And it was time for the battle to start.

"All rise!" cried the bailiff as the judge finally entered, three generous minutes late. "The Pierce County Superior Court is now in session, The Honorable Maxwell Portello presiding."

Talon didn't even try to keep her eyes from rolling up into her skull at the identity of the day's judge. She wouldn't have been able to, even if she'd tried. Judge Portello was the worst judge in the county. Probably the worst judge in three counties. Maybe not the whole state, but only because there were a lot of judges in the state. Talon kept her practice close to home in Tacoma, but she still took the occasional case north in Seattle's King County, or Thurston County to the south, or Kitsap County across Puget Sound. And in all her appearances in all those cases in all those counties, no other judge came as close to the unbearable combination of arrogance, self-importance, and dim-wittedness possessed by The Right Honorable Maxwell Portello.

He'd been appointed by the governor upon the unexpected retirement of the court's oldest judge, James Harrington III. Everyone expected Judge Harrington to literally die on the bench, but the day he almost did—a stroke in the middle of a motion for summary judgment on a multimillion-dollar civil case—was the day he decided that was no way to go. Already almost eighty, he decided life really was too short after all, and he stepped aside for someone younger to take his spot above the litigants and lawyers of Pierce County.

Unfortunately, that someone younger was an unpopular junior partner at the Tacoma law firm that had donated the most money to the governor's reelection campaign. The rumor was that young Maxwell's parents were big clients of the firm, so when he graduated (barely) from law school, the firm took him on as a favor to them—and to keep their business. Then they got rid of him at the first opportunity, with a prestigious appointment from the governor. Win-win for the firm. Lose-lose for those aforementioned litigants and lawyers.

"You may be seated," Judge Portello deigned, with a flourish of his wrist. He was a tall, lanky man, in need of a haircut and some orthodontics. Appearances aside, he had more than taken to being a judge. Always the most important person in the room, people standing when he entered and exited, being addressed with the honorific 'Your Honor.' As if, finally, people treated him with the respect he always knew he deserved. "I see we have members of the law enforcement community with us here in the gallery today." He practically blew them a kiss. "We will start with the case they have come for, so they can hurry and return to their jobs keeping the rest of us safe."

Great. Talon shook her head slightly, again failing to stop herself from the gesture. Of course, a low-I.Q. political appointee who'd never touched a criminal case before being appointed to the bench would love the cops unconditionally, and profess it publicly, oblivious to how that might impact the appearance of fairness when presiding over the arraignment and bail hearing of a young man accused of murdering a cop...by waiting outside in the car. Talon had been hoping to argue there wasn't even probable cause to file the charges. Now, she was just hoping to get a bail that someone who hadn't founded Microsoft could post.

"The parties may approach on the matter of the State of Washington versus Luke Zlotnik," Judge Portello announced. Most judges usually just asked if the parties were ready on a given matter, rather than grant permission to approach the bar. Portello turned to the jailors stationed at the door to the holding cells and with another flourish of his hand ordered, "Bring in the accused."

He has a name, Talon thought with a frown. But she knew better than to say anything. It would only hurt Luke's chances of a fair hearing if she pissed off the judge before he even entered the courtroom.

Talon and Cecilia both approached the bar. The corrections officers opened the door and yelled, "Zlotnik!" A moment later, a very young-looking and even more confused-looking Luke Zlotnik was pushed to his spot next to Talon directly in front of the judge's bench. He was short and skinny, with a mop of black curls on top of his head and his hands still cuffed to the belly chains around his orange jumpsuit.

"Who are you supposed to be?" he asked Talon after giving her a once-over. She couldn't tell if he was trying to sound tough, or just had no idea what was going on.

"I'm your lawyer," she answered in a lowered voice. "My name is Talon Winter."

"So, what? You the public defender?" Luke asked dismissively. "I don't want no public defender."

"I'm not a public defender," Talon assured him. "Your family hired me this morning." *Sort of. Almost.* She recalled the lack of any actual contract, or money, but decided not to get into that right then.

"My family?" Luke asked.

"Your mom," Talon clarified. "Now, pay attention. You're in big trouble."

"But I didn't do anything," Luke insisted.

"That might be important later." Talon put a hand on his shoulder. "But it's not going to matter today."

"You may proceed with the arraignment, Madame Prosecutor," Judge Portello sniffed down at the attorneys beneath him.

Talon was pretty sure she wasn't going to get a 'Madame' in front of her own job description when it came time for her to speak.

"Thank you, Your Honor," Cecilia responded. "The State has charged the defendant with one count of murder in the first degree and one count of robbery in the first degree. I am handing defense counsel copies of the charging papers and would ask her to acknowledge receipt of those on the record."

"I will acknowledge receipt," Talon agreed. "Although I would note that I haven't had a chance to review them yet."

"You will get your chance to review them, counsel," Portello sniped at her. "And your chance to speak. Please do not interrupt again."

Nope, definitely no 'Madame Defense Attorney.' And it was hardly interrupting to respond out loud to a request to acknowledge something out loud. So far, so terrible. She lowered her head and flipped to the probable cause declaration — the factual summary of what her client was alleged to have done to warrant the filing of the charges. The judge was supposed to read it to determine whether there was probable cause for the charges. If there wasn't probable cause, the defendant would be released.

"Please continue, Madame Prosecutor," Portello encouraged.

Cecilia hesitated. "Uh, that's all, Your Honor. We would ask defense counsel to enter a plea to the charges, then we'd like to be heard regarding conditions of release."

'Conditions of release.' Talon would have rolled her eyes except they were busy skimming the probable cause summary. What Cecilia really meant was 'bail'. High bail.

"Very well," the judge replied. He turned to scowl at Talon. And Luke. But mostly Talon. "How does the defendant plead?"

"The defendant pleads not guilty to all charges, Your Honor," Talon answered, without looking up from her review of the charging papers. "And we would ask the Court to release Mr. Zlotnik on his own recognizance pending trial."

Gasps of disbelief and incredulity escaped both His Honor and Madame Prosecutor, along with several other people in the courtroom Talon didn't care enough about to bother looking at.

"Counsel!" Judge Portello admonished. "The Court will hear first from the State regarding conditions of release. And," he added, both unprofessionally and unnecessarily, "I hardly think you should expect to obtain a personal recognizance release on a first degree murder charge. Particularly when the victim is a police officer."

"*Alleged* victim," Talon corrected. Out of turn again, she knew.

"He's dead, counsel," Portello shot back. "That's hardly in doubt."

"The allegation is that he's a murder victim," Talon responded. "That he's dead because of a murder committed by my client. And that, Your Honor, is very much in doubt."

Portello flared his eyes, and his nostrils, at Talon. He didn't reply. Instead, he turned to Cecilia. "Madame Prosecutor, what is the State's recommendation regarding conditions of release?"

"Thank you, Your Honor," Cecilia genuflected. "The State is asking the Court to set bail in the amount of two million dollars. As the Court noted, this is a charge of first degree murder. In addition, the murder occurred during the course of an armed robbery. Most importantly, however, is the fact that the alleged victim was a police officer, killed in the line of duty. This crime was, therefore, committed not just against the fallen officer, but against all of us whom that officer had sworn to protect."

Oh, please. Talon went ahead and let her eyes roll at that too.

"The defendant," Cecilia continued, "therefore, presents a real and substantial risk to the safety of our entire community."

Judge Portello had nodded along to every point Cecilia had made. Then he turned to Talon, his encouraging smile quickly twisting into a scornful frown. "Any response, counsel?"

"My client was sitting in a car," Talon got right to the point. And she left off the 'Your Honor', which was palpable to everyone in the courtroom used to adding those two words to the end of every sentence addressed to a judge. "That hardly makes him a threat to anyone. And putting two million dollars in the court's trust account wouldn't make him any less of a threat—it would just mean he was rich, which he isn't—unless the Court is prepared to enter a finding that rich people are presumptively less dangerous than poor people."

"This has nothing to do with being rich or poor, counsel," Portello shot back. "This is about community safety."

"Then arrest whoever actually shot the alleged victim." Talon didn't back down, "because it wasn't my client." She held up the charging papers. "Even the State's own probable cause declaration admits Mr. Zlotnik never went inside the store. They don't even know who shot the officer. It just says, 'He was shot and killed.' Oh, and by the way, so was my client's best friend, but no one seems to care about that."

"Investigation is ongoing, Your Honor," Cecilia interjected. "But it appears that the defendant's accomplice was most likely armed and engaged in a shootout with the fallen officer."

"Ongoing?" Talon scoffed. "Most likely? What are we doing here, then? Why don't we—oh, I don't know—wait until we actually know what happened before we start putting poor people in cages for sitting in cars near what other people did?"

"That's enough, counsel," Portello interjected.

"Ms. Winter," Talon instructed.

"I—I beg your pardon?" the judge stammered.

"My name is Ms. Winter," Talon explained. "Not counsel. And his name is Mr. Zlotnik, not defendant. You can treat me and my client with the same respect as 'Madame Prosecutor.'"

"Fine, Ms. Winter," Portello fumed. "Mr. Zlotnik is charged with the first degree murder of a police officer."

"Mr. Zlotnik is presumed innocent," Talon replied.

"The jails are full of people who are presumed innocent!" Portello slammed his fist on the bench.

"Exactly," Talon replied calmly. "Because of judges like you."

Portello had very pale skin, so when his face flushed like it did just then, his skin broke out in angry red blotches.

"One more word out of you, *counsel*," he pointed down at Talon, "and I will hold you in contempt of court, and you can join the *defendant* in the jail pending his trial. Am I understood?"

Talon understood. And as much as she wanted to give the judge one more word—or two, actually—she thought better of it and offered just a nod.

"Good," Portello growled. "Bail will be set at two million dollars. The defendant is remanded into the custody of the jail pending his trial. Next case."

Talon finally looked again at her client. His eyes were wide and his jaw open.

"I'm sorry," she whispered a quick apology before the guards could grab him and drag him away. "I should have kept my cool."

"Are you kidding?" Luke laughed. "That was awesome. You're hired."

CHAPTER 4

The cops inside the courtroom disappeared with Luke through the door to the holding cells. That just left the cops waiting on the other side of the bulletproof glass. The judge had definitely moved on to the next case, but the police officers who had come to watch the cop-killer's arraignment were still crowding the gallery, arms crossed and stone faced, blocking Talon's way to the hallway.

The thick blue clot.

She double-checked to make sure she had all of her files, then nodded to the court clerk who buzzed open the secure door to the gauntlet. The best way out was usually through.

There were about half a dozen cops still in the gallery. The first five moved out of her way, albeit just barely, with narrowed eyes and audible huffs. The sixth cop was right in front of the door. He was well over six feet tall, with a big frame, made even larger by the bulletproof vest under his uniform—and years of extra donuts. As Talon made for the door, he didn't move.

Neither did she.

He was bigger, but she had the element of surprise. He didn't actually expect her to smash into him. He was blocking the door, so she'd have to ask his permission to leave. But Talon wasn't really the asking permission type. Especially not to a cop.

She lowered her shoulder into his chest and knocked him back a couple of steps, freeing up her path to the door.

"Watch yourself, young lady!" The cop blurted out, catching his balance but not his temper. He grabbed Talon's sleeve. "It's a felony to assault a police officer."

"Only if he's performing his official duties at the time of the assault," Talon quoted the statute back to him. She pulled her arm out of his fat grasp. "Is trying to intimidate little lady lawyers part of your official duties, Officer Tough Guy?"

That didn't help check the cop's temper. But it drew the gallery's attention and the eyes of the crowd checked the cop's actions. He glanced around at all the people who had turned away from the proceedings in front of them to watch the confrontation unfolding behind them. He took a moment, then pushed a smile onto his face and reached out to open the door for Talon.

"Be careful, counselor," he said through gritted teeth. "You wouldn't want to do anything that could get you arrested."

Talon sneered up at him. "Or shot," she returned. "And don't open the door for me. I'm a woman, not a baby."

Talon could hear the chuckles and a couple of 'you go, girl' as she exited the gallery. She could also feel the cop staring a hole in her back. She ignored them both and got on with the job.

* * *

She ended up having to wait about forty minutes before she could actually get on with that job of hers. That's how long it took for Luke to be transported back to his cell and made available for an attorney visit. There were so many things wrong with the bail system, but one of the more time-wasting ones was how much an attorney had to go through just to be able to meet with her client. If Luke's family were rich, he could have posted the bail and come to her office directly after court. But Luke's family wasn't rich. Rich people don't say, 'We don't even know if we can afford you' to their lawyers.

"Hey," Luke waved weakly as he was escorted into the jailhouse meeting room by the guard of the day. "That didn't go so well, huh?"

Talon shrugged. "It went exactly like it always does: whatever way the judge and the prosecutor want. Get used to it."

"Does that mean I'm gonna get convicted?" Luke's eyes widened and he dropped his gangly frame into the cheap plastic chair opposite the cheap plastic table from Talon's own cheap plastic chair. It was the first time she'd gotten a chance to take a good look at him. He was definitely young. She guessed he hadn't even stopped growing, judging by his overly large feet and hands. Even his nose and ears seemed a bit too big for his face still, with acne scars at the edges of his jaw.

"That depends," Talon answered. "Did you do it?"

Luke shook his head slowly. "I didn't kill anybody. You gotta believe me."

"Oh, I believe you," Talon assured him. "But that might not matter. No one is saying you actually killed anyone. In Washington, you can be guilty of murder even if you don't kill anyone."

"Really?" Luke cocked his head at her. "That's crazy."

Talon nodded. "It sure is. But instead of me telling you the law, why don't you tell me the facts?"

Luke frowned at her. "What?" He looked confused.

Talon sighed. "Tell me what happened," she translated. "We'll talk about the law later."

"Oh." Luke nodded. "Right."

"All of it," Talon clarified. "Everything. Don't leave anything out."

Luke thought for a moment. "Where do I start?"

"At the beginning," Talon huffed. "Come on, Luke. This isn't hard. Just tell me the story."

"Okay, okay." Luke took a deep breath. "It all started when Miguel texted me that afternoon. He was like, 'What are you doing?' And I was like, 'Nothing.' And he was like, 'I need a ride.' And I was like, 'Okay.'"

Talon nodded along. Teenagers and texting. "What time was that?"

Luke shrugged. "I dunno. Like noon or something. I just woke up."

Talon frowned. "You woke up at noon?"

"I was up late," Luke offered.

"Doing what?"

"Nothing," was the answer. Talon believed it.

"Okay, noon or something," she repeated. "Fine. We can get the texts and find out the exact time if it's important. What happened next?"

"So, like, a while later I drove over to his place and picked him up," Luke answered.

"He doesn't have a car?" Talon asked.

Luke shook his head. "Nah. Sometimes he drives his mom's car, but she was at work."

"You guys don't work." It wasn't a question.

"Uh, not really," Luke admitted. "Mostly, we just kinda hang out."

"Smoke pot," Talon added.

"Uh…" Luke didn't know how to reply.

"Don't worry. It's legal," Talon said. "Well, not for you, I guess. You have to be twenty-one for it to be legal. How old are you again?"

"Eighteen," Luke answered. "So's Miguel."

"Great," Talon said. "So, two eighteen-year-old dudes with no jobs, sleeping in 'til noon, going for a drive. What could go wrong?" She looked around the cinderblock walls. "Oh, right. Everything."

Luke took a moment. "Are you always like this?"

"A bitch?" Talon knew what he meant. "Yeah, pretty much. You liked it in court a few minutes ago. Now, keep talking. You pick up Miguel and then what? Did you know where he wanted you to drive him?"

"Uh, no," Luke stammered. "Not at first, I mean. Not when I drove over to his place. But then he was like, 'I gotta go to the check-cashing place, man.' And I was like, 'Cool.'"

"Because you didn't have any other plans anyway, right?" Talon said.

"Yeah." Luke shrugged. "I mean, he needed a ride and he's my friend. So, yeah, whatever."

"Did you go straight there?"

Luke nodded.

"And where was it again?" There were a lot of check-cashing places in Tacoma.

"It was the Check-U.S.A. over by the mall," Luke answered. "Like in that little shopping thing between Thirty-Eighth and Tacoma Mall Boulevard. Right next to the Subway."

Talon nodded. She knew that shopping complex. There used to be a bookstore across the street, before all the bookstores started closing. "Yeah, I know the place."

"Right?' Luke said. "Everybody does. So, we drive over

there and as we're pulling up, Miguel says to park a couple spots down, like not right in front of the check-mart. Then he says, 'I gotta make a withdrawal' and laughs. I thought he meant because it was really a loan and they're not really a bank, but I guess it was 'cause—"

"Because he was gonna rob the place," Talon surmised.

"Yeah," Luke agreed. "But I didn't know that's what he meant. I thought it was just a lame joke."

"It's a lame joke either way," Talon observed.

"Yeah, I guess so," Luke said. "But it's kind of a good place to rob, you know? Lots of cash, but no security guards like at a bank."

"Lots of checks, you mean," Talon tried to correct him. "Not that useful unless they're made out to you."

"No, lots of cash," Luke repeated. "Haven't you ever been to one?'

"Uh, no, actually," Talon felt a little embarrassed to admit.

"Oh, yeah, my mom used to take us all the time," Luke said. "No one ever wanted to babysit us, so we had to go with her everywhere. You write a check, but then they open their drawer and just hand you a bunch of hundred dollar bills. The drawers are all full of them. So, yeah, great place to rob."

"Are you sure you didn't know?" Talon asked. "It kinda sounds like maybe you knew."

Luke shook his head emphatically. "No, no, I didn't know."

"Okay," Talon accepted his protest. "Because that's really important. Absolutely critical. Washington doesn't have an 'accessory after the fact' statute. If you knew beforehand, you're an accomplice and you go down for the exact same crime. But if you didn't know until afterward, and help anyway, they can only charge you with rendering criminal assistance which is way less serious."

"No, no way, man.," Luke repeated. "I didn't know beforehand. I wasn't in for no robbery."

"Good," Talon signaled.

"I mean," Luke went on, "I thought maybe he snuck his mom's checkbook out of her purse or something, but I wasn't gonna get involved in all that. I just figured he was gonna get some cash and then we'd go buy some weed with it or something."

"Is that why you agreed to drive him?" Talon asked. "Because you thought you'd get some pot out of it?"

Luke shrugged. "I dunno. I mean, I woulda driven him anyway. But I wasn't gonna say no to some weed either, you know?"

"Sure," Talon replied. "Of course. Great."

She took a moment. So far Luke had admitted to sort of knowing about check fraud and unlawful possession of marijuana, but not the robbery. She could ignore the other crimes for the moment. It was the robbery that mattered. "So, what happened next?"

"I found a spot over in front of Subway and I parked," Luke answered. "That's it. He ran inside and I waited."

"Did he come out again?"

Luke shook his head and frowned. "No, man. I never saw him again."

Talon took a moment to consider what he'd told her up to that point. It seemed believable enough. To her anyway.

"How long did you wait?"

Luke's mouth twisted into a knot. "I dunno. Five or ten minutes. I'm not sure. Long enough to start wondering what was taking so long. Then the cops started showing up."

"The cops," Talon repeated.

"Yeah, like two or three cop cars whipped into the parking lot, lights flashing, but no sirens. They stopped right by where I was parked and jumped out of their cars. I remember one guy got a shotgun out of his trunk, and the other two went up to the doors of the check-mart like the cops do on T.V. Guns out, pointing down, their back against the wall on either side of the door. Then they rushed inside."

"What did you think was going on?"

"I thought it was a fucking robbery," Luke answered with a nervous laugh.

"Did you think it was Miguel doing the robbery?"

"No way," Luke insisted. "I didn't even remember that stupid joke. I was just worried about him. Like, was he gonna be okay? Was there some crazy guy in there with a gun, making everybody lay face down on the floor, you know?"

"Sure," Talon said. "So, did you do anything? Did you think about going inside, or leaving, or what?"

"I couldn't leave," Luke said. "I was blocked in by the cop cars. And I sure as hell wasn't going inside. I checked my phone to see if he'd texted me. Like, 'I'm being held hostage' or something. But nothing. So, I just sat there, scared and wondering what was going on inside. And then..." he trailed off.

"Then what?" Talon encouraged.

"Then the gunshots," Luke answered. His eyes were wide and distant at the memory. "A lot of fucking gunshots. And screaming. Lots of screaming. It was, just, it was crazy, man."

"I'm sure it was," Talon acknowledged. "What did you think was happening?"

"I thought it was a gunfight. Cops and robbers, man. I was hoping Miguel was okay. I didn't know he was one of the fucking robbers."

"The *only* robber," Talon corrected. "That's going to be really, really important moving forward."

"Right," Luke agreed. "The only robber. I wasn't no robber, man. I was just sitting in the car, hoping I was gonna get high."

"Did you ever get out of the car?"

"Not until the rest of the cops showed up," Luke said.

"How many more showed up?" Talon asked.

"After the gunshots? I dunno, like a hundred?" Luke laughed. "It was a lot, man. Cops everywhere, you know? And fire trucks and an ambulance. It was just crazy."

"And you just sat in the car?"

"I didn't know what else to do," Luke said. "It happened pretty fast. Miguel goes in, cops show up, gunshots, then total craziness. Next thing I know, some cop is pulling me out of the car, asking me if I knew the guy who tried to rob the check-mart."

"What did you say?" Talon asked. This was the important stuff. Whatever Luke told her was attorney-client privileged. Whatever Luke told the cops was evidence.

"I was like, 'I know Miguel.' Is he the guy who tried to rob the place?'"

"And what did they say?"

"They didn't say anything," Luke answered. "They just looked at each other, then they grabbed my arm and put me in the back of one of their cop cars. I didn't know what was going on. But I figured maybe Miguel was the robber after all. That he wasn't joking around about making that withdrawal."

"Did you tell the cops about that joke?" That could be used as evidence of prior knowledge.

But Luke could only shrug. "I don't know. Maybe. Probably. I mean, not right then, 'cause they left me alone. But when they came back, they started asking me a lot of questions, you know.

That might have been one of them."

Talon sighed. She wasn't surprised he didn't remember every detail of what he said. It happened quickly and he was probably freaking out. And it didn't really matter what he remembered right then. The cops wrote it all down, Talon knew. Every word. Whatever Luke said, it would be in the reports, whether or not Luke remembered ever saying it.

"Did they read you your rights before they started asking questions?" She could hope.

"Oh, yeah," Luke remembered that. "The whole, 'you have the right to remain silent' thing? Yeah, they did that."

"But you talked to them anyway?" Hope dashed.

"Well, yeah," Luke answered. "I didn't know I was in any trouble."

Talon surrendered a dark chuckle and she looked around their jailhouse conference room. "Yeah, you're in trouble all right."

Luke didn't laugh. He frowned. "Yeah, I guess so."

"Did they interview you just at the scene?" Talon followed up. "Or back at the station too?"

"At the scene, in the car, back at the station. Everywhere," Luke answered. "They asked me a lot of questions. I was trying to cooperate, you know? I didn't think I did anything wrong."

"You didn't," Talon assured him. "Well, you did one thing wrong. You talked to the cops."

Luke lowered his head into his hands. "I didn't know, man. I thought if I answered their questions, they'd let me go. I thought I'd get to go home. But now I'm charged with murder and I got a two-million-dollar bail." He looked up at Talon. "When am I going to get out again?"

Talon had to shake her head. "I don't know," she admitted.

"But I am going to get out again, right?" Luke tried to

confirm. "I am gonna go home again eventually, right?"

Talon took a moment, then decided to go ahead and tell him the truth. "I don't know that either."

CHAPTER 5

By the time Talon left the jail, all but one of the news crews that had come to film her client's arraignment had vacated the courthouse parking lot. But it only took one.

"Hey, isn't that the cop-killer's lawyer?" Talon heard the reporter ask her cameraman. Followed by, "Grab that camera." Then, to Talon, as the smallish woman rushed toward her, microphone in hand, "Excuse me! Excuse me, ma'am! Could we get a statement from you?"

Talon thought for a moment. Her first instinct was to say, 'No.' She was tired. It had been a draining afternoon, unexpectedly so. She had planned to sit in her office and catch up on email, sipping a latte. She just wanted to be done.

But there was no rest for the wicked. Or their lawyers.

Talon switched on her smile and turned to the onrushing reporter. There was still work to be done. Potential jurors to taint.

"Yes, I'm Talon Winter," she answered. "I represent Luke Zlotnik."

Normally, Talon wasn't one to talk with reporters. It was rare for the media to treat criminal defendants fairly. The reporting generally suggested guilt, the formulaic 'alleged(ly)' losing its effectiveness through overuse. But this was a case with such bad publicity—even Amy Koh had called her 'the cop-killer's lawyer'—that a big part of Talon's job was going to be getting the jurors to see past labels like that and assess the case on the merits of what her client did, not his friend's admittedly terrible actions. She didn't know who those jurors would be, but she knew they would come from the greater community and at least one of them, whoever they ended up being, would probably be watching the news that night.

"I'm Amy Koh with Channel Eight," the reporter identified herself. She was noticeably short, less than five feet tall, with a stylish bob that didn't seem to move even as she skidded to a stop in front of Talon. "Do you have time for a few questions, Ms. Winter?"

Talon nodded, and resisted saying, 'I just told you I did, didn't I?' Instead, she smiled warmly. "Of course."

The cameraman had made his way over to them. He was considerably larger than either Talon or Amy Koh, but he also had a heavy-looking camera on his shoulder, so he didn't run over. Or introduce himself. He just took up his position behind Amy Koh and turned on the spotlight, momentarily blinding Talon and reminding her to look at Amy, not the lens.

"Could you comment on the bail the judge set, Ms. Winter?" Amy Koh asked. "It seems like a higher bail than normal for a murder case. Is that because the victim was a police officer?"

Talon wanted nothing more than to go off on Judge Portello. Oh, the stories she could tell. But there were limits on what she could say about judges. Specifically, the Rules of Professional Conduct, one of which was pretty clear in its edict that lawyers not disparage 'the qualifications, integrity, or record of a judge.' So, despite her desire to do so, Talon wasn't going to attack Judge

Portello.

Instead, she'd attack the prosecutor. Always attack the prosecutor.

Normally, she would have attacked the cops, too, but not when the murder victim was also a cop. Poor form. The potential jurors in her audience wouldn't like that.

"The issue in this case," Talon answered carefully, but forcefully," is not the bail decision by the judge. The issue in this case is the charging decision by the prosecutor. By all accounts, my client, Mr. Zlotnik, remained outside of the business while an acquaintance of his went inside and, unknown to Mr. Zlotnik, attempted to commit a robbery. What followed was a tragedy. It was also a crime. But it was not a crime committed by Mr. Zlotnik."

"But doesn't being the getaway driver make you part of the robbery?" Amy Koh followed up. It was exactly the sort of half-informed common knowledge Talon was going to be fighting against the entire way.

"Only if you know you're the getaway driver," Talon explained. "If you drive someone to a store and wait outside knowing they are going inside to rob it, then yes, you are the getaway driver and you are guilty as an accomplice. But if you drive someone to a store and wait outside not knowing they plan to rob the store, then no, you are not the getaway driver. You're just a friend who got tricked. And you're not guilty of robbery or anything else that happens inside."

"Is that your defense, then?" Amy Koh asked. "Are you going to claim your client didn't know his friend was going to rob the store and kill the police officer?"

"It's not my defense," Talon clarified. "It's the truth. My client had no idea what his friend had planned."

Up to that point, Talon had been facing the reporter to

deliver her answers, but she turned and looked directly into the camera—at all those potential jurors watching at home.

"Luke Zlotnik is one hundred percent innocent," she declared. "And I should know. I'm his lawyer."

She was sort of right, but sort of wrong on both counts.

CHAPTER 6

"Oh, dear, I guess we can't hire you after all," Luke's mother groaned after Talon slid the proposed fee agreement across the table to her and her husband. "We can't afford that."

She looked to her husband. "I mean, maybe if we could make payments," she suggested.

"Thirty years of payments, maybe," Paul Zlotnik put in, glancing at the proposed fee. "With a balloon at the end."

Talon stifled a sigh and pulled the fee agreement back slightly. It was a first degree murder case. There was a lot of work to be done, and she didn't work for free.

"The thing is," she said, "I'm not a bank."

Discussing fees wasn't the worst part of criminal defense, but it was one of the more awkward. Being a lawyer was supposed to be a profession, a calling, not just a job. It was supposed to be above base things like money. It was about justice and law, freedom and rights. But it was also about rent and food, clothes and more rent. Money was a necessary evil. It just felt especially evil when it was based on a person being shoved in a jail cell and needing a lawyer to protect those rights and save that freedom.

"I hate banks," Paul grumbled. "And everybody hates lawyers."

Talon decided to just blink at that. She wanted the case. She'd already cut 25% off her fee. Any more and she would be losing money on it. She was a solo practitioner sharing office space and a receptionist. Her margins weren't that fat. In fact, they were pretty damn thin.

She was about to remind them that Luke could always get the public defender—not as a negotiating tactic, but as a reassurance that he would at least have some lawyer representing him—when Mary spoke up.

"We can put the shop up as collateral for a loan," she suggested. "There's not a lot of equity, but there's some."

"Not the whole amount. Maybe half." Paul glanced again at the fee agreement. "Probably half." He looked up at Talon. "If we can manage half up front, can we do payments on the rest?"

Payments, Talon thought ruefully. When she started doing criminal cases, the first advice she got was: Don't do payment plans. Criminal cases went fast, and when they were over, they were really over. If they lost, the defendant was hardly going to want to keep paying an outstanding balance from prison. And if they won, well, the client had no incentive to pay any more. It wasn't like Talon could put the acquittal on hold until her balance was paid off.

No, best to let Visa or MasterCard work out the payment plan. Full retainer, nonrefundable, paid up front. That's how you ran a criminal practice.

Then again, Luke was charged with first degree murder of a police officer.

He was eighteen years old, looking at thirty years in prison.

And he was innocent. That counted for a lot.

"Sure," Talon sighed. "We can do payments."

* * *

After the Zlotniks left, Talon went to the break room she
shared with the other attorneys in the office. It was too early for a
drink, so she settled for a cup of coffee. But not the old stuff that
had been thickening on the burner. She dumped it down the sink
and started a fresh pot. As she was waiting, Greg Olsen joined her.
He was another attorney in the office share, but he did civil work, a
mix of personal injury, some family law, and occasionally a
bankruptcy.

"Was that the family of the cop killer?" he asked, tipping his
bald head back toward the lobby. He still had a little hair above his
ears and around the back of his head, but it mostly just served to
frame the expanse of pink skin reflecting the fluorescent lights
above them. He kept his tie loose around a thick neck and his belt
even looser under an even thicker gut.

"Accused cop killer," Talon corrected. "And yeah, they just
hired me. Well, sort of."

"Sort of?" Greg glanced approvingly at the freshly brewing
pot, then pulled down a mug from one of the cabinets. What does
that mean?"

"It means I'm on the case," Talon explained, "but they
haven't actually paid me yet. They need to get some financing in
place. And I'm letting them make payments."

"Payments? On a murder case?" Olsen's face screwed up
into an incredulous scowl. "On *that* murder case?"

Talon frowned. "Yeah," she admitted. "That murder case."

Olsen shook his head at her. "You're never going to get rich
doing that."

"I'm never going to get rich doing criminal cases at all." She
reached around him to pour herself the first cup of coffee. "But
that's not why I do them."

"Just be careful," Olsen warned, accepting the carafe from Talon when she'd finished pouring her coffee. "You can't live on 'not guilty' verdicts."

"Yeah, but I can't live without them." Talon grinned. She took a large gulp of the too hot liquid and waited for the burn to subside. "Anyway, I'm hoping to avoid going all the way to a jury verdict. This case is way overcharged. Now that I'm officially hired, it's time to talk with the prosecutor and tell her to dismiss the case."

Olson laughed. "Has that ever worked?"

"No," Talon admitted. "But who knows? Maybe I'll be surprised."

CHAPTER 7

"He confessed?" Talon exclaimed.

It was her first sit-down with the prosecutor, in Cecilia Thompson's office on the tenth floor of the courthouse building. Nice view. Terrible news.

"Yes." Cecilia pointed at the stack of police reports she had just handed to Talon as she dropped the bombshell about the confession.

"To knowing it was a robbery?" Talon clarified.

"Yes," Cecilia repeated.

"My guy confessed," Talon wanted to make sure she fully understood, "to the police, that he knew, beforehand, that his friend was going to commit a robbery?"

"Yes," Cecilia confirmed. "All that."

Talon put a hand to her forehead. "Well, fuck."

"Yes," Cecilia agreed one last time. "Did he forget to tell you that little detail?" she laughed. "I hope you got paid up front."

Talon suppressed a wince. She didn't discuss fee arrangements with prosecutors. Instead, she fanned the edges of the police reports. "Where's the confession?"

Cecilia leaned forward and flipped the pages until she found the transcript of Luke's statement to the police, about halfway down the stack. She set the pages above it to the side, and there were still several inches of paper beneath it. "Right here. It's pretty detailed too. Not just that he knew what his friend was going to do, but he helped plan it, parked in front of a different business on purpose, and knew his friend had a gun when he went in."

That was all they needed. Luke was guilty.

Talon looked down at the double-spaced transcription, formatted like a play script, each speaker identified by initials. Some detectives and 'LZ' for Lucas Zlotnik. Page one was just the formalities: date and time, identity of everyone in the room, *Miranda* rights. She couldn't bring herself to read the rest of it just then. Not in front of the prosecutor. It was going to be bad enough assessing exactly how screwed her client was; she didn't need Cecilia watching her facial expressions while she did it.

Talon put the set-aside pages back on top of the stack. "I'll read it later. Is this everything then?"

"For now," Cecilia answered. "But supplemental reports are still coming in. Autopsy. Ballistics. Follow-up witness interviews. They haven't even finished processing the crime scene. Two bodies and a hell of a lot of blood. It was pretty messy, if the crime scene photos are anything to go by."

"Crime scene photos," Talon repeated. She hesitated, but then went ahead and flipped to those. She was curious how bad they were.

They were bad.

The jury was going to hate those pictures. Or rather, those pictures were going to motivate the jury to hate whoever was responsible for what was in them. And the government was going to put her client in a big red chair with the word 'Defendant' flashing above it in neon lights, so the jury would know exactly whom to hate.

"So, what's the offer?" Talon asked, without looking up from the photos. "Murder Two, plus the gun enhancement?"

"Offer?" Cecilia laughed again. "Oh, Talon. There is no offer. Not on this case. And certainly not Murder Two. He killed a cop."

"He sat in a car outside," Talon raised her gaze to her opponent, "while someone else killed a cop."

"Yeah," Cecilia replied. "His accomplice."

Talon pointed to the photo she was looking at. Miguel Maldonado in a pool of blood on the floor of the check-mart. "I'd say he paid for it."

"Your guy will too," Cecilia returned.

"He's eighteen years old," Talon tried. "He was sitting in the car outside. He didn't know what was going to happen."

"He confessed," Cecilia reminded her.

"To robbery," Talon pointed out. "Not murder."

"It doesn't matter," Cecilia answered. "You know that."

"Of course it matters," Talon responded. "Everything matters."

"No, nothing matters," Cecilia said. "Certainly not whether he knew it was murder or robbery. If he's in for the robbery and somebody dies, that's felony murder. I don't have to prove he knew his friend was going to kill someone."

"But isn't it different?" Talon insisted. "Isn't it different if he agrees to help a murder, rather than just a robbery? Isn't that worse?"

"Not according to the law." Cecilia crossed her arms. "Either way it's Murder One. You premediate a murder, it's Murder One. You commit a serious felony and somebody dies, it's also Murder One. The Legislature made them the same crime."

"Okay, okay," Talon conceded. "But what about you? What about prosecutorial discretion? Not every case that meets the elements of a crime deserves the same punishment. You have to admit that. Every case is different. My guy didn't pull the trigger. He didn't set out to kill a cop. Some people do that. Shouldn't they be punished more than an eighteen-year-old kid who made a bad decision to help his friend do something stupid?"

"Look, Talon." Cecilia unfolded her arms and leaned forward. "The prosecutor exercising discretion in this case isn't me. It isn't even my boss. It's my boss's boss. *The* boss. This is big, Talon. Huge. The cops care about this one. Everyone does. The boss can't cut any deals. That means I can't either, even if I wanted to."

Talon took a moment. "Do you want to?"

Cecilia paused, too, before answering. "That doesn't matter either. Your guy knew it was a robbery. Somebody died. It all adds up to murder in the first degree. Twenty-five year minimum sentence. And I'll be asking for the maximum, thirty-five years."

"Without any consideration for my guy's personal situation?" Talon asked. "His lack of criminal history? Nothing?"

"Nothing," Cecilia confirmed. "No deals. Maximum sentence."

Talon shook her head again. "That's not justice."

"Maybe not," Cecilia admitted. "But it's the law."

CHAPTER 8

"Fuck Cecilia Thompson."

Talon was back at her office, working into the night, reading and rereading the inches of police reports that Cecilia had provided her at their meeting.

She considered how a person could be charged with a murder they never intended and that someone else committed. "Fuck the felony murder statute."

Then she pulled out the 47-page transcript of her client's suspect interview and threw it across the room. "And fuck this confession!"

It wasn't just that Luke had confessed. It was how detailed the confession was. It was like he'd read the police reports first. The kind of knowledge only someone who was in on the crime would have known. It was all over except the crying. And the trial. The lengthy show trial the prosecutor's office was going to put on for the cops and the voters. At least the deliberations would be quick. The jury was going to convict him faster than Talon could say 'payment plan.'

But the worst part was that Luke didn't tell her about the

confession. It sounded like he didn't tell his family either. She never would have agreed to take the case on a thousand-year payment plan if she'd known Luke had confessed. It didn't make him any less deserving of a defense. But it made it a hell of a lot harder for her to be successful in that defense. Losing was bad enough. Losing for free was just stupid.

And Talon hated looking stupid.

She walked over and started picking up the transcript. Maybe she could suppress the confession somehow. Maybe they left out one of his constitutional rights. Maybe they didn't follow all the steps in the confession recording statute. Maybe....

Maybe she was fucked.

"Working late?" came a voice from behind her, even as she was still bent over picking up pieces of her client's confession.

Talon knew the voice. It was Curt Fairchild, a private investigator whose office was on the same floor. They'd worked a few cases together, among other things. She supposed he was a friend. She supposed he wanted more. She supposed she couldn't blame him.

"That's a stupid question," she answered, as she picked up the last of the papers off the floor. She stood up and faced him. "You call yourself an investigator?"

"Depends who's asking," Curt replied. He didn't exactly look like an investigator, but then again that probably made him a better one. Instead of a rumpled trench coat and tousled hair, he wore a crisp blue shirt and khakis over a fit frame, stylishly cut black hair pushed back from a clean-shaven face. "Why? You need one on that cop-killer case?"

"Oh, you've heard about that case?" Talon sat down behind her desk again.

"Oh, yeah," Curt answered. "Everyone's talking about it."

"Everyone?" Talon asked.

"Well, Hannah," Curt clarified. "When I asked her what you were working on."

"Ah." Talon nodded.

"And Greg," Curt expounded. "He was standing there when I asked Hannah."

Talon groaned. "What did Greg say about it?"

"He said you were crazy for taking it."

Talon ran her hands through her hair. "I think he may be right."

"Big case. Good publicity, right?" Curt tried.

"Not when I lose." Talon frowned.

"Lose?" Curt questioned. "That doesn't sound like you."

Talon tapped the transcript. "Well, my client's confession may disagree."

"He confessed?" Curt reached out for the document.

"Apparently," Talon said, handing it to him. "But the worst part is, he didn't tell me about it when I first met with him. He told me everything else, but he never told me he confessed."

"Seems like kind of a big thing to leave out," Curt observed as he flipped through the transcript.

"Yeah, and now I have to go talk to him again," Talon sighed. "It's not going to be pretty. I don't like being lied to."

"Sounds like you could use a witness," Curt suggested. "Or an investigator."

Talon laughed and shook her head. "You really want to work on a cop-killer case?"

Curt shrugged and handed the confession transcript back to Talon. "I bet there's more to it than that."

"There always is," Talon agreed. She took a moment and looked at the reports, then the clock. She sighed. "Okay, I can look at this more tomorrow, before we go pay a visit to my client." She stood up and stretched her back. "You heading out?" she asked Curt.

"Yeah," Curt answered. "I parked right by you."

"Cool," Talon acknowledged. She turned off her computer and her office light, and they headed for the elevators.

It had been a long day. She appreciated having someone else to talk with about the case, even if it was Curt, and even if it was just to complain. A good night's sleep and she'd be ready to attack the case again—even if that meant attacking her own client, rather than her usual targets on the other side, the prosecutor and the cops.

The elevator door opened, and she decided her usual targets would be just fine after all.

There were only two cars still in the garage. Curt's and hers. You could tell which one was Curt's car because it didn't have its windows smashed out and the words 'COP KILLER LOVER' painted down the side.

"Holy shit!" Curt exclaimed.

Talon didn't say a word.

After a moment, Curt looked at her and gestured frantically toward the vandalized car. "We better call the police."

But Talon just barked out a dark laugh. "Who the hell do you think did this?"

CHAPTER 9

"You really should call the police," Curt nagged the next day as they walked into the Pierce County Jail. He had driven. Obviously.

"I'm not calling the police, Curt," Talon answered. "I have insurance. They'll take care of the damage."

"It's not about the damage," Curt pressed. "It's about holding the culprits accountable."

Talon stopped short. "Did you really just say 'culprit'?" She reached up and patted him on the head. "That's adorable. Now shut up. Don't tell me what decisions to make. I can just as easily decide I don't need an investigator on this case. Or If I do, that it's not you."

Curt took the advice. He kept quiet until they'd made it inside the jail and Luke Zlotnik was escorted into the attorney-client meeting room for his cell block.

Talon didn't stand up when they entered. Instead she glared at Luke from her seat at the small plastic table and waited for the guard to leave. When he did, she nodded toward Curt.

"This is Curt Fairchild," she said. "He's here because you

lied to me."

"Uh…" Luke wasn't sure how to respond. He looked at Curt, but didn't say hi, then back to Talon, but didn't seem to know what to say. Finally, he stammered, "I, I didn't lie to you."

"That's two." Talon held up two fingers. "If you lie again, we're done, and you can find yourself a different lawyer. And I'm keeping your parents' money—what I've received so far anyway— so it'll probably be the public defender, who already has way too many cases. Hope you like prison food."

Luke opened his mouth to say something, but Talon cut him off.

"Be careful," she warned. "Do not lie to me again."

Luke closed his mouth, then sat down meekly across from her and Curt. "What are we talking about?"

Talon leaned forward. "We are talking about your confession, Luke," she growled. "We are talking about the single most important piece of evidence the State has against you. We are talking about the thing you didn't even bother to mention to me before I agreed to take your case. That, Luke, is what we are talking about."

"Oh." Luke actually seemed to relax a little. "Okay, yeah. I forgot about that. But I didn't lie to you. I lied to them."

"You lied to them?" Talon repeated. "The cops?"

"Yeah," Luke answered. "That confession, it wasn't true. That's why I didn't tell you about it. They can't use it if isn't true, right?"

"Wrong," Talon pinched the bridge of her nose. "And stupid. And totally unbelievable. No one lies to say they committed a crime they didn't commit. They lie to say they didn't commit a crime they did commit."

"But they told me they'd let me go if I just told them what

happened," Luke protested.

"So, tell them the truth," Talon suggested. "Assuming you're not lying to me again right now."

"I'm not," Luke insisted.

"Then why in the world would you ever confess to murder?" Talon challenged.

"I didn't confess to murder," Luke defended. "I didn't say I killed anyone. They just told me if I cooperated, I could go home. They told me if I just admitted I knew what Miguel was going to do then they could wrap up their investigation and everyone could go home."

"Well, I suppose that was sort of true," Curt chimed in. "They got to wrap up their investigation."

"And they got to go home," Talon pointed out. "But not you, huh, Luke?"

Luke just frowned and shrugged. "No, I guess not."

"I've read the confession, Luke," Talon continued. "You're right. You didn't confess to premeditated murder. But you did confess to felony murder. You admit you helped plan the robbery, drove Miguel to the robbery, and waited outside while Miguel went inside to commit the robbery, so you could drive him away after the robbery. That's a confession to robbery. And because someone besides Miguel died during that robbery, it's also a confession to felony murder."

"I don't even know what felony murder means," Luke protested. "I just—"

"The cops did," Curt pointed out. "They knew what felony murder means."

"Yep." Talon nodded. "They knew exactly what he needed to say."

"What are you guys talking about?" Luke asked.

"The guy who interviewed you," Talon asked, "was he nice or was he kind of a jerk?"

"There were two of them," Luke answered, "and they were both really nice. They brought me McDonald's. They told me what happened to Miguel and the cop who died. They told me they were just trying to tie up some loose ends, and I could help them with that."

"Did you tell them you didn't know what Miguel was going to do?" Talon asked.

"Yeah, a bunch of times," Luke said. "I kept telling them I had no idea Miguel was planning on robbing the place, but they kept saying that didn't make sense, and I had to know. They said they weren't accusing me of murder—because Miguel did that—but no one was gonna believe I didn't know he was gonna rob the place."

Curt frowned at Talon. "The recorder wasn't on for any of that, was it?"

Luke thought for a moment. "No, they didn't even put the recorder on the table until the very end. After they told me everything that happened."

"The Reid Method," Curt recalled from his days of training to be a cop—before deciding to strike out as a defense investigator instead. "Lock down the details first, off the record, then turn on the recorder to get a nice clean confession. No initial denials, no irrelevant tangents, no confusing questions from the suspect."

"And no record of feeding the suspect all the details that make it into the recorded confession." Talon knew the interrogation technique too. And its dangers. "Feed him the info, tell him what to say, and promise him he can go if he'll just say it."

"I shouldn't have said anything, huh?" Luke asked.

"You should never say anything to the cops," Talon

answered. "But it's too late now."

"Is it really too late?" Luke's eyes widened. "Like, that's it, it's over? I'm going to get convicted of murder? I swear, I didn't know Miguel was gonna kill anyone. I didn't even know he was going to rob that place. I just thought we were gonna score some weed and get high. I swear to God. You have to believe me. You have to."

Talon raised a palm. "Calm down. I do believe you. I probably shouldn't, but I do. The problem is, the jury won't. They'll believe your confession."

"We need someone to tell them about the Reid Method," Curt said.

"Right," Talon agreed. "That it's designed to extract confessions no matter what the facts are. That it's been rejected by most other countries as unreliable and rife for abuse. That there are documented cases where people were wrongly convicted based on false confessions."

"Can't you just tell them all that?" Luke asked.

"No," Talon answered. "I'm just a lawyer. I can't say anything a witness doesn't say first."

"So, what are we going to do?" Luke almost pleaded. "They have to understand I was lying. I didn't know."

"We need an expert," Talon knew. "Someone with a bunch of letters after their name to come in and explain to the jury how a person could possibly be stupid enough to confess to a crime they didn't commit."

"Good," Curt interjected with a grin. "Sounds like we have a plan."

"Sure." Talon leaned back in her chair. "A terrible plan."

Curt looked askance. "Why terrible?'

"Because that's going to cost money," Talon complained.

"Money no one has. His parents can't afford to pay me. I can't afford to pay you. I don't know how we're going to pay for a national expert on false confessions."

Curt raised a finger. "Wait. You can't afford to pay me?"

Talon ignored him.

"What happens if we don't hire the expert?" Luke asked.

"What if we don't hire a Ph.D. in psychology?" Talon asked, "To explain to the jury how a person could possibly confess to a crime they didn't commit? To explain why they shouldn't just go ahead and believe your confession since it's filled with corroborating details only a guilty person would know? To explain why they shouldn't just do the easy thing, take you at your word, and convict you of murder in the first degree?"

Luke frowned. "Uh, yeah."

"Simple," Talon answered. "You'll spend the next thirty-five years in prison."

CHAPTER 10

"Can we talk again about that whole 'I'm not getting paid' thing?" Curt asked as he and Talon stepped out of the jail and onto the sidewalk next to the courthouse.

Talon sighed. That was the last thing she wanted to talk about just then. Luckily, she saw an opportunity to change the subject. Literally.

"Hey." She pointed at a crowd gathering on the courthouse steps. "What's that?"

Curt looked over. "It looks like a crowd."

Talon rolled her eyes, then clapped him on the back. "You really are the world's best investigator. Come on, let's go take a closer look. I see someone I know."

That someone was Cecilia Thompson. She was standing on the courthouse steps next to her boss, who in turn was standing in front of a throng of reporters and cameramen, with a crowd behind them. Some of the crowd were identifiable by their dark suits as members of the legal profession, mostly obsequious junior prosecutors sucking up to their boss, but a few defenders like Talon, curious about what was happening. Except Talon could at least guess at the topic. Her little attempt at tainting the jury pool was apparently not going to go unanswered.

"Thank you, thank you," Cecilia's boss started out. His

name was Craig Donaldson. He wasn't the elected prosecutor for the county, but he was only one step down. His official title was 'Chief Deputy Prosecutor for the Criminal Division', but everyone called that position 'Chief Criminal.' Every county prosecutor's office had several divisions, including things like civil litigation, child support enforcement, but the criminal division was the largest and Craig Donaldson had been in charge of it for as long as anyone could remember. He was probably seventy, but looked more like he was in his late fifties, thanks to the type of healthy and clean living you might expect a career prosecutor to pursue in order to have just one more way to judge everyone else on the planet. Thick white hair was combed straight back from tanned skin and bright blue eyes. "Thank you for coming out today. We have an important announcement regarding the case of Officer Todd Dickerson, who, as we all know only too well, recently lost his life in the line of duty while stopping an armed robbery."

Talon and Curt came up and took a position at the back of the crowd. Talon stared intently at Cecilia so she would catch her eye when Cecilia's slow scan of the crowd finally reached Talon. The fact that Cecilia's scan never quite reached Talon confirmed to her that Cecilia had seen her walk up and was going to avoid eye contact at all costs.

"I'm here today," Donaldson continued, "to announce that while we cannot bring Officer Dickerson back, we can make sure that those responsible for his death never get the chance to live in the freedom and peace they denied him. I'm here today to announce that we will be amending the charges against Lucas Zlotnik from murder in the first degree to *aggravated* murder in the first degree, a charge only available in certain limited circumstances. One of those circumstances is when the victim is a police officer performing his official duties."

Agg Murder One. Talon knew what that meant. It meant even thirty-five years wasn't enough.

"The crime of aggravated murder in the first degree," Donaldson explained, "has a mandatory sentence of life in prison without the possibility of parole. We intend to honor Officer Dickerson's memory by holding his killer responsible and seeking the maximum penalty under the law. Thank you."

Talon continued to stare at Cecilia, but the prosecutor avoided her gaze. Instead, she turned to follow Donaldson back inside the courthouse. However much respect Talon might have had for Cecilia Thompson until that moment, it became clear to Talon that Cecilia was just another member of the opposing team. Part of The System. Part of The Problem.

"Can they do that?" Curt asked as the crowd began to dissipate.

"Can they amend the charges up?" Talon clarified. "Yeah, they can do that. They're the prosecutor. They can do whatever the hell they want."

"Oh. Wow," Curt shook his head. "And can they say that about Luke? That he's responsible for Officer Dickerson's death? Isn't he presumed innocent?"

Talon shrugged. "Of course he is. And no one believes that. There's a dead cop. And they're going to say 'dead cop' as many times as they can, so by the time the trial starts, everyone will hate Luke, no matter what the facts are."

"And they can just do that?" Curt complained. "Aren't they supposed to be held to a higher standard or something? I mean, they're supposed to be the good guys, right?"

"I don't know about that," Talon scoffed. "But yeah, there's a special ethical rule just for prosecutors talking to the press. They aren't supposed to say anything that would 'heighten public condemnation of the accused.'"

"They totally just did that!" Curt pointed at the empty spot where Donaldson had just been standing.

"Yes, they did," Talon agreed.

"So, what do you do now? File a bar complaint?"

Talon laughed at that. "I'm not filing a bar complaint."

"Why not?" Curt asked. "Wouldn't that create, I don't know, a conflict of interest or something?"

Talon shook her head. "A bar complaint just isn't my style."

"Winning isn't your style?" Curt challenged.

Talon grinned. "That's exactly my style. And you know it. Which means I know how to do it. Trust me. Filing a bar complaint over a press conference is not how to win this case."

"Really?" Curt asked. "It won't help to take out the prosecutor?"

"Cut off one asshole," Talon answered, "and two more will take its place."

"Wow," Curt said. "Gross."

Talon laughed again. "There will always be another prosecutor," she explained. "I'm not going to win by trying to disqualify their team. I have to win on my terms. And with my team."

Curt just nodded, apparently ready to concede the argument.

"And you're part of my team," Talon reminded him. "Right?"

"Even if I don't get paid?" Curt knew. He sighed. "Sure. But I really would prefer to be paid."

"Me too," Talon agreed. "And our false confession expert will absolutely insist on it."

CHAPTER 11

"We don't even know how we're going to pay for you," Mary Zlotnik said at the meeting Talon called with her and her husband later that week. "How are we supposed to pay for an expert too?"

"And an investigator," Curt put in.

Talon shot him a harsh glance.

"That's why I wanted to meet with you," she explained. "We have some important decisions to make."

"What happens if we don't hire this expert you want?" Paul Zlotnik asked.

"Honestly?" Talon replied. "We'll lose. The jury will accept Luke's confession at face value, and he'll be convicted. Period. And now he's looking at life in prison."

"I still don't understand," Mary interjected. "You say he confessed? Why would he confess? And why didn't he tell us that?"

"That's why we need the false confession expert," Talon explained. "And that's why we'll lose without one. The jury will have the same questions. We have to have an answer for them."

"I thought it was the prosecutor who had to prove everything," Paul said. "Isn't Luke presumed innocent?"

"He is," Talon agreed. "But without the expert, the State will tell the jury he confessed and there won't be anyone to say it's not true."

"What about Luke?" Paul suggested. "He can tell them it wasn't true, that they forced it out of him. Right?"

"He can," Talon agreed again. "But the jury won't believe him. Without a scientific reason to disregard the confession, the jury will think he's just trying to get out of trouble."

"Get away with murder," Curt put in.

Talon gave him another disapproving glance.

"He didn't murder anyone," Mary insisted loudly. "Why won't anyone believe that?"

"Because he said he did it," Paul answered his wife's question. "Or he said he knew it was a robbery, and I guess that's enough. I don't know. That's why we hired her."

He turned to Talon again. "I believe you when you say we need this expert, but you have to believe us. We don't have any more money. It took everything to hire you. There's nothing left."

"Why can't we get a public defender expert?" Mary asked. "Do people with public defenders get to have expert witnesses?"

Talon nodded. "Of course."

"Who pays for those experts?" Mary asked.

"The county," Talon answered. "They have money set aside to hire experts. It comes out of the same budget as the lawyers."

"Then why can't we get an expert at public expense?" Mary asked. "We can't afford one, but you say he absolutely needs one. Shouldn't the county pay for that too?"

Talon thought for a long moment. Curt's body language threatened he was about to say something, so she cut it off with a third harsh glance. Finally, she said, "I can try."

"Really?" Mary asked.

"Really?" Paul echoed.

"It's unusual," Talon said. "And judges hate to do anything unusual. Plus, the public defenders aren't going to want to use their budget on somebody else's client. But you're right. Luke deserves it and he can't afford it. It doesn't hurt to ask."

"Oh, that would be wonderful," Mary said. "Do you think it will work?"

"I can't promise anything," Talon cautioned. "I'll file a motion for an expert at public expense. Hopefully, the judge will understand we can't win this case without one."

Paul leaned forward and shook Talon's hand. "Thank you."

"Don't thank me yet," Talon replied. "No one is going to like giving public money to someone who hired a private attorney. I can't promise this will work. And if it doesn't, we're right back where we are now."

"We understand," Paul said. "But that's why we hired you."

"To do the impossible." Mary smiled.

"We read about you," Paul explained. "We did our research. Everybody said you're the best. They said if anybody could get Luke out of trouble, it was you. It's why we're risking everything."

He looked to his wife, who nodded sadly and looked at Talon with glistening eyes.

"Because without Luke," she said, "we don't have anything."

Talon nodded. "Of course."

No pressure.

CHAPTER 12

It wasn't a difficult motion to draft. The ask was straightforward, and there wasn't a lot of case law on either side. Her client needed money to hire an expert, and the family had used all their resources to pay her (or to promise to pay her... eventually... maybe). The judge simply needed to order the county's public defense office to pay funds directly to Talon's expert.

Technically, the request for public funds was just between Talon and the judge. The prosecutor had no standing to argue against the motion, but she still had to provide notice to the prosecutor since it was under the criminal case number and the State was a named party. The problem was, prosecutors were so used to running everything, they couldn't even conceive of a situation where they didn't get to talk.

That meant a trip to the prosecutor's office to drop off the notice of the hearing. The last thing any defense attorney wanted to talk about with the prosecutor was defense tactics. It was bad enough that the motion would expose at least part of Talon's strategy. She didn't want to get into an off-the-record conversation with Cecilia about it. In court, the opportunities to speak were structured and limited. She could stonewall the prosecutor by simply limiting her answers to the judge's questions. But a hallway conversation with Cecilia might lead to a slip of the tongue that betrayed even more of Talon's plans than the motion was already exposing.

That was what the 'IN' basket at the front desk of the prosecutor's office was for, as far as Talon was concerned. Drop and dash.

It almost worked.

Talon dropped off the notice of hearing in the prosecutor's office on the ninth floor and took the first elevator back down to one. She was halfway across the lobby when she heard Cecilia call out to her. And not in a friendly way.

"Talon! Talon! What is this?"

Talon sighed, then stopped and turned around. Cecilia was waving the notice Talon had just dropped off. Cecilia must have been hiding behind the receptionist or something and run down the stairs after her.

"It's called a pleading," Talon called back. "That's the general term for a document filed by a party to a court action."

"You're going to hire a false confession expert?" Cecilia practically spat as she closed the distance between them. "Really? That's the best you can do?"

"You haven't seen the best I can do," Talon responded. "Not yet anyway. But yes, we plan on hiring an expert to explain to the jury how your cops coerced a false confession from an innocent man."

Cecilia crossed her arms. "I thought he was just a boy."

"And I thought you were a decent, honorable prosecutor," Talon said. "But I forgot. No such thing. Like unicorns. And justice."

"I'm going to oppose this." Cecilia shook the pleading at Talon.

"You don't have any standing," Talon replied. "You can't object to the defendant preparing his defense."

"I can object to a defendant using public money to get away with the murder of a public servant who died protecting the public at large."

"Did you want to say 'public' one more time?" Talon sneered. "Or are we done?"

"We'll be done when the jury says 'Guilty'," Cecilia answered, "and the judge sends your client to prison."

"For the rest of his life," Talon expounded. "For something his friend did."

"We talked about this, Talon." Cecilia put her hands on her hips.

"Yes, we did, Cecilia," Talon responded. "You know, I used to respect you. I still want to. But you're drinking the Kool-Aid on this one, and I don't get it. Did Donaldson promise you a promotion or something?"

Cecilia lifted her chin. "I don't need a promotion to want to see justice."

"Justice?" Talon laughed. "This is vengeance."

Cecilia thought for a moment. "Maybe vengeance is a part of justice."

Talon had a snappy retort ready. Several in fact. But she stopped herself. She really did want to keep liking Cecilia Thompson. There were so few prosecutors who understood what Talon did. She didn't want to lose one. "Think about this, Cecilia. Don't let this case change you. Think about this motion. Let's get an expert on false confessions. Let's see what they say. Maybe they say

Luke was telling the truth and he did know. If so, you can sleep easy knowing you held him accountable for a murder the law says he's responsible for. But if they say it was coerced, that Luke didn't know, that he really was just sitting in his car waiting on a friend — wouldn't you want to know that?"

Cecilia didn't reply immediately. She let her eyes drop from Talon's to the paper in her hand. It had the date and time of the hearing.

"I'll see you next Tuesday, Talon," Cecilia finally said. "Don't expect me to sit back and stay silent on this issue."

Talon frowned. "Honestly, Cecilia, I don't know what to expect from you anymore."

CHAPTER 13

Normally, going in front of a judge who'd spent a career as a public defender before ascending to the bench would have been a good thing for Talon. But on a motion asking for public money for a defendant who apparently had enough money to hire a private attorney? Not so much.

Judge Bryan Gainsborough was one of the defense bar's favorite judges. Although that wasn't necessarily saying much. Judges were elected in Washington State, and it was just good politics to be pro-law enforcement. That was fine for governors and legislators, mayors and council members, but kind of a problem for judges who were the only check on overzealous cops. Gainsborough was one of the few judges who wasn't afraid to rule against the cops if it was appropriate and that usually made him a good draw for the defense. But Talon wasn't asking for a ruling against the cops. She was asking for a ruling against the public defense budget.

The hearing was set on a busy calendar of miscellaneous criminal motions. Nothing that required testimony—those were assigned out to empty courtrooms for half- and full-day hearings. The ones on Gainsborough's calendar were motions the judge could rule on based just on the arguments of the attorneys. Or, Talon hoped, in her case, the argument from just one attorney. Cecilia had, as promised/threatened, appeared for the hearing, so Talon's first order of business was to block her from addressing the judge at all.

"Are the parties ready on the matter of The State of Washington versus Lucas Zlotnik?" the judge read the name of the next case on the docket.

"The defense is ready, Your Honor," Talon spoke up first, "and this motion does not call for any response from the State. The State has no standing."

That wrinkle broke up the monotony of an entire morning of routine discovery motions. Judge Gainsborough looked up from his papers and actually focused on the litigant before him.

"Ms. Winter," he greeted her. "Nice to see you again. Are you saying there won't be a prosecutor here for this motion?"

"I'm here, Your Honor," Cecilia stepped forward. "Cecilia Thompson on behalf of the State of Washington."

Judge Gainsborough nodded to her. "Ms. Thompson. Good to see you as well. So, do you agree with Ms. Winter's assertion that you have no standing on this motion?"

"No, Your Honor, I do not," Cecilia answered. "I believe the State has standing to address any issue in a criminal case, even if only to help inform the Court in its decisions in an effort to assure that the rights of the public are properly considered."

Judge Gainsborough nodded for several seconds. He didn't ask Talon to respond. Instead he took a few moments to read the file. Then he looked up and addressed Talon. "You want public money for an expert even though you're retained privately?"

"Yes, Your Honor," Talon answered. She knew just to answer the question. Gainsborough would give her the chance to make her argument, but she could show him the respect of waiting until he did so.

"You *are* being paid for this, correct?" the judge clarified. "You didn't take the case *pro bono*?"

Talon was tempted to explain the extraordinary financial arrangements she had reached with Luke's parents, but knew not to discuss fees in public. "It's not *pro bono*, Your Honor."

Judge Gainsborough frowned. He turned to Cecilia. "I take it, the State objects to Ms. Winter's motion?"

Cecilia stood up even straighter than she had already been standing. "No, Your Honor. The State does not object. In fact, we join the motion."

Talon turned to look at her opponent and couldn't help but smile. A small smile, hidden in the corner of her mouth. But a smile nonetheless.

Judge Gainsborough cracked a small smile as well. "Is that so, Ms. Thompson? Well, then, that makes my job easy. I will sign the order. But, Ms. Winter?"

Talon looked back up at the judge. "Yes, Your Honor?"

"If the Director of the Department of Public Defense takes issue with his budget being used to assist a private-paying client," Judge Gainsborough pointed down at her, "I'm sending him to you."

Talon nodded. "Yes, Your Honor. That's fair. Thank you, Your Honor."

Gainsborough signed off the proposed order Talon had included with her motion and in a few moments Talon had a certified copy of the order to take down to that same director of the public defender's office to discuss how to make arrangements to pay whatever false confession expert she could now try to find and hire.

But first, she had a question.

"Cecilia!" Talon called once they were both in the hallway. Cecilia was already halfway to the elevators.

Cecilia was making a beeline for the elevators, but she stopped at Talon's voice and turned around. "Yes?"

Talon walked over to her. "Thanks. That was really professional of you."

Cecilia shrugged, but stayed more formal than usual. "Just doing my job."

"Isn't your job to oppose me at every corner or something like that?" Talon teased.

Cecilia shook a serious head. "No. My job is to enforce the law. My job is to hold people responsible for the crimes they commit. And my job is to do that with complete and total transparency. You can hide evidence from me, you can get a client evaluated a dozen times for mental illness and only tell me about the one psychiatrist who says he's crazy. You can conceal, and misdirect, and sandbag. But I can't do any of that."

Cecilia crossed her arms. "My job is to tell you everything up front. To give you every report, every photograph, every last note made by every last cop. My job is to protect your client's rights despite what he did and make sure he is afforded every protection and every opportunity he's guaranteed by both the Federal and State Constitutions. My job is to do all that and win anyway."

She locked eyes with Talon. "And that's exactly what I'm going to do. I'm going to do all that. I'm going to be the fairest, most ethical, most righteous fucking prosecutor you ever met. And I'm going to convict your guy anyway."

CHAPTER 14

The drive back to the office was short, but kind of fun in the rental she was using while her car was being repaired. It was like a new car, without the new car payment. The drive was long enough to let Talon collect her thoughts about what had just happened, and what she needed to do next. Unfortunately, it was also long enough for her to get pulled over.

"Shit," Talon hissed as the cop lights filled her rearview mirror. She knew she'd beat the ticket in court, but it was still annoying to get pulled over. And time-consuming. She had work to do. She slowed down and pulled over to the right at the next available opportunity. She rolled down her window and put her hands on the wheel at ten and two until the cop walked up and asked for her license, registration, and insurance. But her phone was on her lap, just in case.

She didn't actually know what she was being pulled over for. She wasn't speeding. She hadn't run any red lights or even rolled through a stop sign. She wasn't even on her phone, which was actually a little surprising.

The cop stepped up to her window. He was so close, she

couldn't really see his face, just a stocky torso and meaty hands.

"License, insurance, and registration," he instructed.

Talon didn't like the tone hidden in his voice. She slowly extracted her driver's license from her wallet, then leaned over to her glove box to retrieve the other two papers.

"Why did you stop me, officer?" She held the requested documents back for a moment. "I don't think I was speeding."

"Give me the documents, please," the officer repeated.

"Are you going to tell me why I was pulled over?" Talon countered. "Please."

The officer's meaty hand moved to the gun strapped to the side of his stocky torso. "Are you going to obstruct a law enforcement officer?"

Obstructing a Law Enforcement Officer. RCW 9A.76.020. A gross misdemeanor, Talon knew. Arrestable.

She considered her options, then handed her documents to the headless policeman.

"Sorry, officer. Force of habit." She tried to defuse the situation. "I'm an attorney."

"I know who you are, Ms. Winter," the officer responded. He leaned down enough for Talon to see his face. It wasn't the same officer from the gallery at the arraignment, but Talon guessed they were probably friends. "And I know you're representing that cop killer."

Talon's heart sank. She was alone and all the suppression motions in the world wouldn't protect her from a large cop with a gun and a vendetta.

"Is that why I got pulled over?" she managed to ask.

The cop ignored her question. Instead, he said, "I sure hope you don't have anything illegal in your car," foreshadowing the predetermined outcome of the illegal search he was planning.

"I hope you have a warrant," Talon replied coldly.

"I'm going to need you to step out of the car, Ms. Winter," the cop pulled on the door handle, but it was locked.

"Nope," Talon answered. She held up her phone. Washington was a two-party consent state. Recording someone, even a cop, without their consent was a crime. But so was kidnapping, and there was an exception for when a person was threatening the recorder's personal safety. It was time to show the cop who was really in charge.

"I'm going to need you to give me my driver's license back," Talon instructed. "Holding onto it is a seizure under the Fourth Amendment of the United States Constitution. Violating my federal civil rights under color of state law—that means you, Mr. Local Cop—is actionable under Section 1983 of the U.S. Code. That means I can sue. And not just your department will be liable, but I can sue you individually, too, and you won't have immunity for an illegal act. So, you have a choice. You can give me my license, or you can give me your house. And your car. And your pension."

The cop stood up again, his face obscured by the vehicle roof, but he didn't say anything.

"Do I need to go on?" Talon asked. "There's criminal liability, too, for unlawful imprisonment, among other things. Believe it or not, I have friends who are prosecutors. And judges. And reporters."

She kept the camera rolling.

The officer held out her license, registration, and insurance card. "Here's your information back, ma'am. One of your brake lights was flickering. Be sure to check that out when you get the chance. Drive safe."

Talon snatched her documents back. "Fuck you too."

CHAPTER 15

It took a while for the adrenaline and anger to dissipate out of Talon's bloodstream. The anger took longer. The adrenaline was gone by the time she got back to her desk, but the anger lingered. But she could use anger as fuel for Luke's case—and her anger tank was full.

It was almost six and she was still plowing through the police reports, reading, annotating, cataloging, indexing. She knew she needed to understand every last fact, and know them better than Cecilia, if she was going to find the one, narrow path out of the dark, terrible, life-in-prison woods Luke was trapped in. She just needed to work. And think. And focus.

"Hey, there!" Curt's bright face darkened her doorway. "Whatcha doing here so late?"

Talon closed her eyes and took in a long, deep, loud breath. She really didn't want to deal with Curt Fairchild just then. She didn't want to deal with anyone just then. But especially not Curt.

"I'm working," she said through gritted teeth.

"Are you close to wrapping up?" Curt asked. "I was thinking about trying that new noodle place down on Pacific."

"No," Talon snapped. "I'm not close to wrapping up. And I'm not interested in noodles down on Pacific. I have a lot to do."

"Oh," Curt said. Then, after a moment, "Can I help?"

"No, Curt," Talon barked. She caught herself and lowered her voice again. "No, you can't help. There is nothing you can do which would be helpful."

"You seem stressed," Curt observed. "Tough day?"

"Yeah, Curt. Tough day."

"What happened?"

"Fine!" She shoved the file away from her and threw her hands up. "You wanna know what happened today? You wanna know what happened to me today? I got pulled over by a shit-stain cop, and if it hadn't been for me not trusting cops and having my cell phone ready to record his shit-stain ass, I would have been arrested for planted drugs, obstruction, and God knows what else. I'm sure I would have been roughed up for resisting arrest too. That is, if the cop decided to even drive me to jail instead of just putting me in his patrol car and driving me to the base of Mount Rainier to murder me and leave me in a shallow grave for the coyotes to eat before anybody even knew I was missing. That's what happened today, Curt. Okay? That's what happened."

Curt didn't say anything for several seconds. Then he stepped over and put a hand on Talon's shoulder. "I'm sorry."

She slapped his hand away. "Don't touch me. And don't feel sorry for me. I'm not scared, I'm just angry."

"I never said you were scared," Curt pointed out.

Talon's hands were balled into fists and shaking, despite her best efforts to keep them steady. "I'm just angry. And, no, I'm not going to report it to the cops. So, don't even suggest that."

"Of course not," Curt responded. "No, I get that."

He hesitated. "Look, it's getting late. Maybe you shouldn't stay here alone all night."

Talon looked up at him. "Are you seriously hitting on me? Right now?"

"Is there a better time?" Curt joked. "But no. I'm not hitting on you. I just think this is starting to get a little crazy and maybe having a witness around might discourage anything else like that from happening again."

Talon lowered her head into her hands, then ran her fingers through her hair. Angry didn't have to mean stupid. "Yeah, okay. You're probably right."

"Do you have a lot left to do?" Curt asked. "I can order us some food."

Talon sighed. "Yeah, I have a lot left to do. I guess I don't have to get it done tonight, but I want to. These fuckers. They want to put Luke away for the rest of his life. I can't let them do it. I just can't."

Curt took out his phone. "Thai?"

Talon shook her head. "Pizza. Everything. Extra veggies."

"Gross," Curt replied.

When Talon cocked her head at him, he added, "And exactly what you're going to get. Because that's what you want." He turned away to make the call, but Talon heard him mutter, "And I can get some breadsticks."

Once the pizza was ordered, Curt sat down again across from Talon. "So, what are you working on specifically? I'm supposed to be part of the team, remember? Let me help. Even if I'm not going to get paid."

Talon smiled. "You might get paid. Do you take payment plans?"

"Not in veggie pizzas, I can tell you that," he joked.

"Everything pizzas," Talon corrected. "With extra veggies."

"Right," Curt pointed at her. "That. And breadsticks." Then he pointed at the papers pushed around her desk. "What are you working on right now?"

"Like four different things," Talon explained with a sigh. She was glad dinner was on its way. She was also glad to have someone to talk to. It might help her sort out all the various threads in the case. It was starting to blur together, despite her anger fuel. Or maybe because of it.

"I just got the ballistics reports," she pointed to a stapled report with the state crime lab seal at the top. "So, I need to read that. I need to compare the primary officer's written report with the crime scene photos because, of course, there's no video. The owner of the business had all of his cameras pointed away from the main floor and straight down at the teller stations, because their biggest losses come from employee theft. You see Miguel walk up and talk to one of the tellers, but then the teller backs away off screen and so does Miguel. The other cameras show the rest of the employees bailing away from their own stations about a minute later, but none of the cameras caught the shootout."

"Maybe that's good," Curt suggested. "The State won't be able to show the jury the video of what actually happened. Maybe that's reasonable doubt."

"No, it's bad." Talon shook her head. "It means the cop who survived gets to tell the jury whatever the hell he wants, and no one can contradict his version of events."

"Well, maybe he'll tell the truth," Curt tried to joke.

"Don't even try to defend cops in this room tonight," Talon warned. "Not tonight. And not the cop who shot Luke's friend dead. There were three people in that check-mart when the shots were fired: Miguel, the cop Miguel shot, and the cop who shot Miguel. Everyone else bailed out the back when the cops kicked in the doors. That cop gets to say whatever the hell he wants, and there's not a damn thing I can do about it."

Talon gestured vaguely at the papers strewn across her desk. "All of this interconnects somehow, in ways I can't even begin to guess at, and I don't even know where to start."

"Start at the beginning," Curt suggested, flashing a grin.

Talon rolled her eyes. She was in no mood. "Thanks. Since you said that, I'm going to do the exact opposite."

She grabbed the ballistics report that had just arrived that day and started reading. "Now, shut up."

Curt opened his mouth to protest.

Talon raised a hand at him, but not her eyes. "Shut. Up."

He complied, but Talon could still see him shifting his weight in his chair. Finally, he pulled out his phone again and distracted himself. That let Talon relax enough to actually process what she was reading.

She stopped and read it again.

Then a third time.

"Holy shit," Talon said. She finally looked up at Curt.

"What?" he asked, setting his phone down.

She handed him the pages she was examining. "Look at the ballistics report."

"What about it?" he asked.

"The bullets match," Talon explained. "All of the bullets match."

"Okay." Curt shrugged. "That seems kind of expected, right? We didn't think there was another shooter on the grassy knoll or anything, right?"

"No, *all* of the bullets match," Talon repeated. "All of them.

The bullets from Miguel's autopsy and the bullets from the dead cop's autopsy, they all match. They're all from the same gun."

Curt's eyes widened. "It wasn't a shootout."

"No," Talon knew. "It was a slaughter."

CHAPTER 16

"You need to tell the prosecutor," Curt said. "This is huge."

But Talon laughed at his suggestion. "You're right. It is huge. And that's why I don't tell the prosecutor. Not yet anyway. She'll see it when she looks at the ballistics report herself. Then she'll shit her pants wondering if I saw it too."

"She's going to know you saw it," Curt said.

Talon grinned. "She going to know I saw it. And she's going to know I know she knows I saw it. But she's not going to know why I didn't tell her I saw it."

"And why aren't you going to tell her?" Curt asked.

Talon stood up and shook her head. She put a hand on Curt's face and clicked her tongue. "Because I'm playing four-dimensional chess and she's playing tic-tac-toe."

Curt thought for a moment. "What am I playing?"

Talon grinned again and gave Curt's face a light slap. "You're not playing at all, Curt. You're the towel boy. But that's okay. The game needs towel boys too."

CHAPTER 17

Chess was all about setting up the board, moving the pieces into position so the outcome was predetermined before the other side even knew what was happening. It was even more so with four-dimensional lawyer chess.

Talon had some setting up to do.

The first was easy. A quick email to Officer Todd Dickerson:

Officer Dickerson,

I represent Luke Zlotnik in his pending criminal matter. I am writing to request an interview of you regarding the incident which led to his arrest and current charges. Please reply with your availability. I expect the interview to last approximately 4-6 hours.

Sincerely,

Talon Winter

Attorney at Law

Next, Talon drafted the motion and order for the formal deposition of Officer Dickerson when he refused her request for an interview. If he even replied at all.

Of course, when she finally got to ask him questions, she wouldn't want to walk in empty-handed, so next was a field trip to serve a subpoena for Officer Dickerson's personnel file:

> *SUBPOENA DUCES TECUM*
>
> *To: Records Custodian, Tacoma Police Department*
>
> *You are hereby commanded to appear at the office of the undersigned attorney at the date and time below indicated. You are further commanded to bring with you the following documents: the complete personnel file of Police Officer Todd Dickerson, including but not limited to: records relating to any disciplinary actions and any internal affairs investigations.*
>
> *Failure to comply with this subpoena may be considered contempt of court.*
>
> *Herein fail not at your peril.*

Talon smiled one more time at that last line before sliding the subpoena under the bulletproof glass to the receptionist at the Tacoma P.D. headquarters, also on 38th Street, just a few blocks north of where one of their own killed two people with his department issued firearm.

She knew the department's legal advisor would drag his feet and eventually ask a judge to quash the subpoena. But there were other ways to obtain information from government agencies, ways that had very short time limits:

> *PUBLIC RECORDS REQUEST*
>
> *Pursuant to the Washington Public Records Act (RCW 42.56), the undersigned Requestor does hereby request the following information:*
>
> *(1) Any and all information regarding the incident which occurred at Check-Now U.S.A. business located at 2610*

*South 38th Street, Tacoma, Washington, 98409, including
but not limited to: police reports, forensic reports, witness
statements, surveillance audio or video recordings, police
audio or video recordings.*

Talon took a nice drive through the city, delivering individually addressed copies of the same request to the public records officers for the Tacoma Police Department, Tacoma Fire Department, Pierce County Medical Examiner, Washington State Patrol Crime Laboratory, and of course, the Pierce County Prosecutor's Office. The prosecutor's office was already supposed to give her everything under the court rules, but that didn't mean they hadn't held something back, Cecilia's reaffirmation of transparency notwithstanding.

Hence, Talon's last written demand for information, dropped directly into that prosecution 'IN' box on the ninth floor of the courthouse:

SUPPLEMENTAL DEMAND FOR DISCOVERY

Pursuant to Criminal Rule 4.7, the defendant in the above-captioned case hereby demands the following discovery:

the complete personnel file of Police Officer Todd Dickerson, including but not limited to: records relating to any disciplinary actions and internal affairs investigations.

If the demanded material is in the possession of the prosecutor's office, this material must be provided to the defense, pursuant to CrR 4.7(a). If the demanded material is in the possession of another government agency (to wit: the Tacoma Police Department), then the prosecutor must attempt to cause the material to be provided to the defense, pursuant to CrR 4.7(d).

Talon exited the prosecutor's office lobby and pressed the down arrow for the elevator. It had been a full day, and it was only

4:00. She decided to head back to the office to see if Officer Dickerson had left a love e-note in her email. Probably not, but the thought of a trigger-happy cop shooting off a screed for daring to ask for an interview made her smile. Sometimes you have to poke the bear before you can take him down.

* * *

There was no email from Dickerson, of course, but Talon decided she'd earned herself a reward anyway. It was a little late for coffee, but there might be some herbal tea somewhere in the break room. Something that tasted like victory and the tears of her enemies.

But she had to settle for lemon hibiscus. At least there were honey packets in one of the drawers.

"No coffee, huh?" Olsen said as he entered the break room and looked past Talon at the empty coffee carafe on the cold burner.

"Afraid not," Talon answered. "You drink coffee this late?"

"I drink coffee anytime," Olsen answered. "It doesn't keep me up anymore. I just fall asleep without it."

Talon thought for a moment, then accepted the distinction. "I can make you a lemon hibiscus tea with honey," she offered. "Or you can make yourself a fresh pot."

Olsen frowned. "I can't drink an entire pot. And I don't want to clean it afterward. Looks like Hannah already cleaned up."

Talon doubted it had been Hannah but decided not to argue the point.

"How's that cop killer case going?" Olsen asked, opening the fridge and scanning the inside.

"Alleged cop killer," Talon corrected. "And it's going pretty well. I had a fun day today."

"Oh yeah?" Olsen pulled a Coke out of the door and turned his attention to Talon. "Do tell. This job can suck sometimes. We deserve to have fun when we can."

So, Talon explained her day. She left out the chess analogies, but explained that the real cop killer was Dickerson, and she was going after him every way she could. But she had to admit as she finished her story, there was a limit to what she could do.

"Every one of my demands is going to be rejected, at least at first," Talon knew. "Then I'll have to go to the judge and ask for the information to be compelled, but there aren't a lot of judges who have the guts to side with an alleged cop killer defendant over an actual cop-killing cop."

Olsen tipped his Coke can at her. "See, in civil, we can just ask the defendant anything we want, and he pretty much has to answer it."

"But that's the problem," Talon answered. "Dickerson isn't a defendant. He's just a witness. Witnesses have more protections. Judges don't want to see them harassed. As long as he's just a witness, every request for information will be judged by whether it's material to the charges against my guy, the actual defendant. Too bad I can't make him a defendant."

"No, you can't make him a defendant." Olsen took a long, thoughtful drink of his Coke, then lowered the can again and smiled. "But I can."

CHAPTER 18

It wasn't going to work to have Luke or his family sue Todd Dickerson. One, Luke was an accused murderer, a cop killer. Two, he didn't have any damages. If he were convicted, then he was a murderer, legally responsible for Dickerson's actions because he helped set up the fatal scenario in the first place. If he was acquitted, well, what harm did he have? Miguel was only his friend. You couldn't sue because someone killed your friend.

But you could sue if someone killed your child.

Luke knew Miguel. That meant Luke's parents knew Miguel's parents. That meant Talon could reach out to Miguel's family through Luke's family. And that meant a very large meeting of both families in the conference room she shared with Olsen, which made sense since she and Olsen were about to share the case too—or parts of it anyway.

"Thank you all for coming," Talon started once everyone had found a seat. There were just enough chairs for everyone: Mary and Paul Zlotnik, Elisabeth and Javier Maldonado, Talon, Olsen, and Curt. Curt wasn't sure why he was there—he'd said as much when she'd invited/instructed him to sit in—but he was key. "Please let me start by acknowledging your loss, Mr. and Mrs. Maldonado. I can't imagine what you're going through, but please know you have my deepest sympathies."

Talon knew enough to know there wasn't really anything she could say to make them feel better. But if she didn't say anything at all, it would make them feel worse. Still, her area of expertise was getting people out of trouble they'd brought on themselves, one way or another. Olsen was the expert on getting other people into trouble for what they'd done to the people who eventually became his clients.

"My job is to make sure the tragedy of your son's death isn't compounded by the unjust conviction of his friend," Talon continued. "But I can't bring Miguel back. No one can."

That was the cold, hard reality of it. Even if Cecilia Thompson, with all her justice this and blue eyes that, managed to get a conviction, it wouldn't bring Miguel or the other officer back to life. It would just inflict more violence, forcing Luke into a series of cages for the rest of his life.

"I also can't hold his real killer responsible," Talon went on. "That's not what I do." She turned to Olsen. "But it is what this man does. This is Greg Olsen. He's the man I invited you here to meet."

It was a grand introduction. But Olsen wasn't really a grand sort of person. He just raised his hand in a small wave. "Hi."

Talon managed, barely, not to roll her eyes. She was hoping Olsen would take over at that point, but apparently, she was going to need to talk more. They should have rehearsed the pitch.

But then Olsen stood up slowly, put his hands in his pants pockets, and started walking, slowly, around the room.

"I agree with most of what Ms. Winter just said," Olsen started, looking down at his feet.

'Most'? Talon couldn't keep an eyebrow from shooting up.

"She's right," Olsen continued, "that we can't bring Miguel back. And whether Luke is acquitted or convicted, Miguel's real killer will still be free. But I'm not sorry about it." He stopped, right next to Mr. and Mrs. Maldonado. He looked down at them, at once a kindly neighbor and a killer litigator. "I'm angry."

He looked angry too.

"I'm angry your son was murdered. I'm angry they charged his friend for it even though he had nothing to do with it. But most of all, I'm angry that the person really responsible is going to walk away without so much as a suspension." He held up his index finger. "Unless *you* decide to hold him responsible. And you let me help you. The prosecutor's office may want to whitewash what this police officer did, but the courts are open to everyone. The courts are open to *you*. And I would be honored to walk into the courthouse at your side to demand justice for Miguel."

Talon was impressed. It was part sales pitch, part opening statement. She'd suggested Olsen to the Maldonados solely because of his proximity to her, but she was starting to think he might actually do a good job too. *Bonus.*

Olsen gestured to Talon." If you're interested in talking more about what we can do to hold Miguel's killer—his *real* killer—responsible, then we should ask Ms. Winter and the Zlotniks to leave. The cases are related, but separate. Ms. Winter needs to do whatever she can to help her client, just like I will do whatever I can to help you. I expect to coordinate our efforts as we seek justice for both Miguel and Luke, but we will want to avoid even the appearance of a conflict of interest. So," he gazed down again at the dead boy's parents, "should we talk further?"

It was an easy decision. Mr. Maldonado looked at his wife, who gave him a quick but solid nod. "Yes," he answered for both of them.

And that was Talon's cue to leave. When Curt started to stand up, too, she put a hand on his shoulder and pushed him back into his seat. "No. You stay," she whispered to him. "I already talked to Greg about this. He's going to hire you as his investigator."

Then, to make sure he understood, she added, "I expect you to report back to me on any and all developments."

Curt frowned, Olsen's exhortation against conflicts of interest still lingering in the air. "Is that ethical?" he whispered back.

"Ethical?" Talon patted his shoulder. "A young man's life is at stake, Curt. Everything is ethical."

CHAPTER 19

Four-dimensional chess meant lots of pieces to move. The cop was an important piece, but he wasn't the only one. Even if Talon demolished him on the stand, it wouldn't matter if the jury believed Luke's confession. Talon needed to add Queen's False Confession Expert to the board. And just as a true queen would want the strongest stallion for her knight, the most impenetrable fortress for her rook, or the cleverist priest for her bishop, Talon wanted the best false confession expert in all the land. That meant a quest to the Kingdom of California.

Normally, that quest might have been accomplished by two coach tickets to Los Angeles on any of the dozen daily commuter flights between Seattle's SeaTac airport and LAX. But they were on a budget. Somebody else's budget, even. Every dollar they spent on airfare and hotels was a dollar they couldn't pay the premier expert of false confessions on the West Coast.

'NATALIE ROSS'

The name popped up on Talon's incoming call notification

just as she and Curt had gotten themselves situated in front of Talon's computer monitor, squeezing in to make sure the good doctor would be able to see them both for the Skype interview.

Talon clicked the green phone receiver icon and Dr. Ross's face popped onto their screen. Talon had expected a professor's office backdrop, a brown and gold palette of dimly lit bookshelves and stacked papers. Instead, it was the bright taupe of a home mudroom, children's drawings taped to the wall behind the casually dressed Natalie Ross, B.S., M.S., Ph.D., Psy.D., B.F.D.

"Sorry about the venue," Ross started, with a wave at her surroundings. "My wife is using the home office right now, so I'm at the workspace next to the kitchen. But the kids are at the park with the sitter, so it should be quiet enough."

"No problem at all," Talon was quick to answer. She couldn't have cared less about the backdrop. She cared about the woman. And how she would present to the jury. So far, so good. She looked the part of competent professional: in her late 40s, with curly, shoulder-length brown hair, smallish glasses, and a calm confidence, even in the workspace by the kitchen. "Thank you for taking the time to speak with us about our case."

"No, thank you for contacting me," Ross replied. "I've had a chance to review the materials you emailed me. This looks like a really interesting case. Usually, the alleged confessions I see pertain to the actual crime charged, not a different predicate crime."

"It's definitely interesting," Talon accepted that description, although she had a few others. "It's also frustrating. My client tells me that part of the reason he agreed to say what he said was because he thought he wouldn't be confessing to murder. He didn't understand Washington's felony murder rule."

"I'm not surprised," Ross said. "It seems a little unfair. I haven't encountered it before."

"Archaic is more like it," Talon replied, "About half the states have it still, mostly in the west. A lot of Eastern states have gotten rid of it. Canada too. But we're stuck with it."

"Well, I think I may be able to help you out then," Ross offered. "In fact, I think we can use this felony murder rule to bolster the argument that your client gave a false confession. It's even more likely that he would have told the police what they wanted to hear if he didn't understand the most serious of the potential consequences."

"Go on," Talon encouraged. "I like where you're headed with this."

Curt nodded his encouragement as well, but minded Talon's pre-interview admonition to resist jumping in at every opportunity.

"The psychology of false confessions is both fairly complex and surprisingly simple," Ross explained. "It's simple to understand that a person in a stressful situation will do whatever he or she can to get out of it, especially if it requires pleasing another person who has all the power in the situation. We will say what we think the other person wants to hear. We actually do this all the time in different situations. Little white lies to avoid hurting someone else's feelings, flattering a boss or supervisor to get a project approved, admitting fault just to end an argument even when we don't really think it's our fault. It's a very normal, very common social skill, and one that can be very useful in a whole host of circumstances.

"The complex part," Ross continued, "is understanding why a person would do it when it would seem to actually get the person in more trouble, not less. That is, when the apparent result of the false statement is a detriment to the speaker, rather than a benefit."

"Which is why I knew we needed to hire someone like you," Talon interjected. "I can try to explain that to the jury, but I'm no expert."

"And you're a lawyer," Curt finally jumped in. "No one is going to believe the defendant's lawyer."

Talon looked sideways at him. But he wasn't wrong. "They will," she pointed at the screen, "if I'm telling them the same thing Dr. Ross told them."

"Exactly." Curt nodded to himself.

"So, what are we going to tell them?" Talon asked the psychologist.

"We're going to tell them that Luke's false confession isn't any different from any other false statement," Ross answered. "He believed it would benefit him. He was just wrong. Very wrong. The trick will be explaining to the jury how he could have genuinely believed it would benefit him to claim advance knowledge of the robbery when, in fact, he didn't know."

"That seems like a tall order," Talon had to admit, "when I hear someone else say it."

"I'll say it better on the stand," Ross assured her. "I've done this before. Many, many times."

"And did you win all those times?" Curt asked, a bit impolitely. "Did the jury always believe you?"

The relaxed smile Ross had been wearing throughout their interview faltered. "Not always, I'm afraid," she admitted. "Every case is different. I can't promise a specific result. I can only promise to explain it to them to the best of my ability. It's my professional opinion, based on everything you've sent me, that Luke's confession was false. It was an attempt to gain favor with the police officers who controlled his freedom. And I will tell the jury that."

"That's all we can ask for," Talon said. "So, do you want on the case then?"

Ross nodded. "I do. I think your client is most likely

innocent, and I'd like to help him."

"Great," Talon answered. "You're hired." Then she offered her own, less relaxed smile. "But let's just try to drop that 'most likely' when you testify for real."

CHAPTER 20

With the False Confession Expert placed on the chessboard, Talon could focus her attention back to the opposing Queen's Constable piece. Not least because her opponent had also had her attention drawn to Officer Dickerson.

Talon recognized the caller ID when her desk phone rang. Actually, the screen just said 'PIERCE COUNTY' but Talon knew who was calling from the semi-blocked number.

"Hello, Cecilia," Talon answered. "What can I do for you?"

"What the hell are you doing, Talon?" Cecilia came out swinging.

"My job," Talon answered. They both knew what Cecilia was talking about.

"Your job is to defend your client," Cecilia shot back, "not go after my cop."

"Same thing," Talon countered. "Or two sides of the same coin anyway. And he's not *your* cop. He's *a* cop. A cop who killed someone. Two someones, it appears."

"Your guy is the one charged with murder," Cecelia returned. Then, "Wait. Two someones?"

Talon smiled. "Are you surprised it's two?" she asked. "Or surprised I figured it out?"

"What are you talking about?" Cecilia avoided the question.

"The bullets," Talon answered. "They're all from the same gun. The ones extracted from both Miguel and the other cop. They all came from the same gun. And I'm pretty sure Miguel didn't shoot himself three times in the chest."

Cecilia didn't say anything.

So Talon did. "There was only one gun, Cecilia. And it was your cop's."

"Oh, so now he's my cop?" Cecilia deflected.

"Now you don't want him to be?" Talon countered.

Again, Cecilia didn't have a reply ready.

"Why are you calling exactly?" Talon asked. "I'm kind of busy defending the innocent and all that."

"You're going after his personnel file," Cecilia finally said.

"Damn right I am," Talon confirmed. "He killed two people. I want to see if he's had any prior complaints of excessive force. I can't believe this is the first time he's overreacted. I'm betting he's been investigated before, even if it was ultimately just covered up by his superiors."

"If there are any prior investigations," Cecilia said, "and I'm not saying there are, but if they were found unsustained, you aren't entitled to them."

"You're trying to put my client in a cage for the rest of his life for something your cop did," Talon growled. "Don't tell me what I'm entitled to."

"You're not getting his personnel file," Cecilia asserted.

"And you're not getting in my way," Talon responded. "You don't have standing, Cecilia. Again. Dickerson's a witness. He doesn't belong to you."

"I thought he was my cop."

"He's your cop when he's killing people," Talon answered. "He's everybody's cop when I'm trying to see if he's done anything like this before."

Then Talon asked Cecilia the question she really cared about. "Why are you fighting this? Don't you want to know if he's done this before? Don't you want to know what really happened?"

"I know what happened," Cecilia claimed. "Two people are dead because the police had to respond to a robbery your guy was an accomplice to. That's murder."

"No," Talon answered. "Murder is shooting an unarmed suspect in the chest three times. Murder is shooting so recklessly, you accidentally hit your partner who was standing too close."

"Your guy is the one charged with murder," Cecilia reminded Talon.

"And your guy is the one who actually did it."

"You can't prove that."

"I shouldn't have to," Talon complained. "My guy is innocent."

"I guess we'll see what the jury says," Cecilia answered.

"And that's justice?" Talon asked. "Throw it at the jury and hope they make the right decision? I thought that was your job. Aren't you supposed to seek justice?"

"I'll get justice," Cecilia replied, "when I convict your client of murder."

CHAPTER 21

The next major development—or non-development—came when Talon received the police department's response to her public records request. The Public Records Act required every public agency to produce the requested documents, but it also allowed the agency to redact certain information that fell into any of a dozen or so exceptions. So, Talon got 114 pages from the police department, and every one of them had been redacted to complete uselessness. The only pages that weren't filled with a single, page-sized black box were pages filled with a half-page-sized black box with the rest of the page blank.

Even the officer's name had been redacted, which seemed especially ridiculous to Talon since her request was for Officer Dickerson's records, no one else's, and the blotted-out pages were provided in response to that specific request.

Talon wasn't surprised by the response from Dickerson's department. In fact, she'd planned for it. She could use it to bolster her efforts to receive the records, unredacted, through the prosecutor's office.

First, the provided pages, even if blacked out, confirmed

that Dickerson's personnel file did in fact contain some sort of disciplinary records; it wasn't just a 'fishing expedition'—the term prosecutors always labelled any effort by the defense to obtain information being hidden by those selfsame prosecutors. Second, the exceptions in the Public Records Act that permitted redactions didn't apply in the context of a criminal defense attorney receiving reports on a particular case. She was entitled to all relevant information, unredacted.

Therefore, Talon concluded, proof that the disciplinary records existed combined with Talon's inability to obtain them through public channels would force the judge to order the prosecutor to provide the records to her.

She was wrong.

CHAPTER 22

Judges didn't like to be forced to do things. That's why most of them became judges—so they could force other people to do things. If anything, telling a judge they *had* to do something was pretty much a guarantee they wouldn't do it. Talon eventually remembered that, but not until it was too late.

And she had an audience for her mistake. Of course. Her client was present, of course, as required for every criminal hearing. Curt had come along too. Not because Talon needed him there; she didn't. But, as Curt explained it, his younger cousin, Meagan, was job-shadowing him or something that day for her criminal justice class, and he thought she'd find the hearing more interesting than sitting in his office. Talon hadn't cared enough to object. Her focus was on winning her motion, or rather obtaining Officer Dickerson's disciplinary file through whatever means effectuated that result. Her motion was simply the current path to that goal.

She hadn't given up on the other paths, but they were farther down the road, and slower to trod. She could challenge the redactions in her public records request, but that would require a whole new lawsuit and take far longer than the criminal case would last. She had subpoenas out to the department, but enforcement of those could also be dragged out by the civil legal advisor to the department. Only the criminal case had a clock ticking, and Talon was going to use that clock to accelerate the result she needed.

But Cecilia Thompson had other ideas.

They drew yet another judge for the hearing. Talon had hoped to get back in front of Judge Gainsborough, but she was relieved not to be dealing with Portello again. Gainsborough was supposed to be hearing criminal motions still, but he had taken the week off, and the motion ended up in front of Judge Kristina Kirshner. Talon had been in front of her before, with mixed results. Judge Kirshner was no nonsense and super prepared. That was good when the facts and the law were both on your side. It was less good when your request was more in the gray area of judicial discretion.

"All rise!" the bailiff called out. "The Pierce County Superior Court is now in session, The Honorable Kristina Kirshner presiding."

Judge Kirshner emerged from her chambers and took the bench. She had her blonde hair in a loose bun, her reading glasses on top of her head, and a serious expression on her face.

"Be seated," she instructed before glancing down at the attorneys, both of whom she knew. "Ms. Thompson. Ms. Winter. Are the parties ready to proceed?"

"Yes, Your Honor," Cecilia jumped in to answer first, even though it was Talon's motion. Prosecutors were used to answering first, always trying to run the courtroom. "The State is ready."

Talon took a moment to stare her disapproval at her opponent, before raising her eyes to the judge. "The defense is ready to proceed with its motion, Your Honor."

Kirshner gave a slight nod to Talon. "Proceed, counselor."

Talon returned the nod. "Thank you, Your Honor. This is a motion to compel the State to provide a copy of Officer Todd Dickerson's police personnel file, and specifically any disciplinary information that may exist therein. As the Court is aware, Officer Dickerson is the State's primary witness. The court may not be aware, however, that it was Officer Dickerson's weapon which fired all of the fatal shots in this case."

"I read your brief, Ms. Winter," Judge Kirshner interrupted. "I'm aware of that allegation."

"Then Your Honor will also be aware," Talon responded, "that means Officer Dickerson shot an unarmed young Hispanic man, despite reports to the contrary promulgated by the police department and prosecuting attorney's office."

"Objection, Your Honor." Cecilia interjected. "Is this a motion for discovery or simply a forum to attack the motives of law enforcement and my office?"

"It's a motion and a forum to seek information about the motives of law enforcement," Talon returned. "Specifically, the motives of the police officer who killed an unarmed Hispanic man."

"You can stop saying 'unarmed young Hispanic man', Ms. Winter," the judge stated. "I'm aware of the facts. And I'm aware of what you're insinuating. What I'm not aware of is any basis to believe this officer had any animosity toward young Hispanic men, or any other demographic group."

"Which is precisely why I need to see his personnel file, Your Honor," Talon explained. "If such a predisposition exists, it has probably surfaced before and would have been the subject of some sort of internal investigation, even if it was ultimately deemed unfounded by a department eager to cover up that sort of thing."

"You are throwing around a lot of accusations, Ms. Winter," Judge Kirshner pointed out. "But I'm not seeing anything to support them."

"Then it's a lot like the State's case against my client," Talon returned. "Yet, they get to keep him locked up in a cage pending trial, despite him allegedly being innocent until proven guilty. If they can do that, the least the Court can do is allow me to see the personnel records of the person who actually pulled the trigger."

"Your client confessed." Judge Kirshner frowned.

"He was tricked into confessing, Your Honor," Talon answered. "We will show that at trial as well."

But Kirshner just harrumphed at that. "We're getting too far afield, counselor. The point is, Officer Dickerson has important privacy rights in his own personnel file. It is important that his department and his supervisors be candid in their appraisal of him without having to fear that their comments will be turned over to every defense attorney on every case he works on, which I'm sure numbers in the hundreds, if not thousands. Unless you can show me some reason, beyond a hunch, that there would be something in the records relevant to bias or improper motivation, I can't just hand them over so you can rifle through them, hoping to find something useful."

"But I can't show you what's in them," Talon complained, "if you don't let me look at them. We know the records exist, Your Honor. And we know the police department doesn't want me to see what's in them. That's why I got over a hundred pages of black redaction boxes. I've shown the records exist and I've shown Officer Dickerson shot an unarmed Hispanic man for no apparent reason."

"He was robbing a store!" Cecilia interjected.

"Allegedly robbing a store," Talon answered. "And now I'm not so sure."

"Well, I'm not sure either, Ms. Winter," Judge Kirshner said. "And if I'm not sure there is something material in the officer's personnel file, then I am not going to order the State to hand it over to you just to satisfy your curiosity."

"But, Your Honor," Talon started to argue, "you can't—"

"Actually, Ms. Winter, I can," Kirshner cut her off. "Your motion is denied."

Talon just stood there for a moment, unsure how to keep her queen from toppling off the board. "Your Honor," she fumbled, "you haven't heard from the State yet."

"I don't need to," Kirshner replied. "I'm denying your motion on its own merits." She turned to Cecilia. "Unless the State wishes to be heard, for the record."

Cecilia was smart enough not to snatch defeat from the jaws of victory. "No, Your Honor. Thank you. We agree with the Court's ruling."

Of course you do, Talon fumed in her head.

And that was that. Kirshner called the next case and two new lawyers stepped forward to address the Court. Talon barely had time to turn to Luke to offer a "Sorry" before the guards pulled him away so they could fetch the next defendant to be ground beneath the wheels of justice.

"That's bullshit you didn't even have to say anything," Talon hissed at Cecilia once they'd both stepped away from the bar.

"It just shows how weak your motion was," Cecilia countered.

"It shows how biased the system is," Talon returned. "If there's nothing in his personnel file, let me see it."

Cecilia shook her head. "That's not how it works."

"I know how it works," Talon growled. "And I know who it works for. The cops, you, but never my clients."

"At least he's not Black," Cecilia practically sighed. "Then I'd have to listen to another lecture about that."

Talon tipped her head at her opponent. "Really? Your concern about systemic racism in the criminal justice system is that you might have to listen to someone point it out to you? Maybe ask you to do something about it? Well, my client might be white, but he's poor. And the system is biased against poor people too."

"He can't be that poor," Cecilia sniffed. "He hired you."

"You'd be surprised," Talon returned.

"You're not doing this one *pro bono*, are you?" Cecilia asked, her own head tipped slightly. "That doesn't sound like the Talon Winter I know."

Talon knew Cecilia was right. But she wasn't going to let her know that. "Maybe you don't know me as well as you think you do."

Cecilia nodded. "That's probably true. This case is starting to show me that."

"Yeah." Talon sized up her opposite part. "Me too you."

Then it was just awkward. Cecilia snatched up her files and said something about going to her next hearing. Talon took longer but gathered up her things and made her way to the back of the courtroom, where Curt and Meagan were waiting for her.

"Well, that went terrible," she said as she walked up to them.

"I don't get it." Curt shook his head. "How can you show what's in his file if they don't let you look at his file? Seems like it's just designed to never let anyone look at a cop's personnel file."

Talon pointed at her nose with one hand and Curt with the other. "Bingo. He could have beaten somebody into a coma, but I wouldn't know it unless charges were filed, and of course, charges would never be filed. It's all one big cover-up. I would need him to voluntarily expose himself, and he's never going to do that."

"I'm not so sure about that," Meagan spoke up. She looked

exactly like Curt, except a little younger, a little shorter, and a lot more female. She held up her phone. "Have you seen his Facebook?"

CHAPTER 23

"I don't have a Facebook account," Talon admitted, even as she squinted at Meagan's phone to see what she'd found.

"What?" Curt was shocked. "How do you stay in touch with your school friends?"

Talon glanced sideways at him. "I don't."

"Well, Officer Dickerson has an account," Meagan said. "And he doesn't know how to set his privacy settings to 'friends only.' I can see everything."

"What do you see?" Talon turned back to Meagan.

"At the top of his feed, nothing," Meagan answered. "Just stupid pictures of his last vacation and where he ate dinner last week. But if you scroll back far enough..."

"How far?" Talon asked.

"Pretty far," Meagan admitted. "A few years. But it looks like he's never cleaned out his feed. And like I said, his privacy settings are public. I can see who he was hanging out with years ago before he even became a cop."

"And who was he hanging out with?"

"Racists," Meagan answered, holding up a photo of a

younger Todd Dickerson with a group of other white men, holding beers and posing, all smiles, in front of a white supremacist flag.

Talon took the phone from Meagan to get a better look. It was definitely Dickerson. And that was definitely some variation on the Nazi flag, the swastika replaced with some new, but similarly designed, symbol of racial hatred. She scrolled through the adjacent photos. It looked like a typical Friday night get-together at any local tavern, except for the flags and the white power hand signs people were throwing up. Dickerson himself wasn't flashing the signs, but the woman he had his arm around in about half the pictures sure did.

"Are you going to renew your motion?" Curt asked. "This shows predilection, right?"

Talon nodded. "Right. But no."

"No?" Curt asked. "Why not? This is huge."

Talon nodded again, still looking at the photos of Todd Dickerson and his racist girlfriend before Dickerson decided to become a cop. She knew what the arguments would be. He was just dating her. He didn't know her politics. He didn't recognize the obscure symbol on the flag. They broke up right after this. It was ages ago. Too distant. Too attenuated. Too bad.

"It is," Talon agreed. "The police aren't going to want anyone to see these."

"So, let the judge see them," Curt suggested. "Let everyone see them."

"No, that's not the play." Talon handed the phone back to Meagan. "I want Dickerson's personnel file. The judge is just the middleman. I'm going to take these straight to the source."

CHAPTER 24

"I'll see if Mr. Fassbinder is in," the receptionist at the Tacoma Police headquarters said. "What did you say your name was again?"

"Winter. Talon Winter," she answered. "I'm a defense attorney. But just tell him it's about *Kommandant* Dickerson."

When the receptionist furrowed her eyebrows, Talon explained, "It's kind of a joke. He'll get it."

The receptionist didn't seem convinced. She called Fassbinder's extension and after a moment, gave him Talon's name and occupation. She did not mention '*Kommandant* Dickerson.'

"Have a seat in the lobby," the receptionist instructed after she hung up again. "Mr. Fassbinder will be out shortly.

Martin Fassbinder was the legal advisor to the Tacoma Police Department. Another lawyer, but in-house with just one client. His job wasn't to secure a conviction, or champion the rights of any individual officer. It was to protect his client—the department.

Talon had never met him before, but when he entered the lobby there was little doubt that he was a lawyer and not a cop. He was short, probably 5'6", with a receding hairline and thick glasses. He also had a pleasant face and a warm smile for Talon as he strode over and extended a hand.

"Ms. Winter? Hi. I'm Martin Fassbinder."

Talon stood up and reached down to shake his hand. "Thanks for taking the time to meet with me, Mr. Fassbinder."

"Please. Call me Martin," he said. "I'll show you back to my office, and we can discuss whatever it is you've come to see me about."

Talon suspected he already knew, but she appreciated that he wasn't going to be the first to tip his hand.

"Ah, yes, Officer Dickerson," Fassbinder nodded after they were seated in his office and Talon began the conversation. "I suspected that was why you'd come. Ms. Thompson called me shortly after your hearing the other day to let me know I didn't need to produce the records. I believe she may have mentioned your name."

Of course she mentioned my name, Talon knew. But it was a dance. Talon could dance.

"How nice of her," Talon replied. "Then I'm sure she mentioned my client's name and Officer Dickerson's as well. It turns out my client is charged with a murder Officer Dickerson actually committed."

Fassbinder's smile faltered for a moment, but he caught himself. "You're not here to argue when a homicide is a murder, or who can be held responsible under the law."

"No, I'm not," Talon agreed. "I'm here to get Officer Dickerson's personnel file. Specifically, his disciplinary file."

Fassbinder folded his hands on the desk in front of him. "You know I can't do that, Ms. Winter. The judge already denied your motion."

"Please. Call me Talon," she replied. "And yes, I know the judge denied my motion. But I definitely do not know that you can't provide me the information anyway. In fact, I know you can, if you want to. Nothing in the judge's ruling prohibited the release of Officer Dickerson's file. It just didn't compel it."

"And what if I don't want to release it?" Fassbinder asked. "Because I can tell you, Talon, I do not want to release it. Not to anyone. But certainly not to you, under the circumstances of this case."

Talon smiled. "Believe it or not, Martin, I understand that. In fact, I would expect nothing less. That's why I've come here. To change your mind."

Fassbinder's hands were still folded calmly in front of him. "And how do you expect to do that, Talon?"

Talon reached into her briefcase and extracted the 8.5 x 11's of Officer Dickerson's white supremacist past. Mostly the photos Meagan had found, but also screenshots of some attendant posts and shares, all suggesting more than a passing interest in the alleged superiority of the White Race. "With these."

Fassbinder scanned the documents, his smile completely forgotten. After a moment, he looked up again. "I'm sure there's an explanation for this."

"I can certainly think of one," Talon answered. "But let's cut to the chase, shall we?"

Fassbinder didn't respond audibly, but he gave Talon a nod.

"Great." She pulled the photos from Fassbinder's hands to put them back in her briefcase. "These photos are from a long time ago. Long enough that there's a good chance the judge would never let the jury see them in the actual trial. You and I both know that, right?"

Talon wasn't sure Fassbinder actually knew that. He was an

in-house police legal advisor, not a trial attorney. But he seemed smart enough to know that she knew it.

"The only way they're really useful is to show the judge that Officer Dickerson might actually have some predisposition to racial animosity. Did I mention my client's friend, the one Officer Dickerson shot dead, was Hispanic?"

"I'm aware of Mr. Maldonado's ethnicity," Fassbinder replied. That smile was long gone.

"Are you also aware of the recent survey that showed one in five police officers have online connections to hate groups?" Talon asked. "What about the FBI's 2006 study that concluded there was an intentional and concerted attempt by white supremacist groups to infiltrate local police and sheriff departments?"

Fassbinder said nothing.

"Ok, good. We understand each other," Talon said. "So, these photos of Officer Dickerson at the white hate rally? Yeah, they're really old. No way the trial judge lets me tell the jury about something that happened that long ago. They're really only useful if I want to go back in front of Judge Kirshner and ask her to reconsider her ruling. To do that, though, I would have to file these photos. And once something is filed with the court, it's an open court record. Anyone who wants to can just open the court file and look at them. Heck, they can even get copies. And they're court records, not just public records, so there are no redactions, no hiding the truth. You know all that, too, right?"

"I know how the Public Records Act works, Ms. Winter."

"Talon. Remember?" Talon was having no trouble smiling. "So, you see, if I have to go back to Judge Kirshner to get Officer Dickerson's personnel and disciplinary files, then I will have to file these photos and they will be available to any Tom, Dick, and reporter who wants to thumb through the court file. Or..."

Fassbinder took up the invitation, but still with a stony expression. "Or I could agree to give you the records and you wouldn't need to file a motion to reconsider."

Talon grinned for both of them. "I knew you'd understand. I just want the records, Martin. Give them to me and there's no reason for any of this old stuff to be dragged up. Unless..."

Fassbinder sighed. "Unless there's something similar in his disciplinary files."

Talon nodded. "You know what's in those files, Martin. I know you've read them. Cecilia Thompson says there's nothing in there that will help my client. So, is she right? Are you going to hand them over quietly? Or am I going to have to make a scene? Amy Koh from Channel Eight owes me a favor."

Fassbinder leaned back in his chair and steepled his fingers. "You don't play around, do you?"

"I don't have the time," Talon agreed. "Or the patience. So, what are you going to do, Martin? Or rather, what am I going to do?"

Fassbinder took a deep breath, then exhaled through his nose. "Fine," he conceded. "I'll produce the records. But you're going to have to find at least a little patience. It's going to take me a few days to pull everything together."

"You mean you didn't have them all ready to hand over in case I won the hearing?" Talon teased.

"We both knew you were going to lose that hearing," Fassbinder asserted.

Talon didn't admit to her overconfidence prior to the hearing. Instead, she stood up and smiled down at him. "But I kinda did win in the end, didn't I? I'll expect the file by Friday, Martin. I have work to do."

CHAPTER 25

A lot had happened since the last time Talon had actually seen Luke, as he was being led away after the judge denied her motion to get at the cop's personnel file. He was too young and ignorant to be making the important decisions on his case, but it was still his case and Talon needed to apprise him of developments at least occasionally.

Which was always easier to do when she had good news to share.

"Good news," she began when Luke entered the jail conference room. It was near lunchtime. The whole wing smelled like cafeteria food and astringent.

"Yeah?" Luke asked, but almost disinterestedly. As if he didn't believe her. Or he didn't think it would matter. He sat down opposite her, but didn't look at her. Talon took a moment to appraise him before she shared her news.

"What's wrong?" Talon asked.

"What's wrong?" Luke repeated. "I'm in jail, and I'm probably never getting out again."

"Who's telling you that?"

A thumb jerked back toward the cells. "Everyone in here. They all say I'm screwed. I killed a cop. That's it. I'm never getting out again. We're all gonna be convicted. Every one of us. And we're all going to prison. That's how the system works."

"That may be how it works for them." Talon nodded toward the door. "But not for you."

Luke finally looked her in the face. "Why not for me?"

"Because," Talon answered, "you hired me."

CHAPTER 26

Confidence was good. Bravado even had its place. But the true currency of success in any endeavor was hard work. And for lawyers, that meant reading. A lot of reading. And Talon's 'to-be-read' pile increased significantly that Friday afternoon when Lieutenant Avery Johnson of the Tacoma Police Department arrived at her office with a banker's box full of papers.

"There's a Lieutenant Johnson here to see you," Hannah informed Talon over the phone. "He says he has a delivery for you."

Talon smiled to herself. "Right on time."

She hung up the phone and strode out to the lobby to accept her delivery from Fassbinder. She was surprised by the size of it.

She nodded at the document box Lt. Johnson was holding in front of him. It looked heavy. "I thought the report was only a hundred and seventeen pages."

Lt. Johnson smiled, then set the box on the floor. It sounded heavy. "This is everything. Every scrap of paper with his name on it. Even the public records request you made. I read it. You didn't ask for all of the records with the exact right language."

Talon crossed her arms. "I bet I did. But again, how can I know what's being hidden when it's, well," she gestured again at the box, "hidden?"

"Not my department, ma'am," Johnson replied. "You lawyer folk figure that out. I'm just producing the results."

Talon smirked at the 'ma'am'. She wasn't a fan of the tradition of women's salutations being divided into young and old, married and unmarried, etc. And she wasn't that old. But Lt. Johnson seemed to mean the term with genuine respect, even as he was unaware of its troublesomeness.

"Thanks for the results, Lieutenant," she said.

"Do you want me to carry it back to your office?" he offered.

"Is it really that heavy?" she asked.

Avery thought about it for a moment, then looked at Talon. "I bet you can manage it."

Talon smirked again. "I bet you're right."

* * *

It was official: Todd Dickerson was a jerk. Hardly a surprise to Talon. In her estimation, anybody who actually wanted to be a cop should automatically be disqualified from becoming one. What kind of person wants to exert that kind of physical control over another human being? But Dickerson was a cop's cop. A jerk's jerk. He butted heads with command staff and routinely got in trouble for things like turning in his reports after his shift—an overtime violation—because he wanted to use every minute he was on the clock 'chasing the bad guys,' as he put it in one disciplinary interview.

But there were no sustained findings of excessive force, although there had been complaints. Then again, every cop got those. The judge wasn't going to let Talon smear Dickerson's reputation with unfounded accusations by criminals Dickerson had pushed a little too hard into the back of his patrol car. No prior incidents of shooting unarmed suspects either. Just a hard-charging, overconfident meathead of a cop.

And Talon Winter knew overconfident.

But there were nuggets. Small indications of incidents that might have been more than they seemed in the whitewashed language of an internal review. She hadn't been there during those investigations, of course, to ask Dickerson incisive questions about his conduct, in order to draw out anything that might help Luke Zlotnik. Which confirmed she needed to interview Dickerson. And now that she had his file, she could prepare to do that in the most effective way possible.

She opened her desk drawer and took out a selection of highlighters and page tabs. It was going to be a long night.

CHAPTER 27

Talon wasn't the only one who'd had a late night, it turned out, as she discovered when she arrived at her office the next morning and walked into a lobby full of police officers.

"What the hell is going on?" she demanded.

"Talon!" Hannah called out from behind her desk. "We were robbed."

Talon frowned. "Was anyone here? Or did it happen overnight?"

"Uh, overnight," Hannah answered.

"Then we were burglarized, not robbed," Talon corrected.

"Fine." Hannah crossed her arms. "*You* were burglarized."

"Me?" Talon's eyebrows shot up. "Just me?"

"Just you," Hannah confirmed, with a nod toward Talon's office.

"Oh, hell no." Talon pushed past the officers in the lobby to the one standing in her doorframe, camera pointing inside her office.

"Get out," she commanded, physically pulling the officer away from his task. "Do not take photographs of my office. I'm a criminal defense attorney. There's attorney-client privileged matters in there."

"Not unless they're on the floor," the photographer-officer replied. "With everything else."

Talon turned away from the officer to scan her office. The cop was right. Everything was on the floor. Books, papers, pens. Everything had been turned over and spilled out. But even in the mess, it didn't look like anything was actually missing. Certainly not anything a burglar would normally consider worth stealing, like computers or other electronics.

Talon's heart sank. The most valuable commodity in her line of work wasn't electronics. It was information.

She pushed the officer aside and kicked her way through the mess to her desk. To her computer.

"You can't go in there!" the officer protested. "It's a crime scene."

"The hell it is," Talon shot back. "I'm the alleged victim. It's not a crime scene unless I say it is."

"Uh," the officer rubbed the back of his neck, "I'm not sure it works that way."

"Yeah, well I am," Talon answered. She pointed to the framed diploma, hanging askew on the wall. "And I'm the one with the law degree. Now be quiet while I figure out whether whoever did this did anything more than make a mess for me to clean up."

The officer opened his mouth to reply, but then thought better of it. Instead he walked back toward the lobby, presumably for reinforcements.

Her computer was still on, which was worrisome in itself because she always turned it off when she went home at the end of the day.

Her password still worked, which meant they hadn't

changed it. They'd cribbed it somehow, or bypassed it.

Once her desktop appeared, it only took a few mouse clicks to confirm what she already knew. Everything on the Zlotnik case was gone. Every file, every photo, everything she'd had scanned and digitized before destroying the paper copies provided by the prosecutor. Plus, the things she had created and collected herself. All of her motions, all of her notes, and all of her materials about and from Dr. Natalie Ross, Ph.D.

They had it all.

And they wanted her to know it.

She raised her head and did another scan of the office. The one thing missing was the one thing so new she hadn't gotten used to it being in her office. The box of documents from Lt. Johnson. It was definitely gone. Everything from the Zlotnik case was gone.

"Excuse me, miss." It was one of the officers from the lobby. He had stripes on his sleeves, and the photographer officer peering over his shoulder. "Officer Greene says you entered the crime scene without permission."

"No crime here, Sergeant." Talon masked her thoughts with a smile. "Certainly nothing I want the police to investigate. Just a very messy office that I'll spend the day cleaning up. My receptionist seems to have overreacted."

The sergeant frowned, eyebrows furrowing. "Are you sure, miss?"

"I'm sure," Talon confirmed. "And don't call me 'miss'."

CHAPTER 28

"Wait, I'm confused," Cecilia Thompson said after Talon explained why she had come to the prosecutor's office unannounced. "Was your office burglarized or not?"

Talon sighed. "It's complicated. I just need replacement copies of the police reports you provided. And maybe a phone call to Martin Fassbinder, to let him know it's okay for him to give me another copy of Dickerson's file."

Cecilia thought for several seconds, then leaned back in her chair and crossed her arms. "No."

"No?" Talon was taken aback. "No, you won't call Fassbinder?"

"No, I won't call Fassbinder," Cecilia confirmed. "And, no, I won't give you new copies of the police reports."

"I can understand you not wanting to vouch for me with Fassbinder," Talon conceded, "but you have to give me new copies of the police reports."

"Not if you lost them," Cecilia returned, her arms still crossed. "That's not my fault."

"I didn't lose them," Talon answered through gritted teeth.

"Were they stolen?" Cecilia asked. "If they were stolen, you should call the police."

"I can't call the police," Talon said. "You know that. And you know why."

"I know nothing of the sort," Cecilia insisted. "It's not my fault you're paranoid."

"When they're really after you," Talon replied, "paranoid is just smart thinking."

"No one is after you, Talon," Cecilia scoffed. "Least of all the police."

"Most of all the police," Talon asserted. "First my car, now my office. What's next?"

"Then report it," Cecilia said.

"To who?" Talon threw her arms wide.

"The police," Cecilia answered.

"Right," Talon said. "So, you see my problem."

Cecilia uncrossed her arms. "No, Talon, I don't. This is serious. You don't have to handle it by yourself. But you have to make it official."

"And let the cops investigate themselves?" Talon posited. "Let them into my office, onto my computer, into my car, all so they can say they just can't quite figure out how to solve the case, 'Gosh, sorry, miss or ma'am'? No, thanks. They can't help me."

"Then I can't help you," Cecilia answered.

Talon just stared at Cecilia, then shook her head.

"I understand you don't want to believe any of your cops would have done this," Talon said. "I can even understand why you won't call Fassbinder to help me get copies of reports I was able to get behind your back. But I don't understand why you won't at least give me a replacement copy of what you already provided."

"If you don't understand that," Cecilia responded, "then

you don't understand my job."

"Or I do understand it," Talon countered. "And so do you. But you just don't care anymore."

CHAPTER 29

It was going to take a while to reconstruct what had been taken. The easiest was the stuff from Dr. Ross regarding the false confession. That took a single email and the good doctor resent everything she had already provided, including her expert report about why she believed Luke's confession was coerced and false.

Talon filed a motion to compel Cecilia to provide replacement copies of the police reports and had scheduled it for five days later, the minimum notice required under the court rules. Talon knew she would win that—and so did Cecilia. Even if Talon had just lost the materials, the judge wasn't going to punish the defendant for that. Not when it was so easy for the prosecutor's office to just make another copy. Although she would probably have to pay copying costs. And provide her own disks.

Dickerson's personnel box was going to be more difficult, it seemed. Fassbinder was simply ignoring her calls and emails. She'd left more than several, but received back not so much as an 'out of office' autoreply from the police department's legal advisor. No wonder a cop had delivered it personally. No wonder he'd offered to carry it to her specific office.

Luckily, Talon wasn't the only one trying to scrape up dirt on Todd Dickerson. Talon had been too busy to really keep tabs on what Olsen was doing, but after her failure of a meeting with Cecilia, Talon had checked in with Hannah to review Greg's calendar.

He had a 'Hearing on Plaintiff's Motion to Compel Deposition of Defendant' scheduled at the same time as a 'Hearing on Defendant's Motion to Suspend Discovery.'

"Perfect," Talon said.

"Perfect?" Hannah questioned. "That sounds incredibly dull."

Talon grinned. "Yeah. Let's see if I can't liven it up a little."

* * *

As it turned out, no, Talon could not liven it up.

Talon had almost forgotten how boring civil law was, even the stuff they called 'litigation.' She'd realized, after she switched to criminal, that the civil attorneys called it 'litigation' instead of 'trial work' because they never went to trial. Not real trials. Not juries and exhibits and lives in the balance. Instead, they 'litigated', and mostly lengthy motions about what information they could or could not pry out of the other side's hands before finally reaching some settlement that cost both sides a lot of money but made the lawyers a little richer.

But even if he wasn't a trial lawyer, Talon still liked Greg Olsen as a person, and she had a personal professional interest in the litigation she had gifted him, so she made her way to the courthouse and snuck into the back of the courtroom he was appearing in to see if he could perhaps accomplish what had eluded her to that point, namely an interview of Todd Dickerson.

The hearing had already started, but no one else was in the courtroom save the lawyers, so when she opened the door at the back of the courtroom, everyone took a moment to look back at her, even the judge. He was one of the old guard, Judge Hightower, an elderly African American man who'd taken the bench well before Talon had even graduated from law school. Talon hadn't appeared before him yet as a criminal defense attorney because he'd been in the civil rotation for a while, but she recalled arguing a few 'litigation' motions in front of him back in the day. She wondered if he remembered her. If so, he didn't show it when he glanced at her entrance, then sniffed at it, and returned his bespectacled gaze to the lawyers actually before him.

"As I was saying," Olsen resumed, "there is no reason to delay discovery in this case. My clients are eager to proceed, and the next step is formal discovery. We intend to serve a full set of interrogatories on the defendant's counsel, together with demands for productions and requests for admission. We expect counsel for Officer Dickerson to do the same. After the documentary phase of discovery is complete, we intend to depose Officer Dickerson, but as the Court can understand, we do not want to conduct that deposition until after the written discovery has been fully exchanged. That's what makes it so important to allow discovery to proceed forward. There is much to be done, and an order for it to be done in. We need to get started."

Judge Hightower sniffed again at Olsen, then turned his white-haired head ever so slowly to the opposing lawyer. "And you want me to halt all discovery, is that right, Mr. Nargle?"

"That is correct, Your Honor." Nargle stood to answer the judge's question even as Olsen sat down again. Nargle had a high-pitched, nasally voice, with thinning black hair and slight frame. He wore a light-colored suit and caramel-colored shoes. "The incident which gave rise to this lawsuit also gave rise to a criminal matter, and specifically, a murder case. That case is still pending and my client, Officer Todd Dickerson, is the star witness for the prosecution. Forcing him to answer any questions, even in writing, let alone in a deposition, would have the potential, even likelihood, of prejudicing the results of that criminal trial. The Court should stay all discovery until the criminal trial is complete. The defendant in that criminal trial is not a party to this civil matter, so there would be no prejudice to him in that case by delaying discovery in this case."

Judge Hightower nodded and thought for several moments, before returning his attention to Olsen. "Any response, counsel?"

Olson stood again to address the Court. "Yes, Your Honor. The question is not whether there is any prejudice to a criminal defendant in another case. The question is whether there is any prejudice to the parties in this case. There is no prejudice to allowing us to proceed with discovery in the normal course, including the standard practice of deposing the opposing party, Officer Dickerson, after all other investigation has been completed. On the other hand, there is grave prejudice to my client, the Maldonados, to have to wait for their day in court to seek justice for the killing of their child."

"The prejudice to my client, Your Honor," Nargle stood up and interjected, "is having to discuss a terrible and tragic incident, under oath, prior to giving testimony about that incident in open court in the murder trial of the person who was the accomplice to the Maldonados' son. If Mr. Olsen wants to know what Officer Dickerson is going to say about the incident under oath, then he should just wait until the criminal trial commences and sit in the gallery when Officer Dickerson is called by the prosecution."

"I might, Your Honor," Olsen replied, "if I were allowed to

ask questions in the criminal trial. But somehow," he glanced back at Talon momentarily, "I doubt that will be permitted."

Judge Hightower was a quiet man, but that sometimes led to the attorneys getting out of hand and not waiting their designated turns to speak.

"If Mr. Olsen is going to get to depose Officer Dickerson before the criminal trial," Nargle sniped, "then I would want an order allowing me to depose the criminal defendant, uh, Marcus Zollnick, I believe his name is."

Talon stood up. "Lucas Zlotnik," she corrected from the gallery. "My client's name is Lucas Zlotnik."

Judge Hightower raised his gaze again at Talon and smiled. "Ms. Winter. Nice to see you again. I hear you're in a new line of work."

Talon stepped into the walkway and approached the front of the courtroom. "That I am, Your Honor. I'm finding it both challenging and rewarding."

"We can't ask for more than that," Judge Hightower replied. "You represent the man accused of murder out of this incident?"

"I do, Your Honor," Talon confirmed. "Lucas Zlotnik. The State has charged him with aggravated first degree murder for waiting in a car in a parking lot while his friend went inside a store and was shot to death by Mr. Nargle's client."

"Now, wait a minute," Nargle protested. "This is highly unusual. I object to this lawyer addressing the Court on a case she is not a party to."

"You want to interview her client?" Judge Hightower asked rhetorically. "Then she's party enough for me."

He frowned slightly and nodded at Talon. "Is there any way you would let your client be deposed by Mr. Nargle prior to the trial?"

Talon and Hightower both knew what her answer would be. "There is absolutely no way at all I would ever allow that, Your Honor."

Hightower's frown curled into a knowing smile. "I suspected as much. When is the trial?"

"It is fast approaching, Your Honor," Talon answered. "Although I have some discovery issues of my own which have recently popped up."

The judge raised a curious eyebrow at that, but knew better than to open another can of worms just then. Instead, he asked, "Do you expect Officer Dickerson to testify at the trial?"

"He has to, Your Honor," Talon answered. "Every other witness to what happened inside is dead. Thanks to Officer Dickerson."

"I will not stand here and permit my client to be maligned like this!" Nargle squeaked.

"You will stand where I tell you to stand and permit whatever I permit to happen," Judge Hightower boomed down at him. "Is that understood?"

Nargle visibly wilted. "Yes, Your Honor."

"Good," Hightower boomed again. "Now sit down, be quiet, and let me grant your motion. I agree that it would be unfair to allow depositions of one witness to this incident without allowing depositions of all witnesses to this incident. Mr. Zlotnik has an absolute right to remain silent, and the choice whether to testify is one he will make with his attorney, Ms. Winter. It will not be made by this Court. That being the situation, I will grant Mr. Nargle's motion to halt any further discovery on this case until such time as the criminal case against Mr. Zlotnik has concluded."

"What if he's convicted, Your Honor, and appeals?" Olsen asked. "Will discovery still be stayed pending any appeals in the event that Mr. Zlotnik is successful and gets a new trial? That could take years."

Hightower chewed his cheek for a moment as he considered that wrinkle. He nodded at Talon. "Ms. Winter? What say you to that?"

Talon smiled. "I'll tell you what, Your Honor. Why don't I make it easy on everyone? I'll just go ahead and win the trial."

CHAPTER 30

It was the end of the workday before Olsen finally came to Talon's office to comment on her performance in court.

"You seem very confident," he said, leaning against her doorframe. "I can't tell if it's an act."

"If you can't tell, then it doesn't matter if it's act," Talon responded, looking up from the papers on her desk. She had a red pen in her hand. "Ninety percent of what we do is bluster and mind games. If you think that I really think I might win, you start to wonder why I think that and if maybe I'm not right."

"So, do you really think you'll win?" Olsen asked.

Talon smiled and shook her head slightly. "Really, it doesn't matter."

"It matters if I can't proceed with my case for years while your case is tied up in appeals," Olsen pointed out. "I thought we were in this together. You didn't exactly help me out today."

Talon's eyebrows knitted together, and she tilted her head to the side. "We're not in this together. That's ridiculous. Why would you think that?"

Olson surrendered a surprised laugh. "Oh, I don't know.

Maybe because you crafted my case out of thin air. You recruited the family to sue, then you recruited me to take the case. And you put Curt on both cases to make sure you always knew what was happening on both cases."

"Don't forget Hannah," Talon answered. "She showed me your schedule."

Olson nodded. "Right. See? That. All that. Clearly, we're all working on this together."

"Oh, no, no, no." Talon shook her head and waved the suggestion away. "I'm monitoring everyone else so I can get the best possible result for my own case. I represent Luke Zlotnik, not the Maldonados or anyone else." She paused. "I thought that was obvious."

"It was sure obvious today," Olsen laughed darkly. "I think Hightower would have let me depose Dickerson if you would have made your guy available."

Another surprised expression from Talon. "That's ludicrous. You don't make a criminal defendant available for a deposition. And certainly not by some lawyer representing the cop who's trying to put him away for life. No defense attorney would do that. I'd lose my license."

"Why?" Olsen challenged. "He already talked once, right?"

"He gave a false confession," Talon expounded. "And that's already one statement too many. I had to hire an expert to try to explain that one away. I can't afford a second expert to explain away his deposition. Hell, I can't even really afford just the one."

"What's to explain away?" Olsen pressed. "Just tell the truth. If he tells the truth in the deposition and tells the truth again when he testifies, then the story will stay the same."

Talon just stared at Olsen for several seconds. "He's not going to testify at the trial. Are you insane?"

"He's not going to testify?" Olson eyebrows lifted. "Why not?"

"Why would he?" Talon returned. "He has the right to remain silent. The judge will tell the jurors they can't use it against him if he doesn't testify."

"They will," Olsen posited.

"They aren't supposed to," Talon insisted. "But they will definitely use it against him if he testifies and the prosecutor shreds him on the stand. It's never pretty when a seasoned prosecutor dissects an inexperienced defendant. But with a full confession in hand, it'll be a bloodbath."

"So, if he's not going to testify," Olsen asked, "what are you going to do?"

Talon gestured at her cluttered desktop. "This. I'm going to go after everyone and everything else. This case isn't really about Luke. It's about Dickerson. It's about what happened inside that check-mart, not what happened out in the parking lot."

Olsen nodded at the papers. "What is all that then?"

"This is all the discovery motions I've filed already or am about to file," Talon explained. "They're hiding everything from me, but I'm going to get it anyway."

She picked up the pleadings in turn. "Motion to compel interview of Officer Todd Dickerson. Motion to compel deposition of Officer Todd Dickerson. Motion to produce personnel file of Officer Todd Dickerson—again. Motion to provide police reports—again. Motion to allow independent examination of ballistic evidence. Motion to release ballistic evidence to defense expert. Motion to appoint defense ballistics expert at public expense. Motion, motion, motion, motion."

"Wow." Olsen nodded approvingly. "Are you going to win any of them?"

Talon cocked her head at him again. "I'm going to win all of them."

Olson laughed. "Of course. Right. I forgot." Then, "Do you really believe that?"

"I already told you." Talon smiled. "It doesn't matter."

But it kind of did.

CHAPTER 31

Talon was right: trial was fast approaching. And she had a lot of information still to get if she was going to be as prepared as she needed to be to save Luke Zlotnik's life. As a result, she requested, and the court administrator granted, her request to have all of her various discovery motions scheduled for the same day in front of the same judge. Even better, they were set in front of Judge Gainsborough. If anyone would understand how important her motions were, it was a career public defender turned judge.

But Luke didn't understand any of that. He just looked scared when the guards brought him into the courtroom for the hearing. Scared and thin. Sickly, almost.

"Are you okay?" Talon asked as her client sat down next to her. The guards unfastened the handcuffs, but kept the leg chains on his ankles, lest he think about making a run for it. "Are they feeding you enough?"

Luke shrugged. "The food's not very good," he replied dully. Then, "What are we doing today? It's not the trial, right?"

"No, it's not the trial," Talon confirmed. "If it were the trial, they would have dressed you out in street clothes. The jury can't see you in your jail garb. Otherwise they might think the judge thinks you're guilty."

"Doesn't he?" Luke asked. "Doesn't everybody?"

"I don't," Talon reassured him. "And I don't think this judge necessarily does either. They're just doing their jobs."

"Like you, right?" Luke questioned.

Talon didn't answer immediately. Instead, she repeated her first question. "Are you okay?"

"No, I don't think so," Luke admitted. "I'm going to go to prison for the rest of my life for something I didn't do. And now I'm in court again, but I don't really understand what's going on. It's just another hearing about lawyer stuff. You fight them so you can get ready to fight them again later. And at the end of it all, I'm just gonna get convicted anyway. So, what's the point?"

Talon took another moment before responding. She'd been so focused on the legal aspect of the case, she'd neglected the human part. It wasn't really her strong suit. The best thing she could do for the human client was win the legal case. Still, she needed Luke on board, if only for the optics. The jury needed to see him look appropriately worried, but not despondent.

"The point," she put her hand on Luke's shoulder, "is that you didn't do anything wrong. You gave a ride to your friend. That's all. And now two people are dead, and The System wants to blame you instead of the person really responsible. The point is, you're only eighteen years old. You have seventy or eighty years left on this planet. Years to get a job, meet someone, have babies, travel and learn and grow, eat and drink and smoke, watch sunsets and stay up all night to see the sunrise. The point is, you don't go down without a fight. *I* don't go down without a fight. We're going to fight these bastards, and we're going to win. And you're going to meet that someone, and you're going to have that baby, and someday you're going to watch a sunset with them and think back on how close you came to losing everything, but didn't. Because you chose to fight. Because you chose to win."

Luke just looked at her for several seconds, his face trying to hide the thoughts behind his widening eyes. Finally, he released a nervous laugh and shook his head. "Shit. You're good. You gonna do that to the jury for me?"

Talon let out a sigh and grinned. "Damn right I am. But first I'm gonna do it to this judge."

"All rise!" Judge Gainsborough's clerk called out as the judge emerged from his chambers. "The Pierce County Superior Court is now in session, The Honorable Bryan Gainsborough presiding."

Talon nodded. "Here we go," she said. Partly to Luke, but mostly to herself.

Gainsborough took a moment to size up the courtroom. The lawyers, the defendant, the guards, the otherwise empty gallery. He nodded to himself, then sighed. "Okay, everyone. We have a lot to go through. Normally, I would let the parties decide the order the motions are heard, but I think it will be more efficient if I set the order. Are there any objections to that procedure?"

Talon thought for a moment, then shook her head. "No objection from the defense, Your Honor."

Cecilia echoed her agreement. "No objection from the State, Your Honor."

Another audible exhale from the bench, but one that sounded more of relief than concern. "Okay, good. Let's start with the motion for the State to provide replacement copies of the discovery stolen from Ms. Winter's office. That seems the most straightforward of the—"

"The State will concede that motion," Cecilia interrupted. "In fact," she gestured to a document box sitting on a chair behind her. "I've brought the new copies with me to court today. Ms. Winter can have them as soon as the hearing is over."

"Or now," Talon suggested with a snarl.

"Or now." Cecilia forced a smile. "They are here for the taking."

Talon looked at Judge Gainsborough for approval, who gave it in the form of a short nod. She walked over and retrieved the box, dropping it on the defense table a little louder than necessary.

She was tempted to make a scene out of why a formal motion had been necessary in the first place. Why Cecilia couldn't have just given her the damn box of reports when she'd first asked for it. But there was no advantage to wasting time on it. She'd won, and judges hated listening to whiny complaints and veiled personal attacks, especially when there was no point anymore.

Instead, she simply looked up to Judge Gainsborough and inquired, "Next motion, Your Honor?"

Gainsborough nodded. "The next logical motion, I believe, is the motion for the State to produce a new copy of the personnel records of Officer Dickerson which were provided directly to Ms. Winter by the police department."

Talon looked over at the prosecution side for another box of records, but there was none.

"I'm going to deny that motion," Judge Gainsborough announced.

"What?" Talon blurted out. "Without any argument?"

Gainsborough let the outburst pass. "You can make your argument, counsel, but I'm trying to be efficient here. You didn't get the records from the prosecutor's office. You got them from the police department."

"And had them stolen back by that same police department," Talon asserted.

Gainsborough frowned. "I don't know about that. But I do know I can't order the prosecutor to provide you something she herself never had possession of. You need to address your request to the police department."

"I've tried, Your Honor," Talon explained. "They won't answer my calls."

Gainsborough nodded. "I'm not surprised. But I'm also not in any position to force them to do something that a previous judge ordered they didn't have to do. I'm not sure how you managed to convince them to provide the records despite Judge Kirshner's ruling, but whatever you did, you're going to have to do it again. I don't have the authority to order the production of those records. At least not on the record before me. And certainly not from the prosecutor's office. The motion is denied."

Talon suppressed another outburst. She had expected that particular request to be the most difficult of her motions. She didn't expect Gainsborough to make a finding that the Tacoma Police Department had burglarized her law office, but she had hoped the judge might set up some sort of structure to get the records eventually. Require the prosecutor to ask for the records, then set a hearing if they were not produced, and require Fassbinder to appear personally to explain why he couldn't provide a second copy of records he was willing to part with only a few weeks earlier. But no such luck. She was going to have to figure out a new way to threaten Fassbinder. She'd think of something.

"The next motions I'd like to address," Judge Gainsborough powered on, "are the motions to compel a witness interview or a deposition of Officer Dickerson. Ms. Winter, I'm a bit confused as to why you've filed both of these motions. Usually, depositions are only ordered in criminal cases if the witness refuses to agree to an interview. Has that happened here? Has Officer Dickerson refused an interview?"

"All of my efforts on that front have been ignored, Your Honor," Talon answered. "I believe Officer Dickerson would very much like to avoid speaking with me about this incident."

"That's simply not true, Your Honor," Cecilia interjected. "In fact, it is my understanding that Officer Dickerson's personal attorney offered to allow his client to be deposed."

Talon cocked her head at Cecilia. Then she shook it and looked up to the judge. "Yes, Your Honor. Deposed by a different lawyer. And only if I allowed my client to also be deposed, notwithstanding the pending murder case and my client's constitutional right to remain silent."

Cecilia didn't look over at Talon during her reply. She simply kept her eyes on the judge and shrugged. "Sounds like standard negotiations to me, Your Honor. I'm sure they'll work something out."

"I'm not working anything out with Dickerson's civil defense attorney," Talon snapped. "I'm going to interview him as part of this criminal case. He's your star witness. I get to talk to him prior to trial."

Cecilia again didn't look over at Talon. She kept her eyes on the bench and shrugged again. "I'm not sure the case law supports that absolute of a position. The witness is entitled to certain considerations as well. Especially when he is facing potential liability in a related civil action, filed—coincidentally, I'm sure—by one of Ms. Talon's office mates."

Gainsborough's eyebrows lifted for that piece of information. "Is that accurate, Ms. Winter?"

"I referred an inquiry by the parents of my client's slain friend to another attorney who handles civil litigation," Talon responded carefully. "And yes, he and I share office space, along with four other attorneys. But nothing more than that, Your Honor."

"Enough more, Your Honor," Cecilia added, "that Ms. Winter went to the discovery hearing in the civil case to discuss her office partner deposing Officer Dickerson."

Gainsborough's other eyebrows raised. "Is that true?"

Talon twisted back a frown and nodded. "Yes, Your Honor," she admitted. "But I went only to observe. I may not be involved directly in that case, but I would obviously want a copy of any statement Officer Dickerson might make regarding this incident. Especially when," she finally turned it back on Cecilia, "the officer won't talk to me directly."

Gainsborough raised his hand at both attorneys to tell them to stop talking and let him think. After a few moments, he rubbed his chin and frowned. "This is more complicated than usual," he began. "The State's key witness is being sued for the same conduct he will testify about at trial. He is represented by counsel in the civil matter, who would understandably want to be involved in any interview or deposition. I don't think he can refuse to testify at the trial—or rather, he could, but the State's case would fail, and the criminal case would be dismissed. I doubt that's an outcome either Ms. Thompson or Officer Dickerson's attorney would want. So, I expect he will show up at trial, and he will testify under oath as to what happened that day. And when he does that, Ms. Winter, you will have the absolute right to cross examine him, under oath, on the record, and in front of the jury."

Talon's jaw would have dropped if she hadn't clenched it as Gainsborough began explaining his thought process.

"I'm entitled to interview witnesses *before* they testify, Your Honor," Talon protested. "It's part of being fully prepared and Mr. Zlotnik has a constitutional right, not just to an attorney, but to a prepared attorney."

But Gainsborough shrugged. "I'm not sure about that, Ms. Winter. I mean, I agree that your client has to the right to prepared counsel, but he doesn't have a right to perfectly prepared counsel. Perfection isn't the standard. It couldn't be. No attorney is perfect, not even you. I assume Officer Dickerson wrote a report about the incident, and I just ordered the State to provide you a second copy of that report. So, you won't be completely unprepared. If he testifies consistent with his report, then you'll be ready for that. If he changes his story, I feel confident you will point that out to the jury, to the benefit of your client."

Talon looked down at Luke to see if he was digesting what was happening. Luke might not have been a lawyer, but it was pretty obvious to anyone watching that she had just lost two motions in a row. And the ones she cared about.

She looked back up at the judge, aware of his decision, but still stung by it. "I take exception to Your Honor's ruling," was all she could think to say.

"I appreciate that, Ms. Winter," Judge Gainsborough replied evenly. "And I'm sure I would have, too, back when I was still doing your job. But I have a different job now. So, with that in mind, let's move on to your next set of motions. The ones regarding the ballistics evidence."

Talon suddenly had a very bad feeling in the pit of her stomach. She had expected to win every motion up to that point. But the combination of losing motions she thought she'd win and the judge grouping her next three motions together, rather than taking them one at a time, left her bracing for the worst.

The motions built on each other. First, the State's ballistics evidence should be examined by an independent (that is, defense) expert. Second, the evidence needed to be released by the police property room for that independent (defense) expert to do that examination. Third, somebody was going to have to pay that independent (defense) expert, and as her motion regarding the false confession expert had shown, it sure wasn't going to be Luke Zlotnik's family.

Instead, before Talon could even argue, the judge attacked the very basis of all three motions. "Why do you need to examine the ballistics evidence, Ms. Winter? I thought your defense was that your client didn't know what was going to happen inside. Isn't that why you needed public defense money to hire a false confession expert?"

Ah, Talon thought. *He's still upset about ordering public money to benefit a private client.* And here she was again, asking for more of that money.

"That is our defense, Your Honor," Talon acknowledged, "but what happened inside the check-mart is vitally important."

Gainsborough narrowed his eyes a little at her. "Vitally?" he questioned. "Why does it matter what happened inside? If your client didn't know it was a robbery, as you will argue, then he's not responsible for anything that happened inside. But if he did know, as Ms. Thompson will argue, then he's responsible for everything that happened inside, no matter who did the shooting. Don't you agree?"

"No, Your Honor, I don't agree," Talon answered. "First of all, I don't believe I'm required to put all of my defense eggs in one basket. I certainly will argue that Mr. Zlotnik did not know what his friend was going to do inside the check-mart, but as you yourself just pointed out, Ms. Thompson is going to argue that he did. In the unfortunate event that the jury chooses to believe Ms. Thompson, then I am entitled to present another defense, for which the ballistics are exceedingly important."

"Vitally important," Judge Gainsborough reminded her.

"Yes, Your Honor." Talon nodded.

"And what is this other defense?" Judge Gainsborough inquired, "for which ballistics are so exceedingly, vitally important?"

Talon stood up a little straighter as she presented her fallback theory. "Intervening actor, Your Honor. Officer Dickerson may have been responding to a robbery, but if he shot the people inside the check-mart for reasons unrelated to stopping the crime, then the deaths did not occur 'in the course of' the robbery, as required by the felony murder statute. Officer Dickerson would be an intervening actor, and his actions would be superseding events which break the chain of proximate cause between my client and the deaths."

Judge Gainsborough's eyebrows knitted together. He leaned forward. "And just what sort of reasons are you suggesting, Ms. Winter, that would be unrelated to stopping the robbery?"

Talon needed to keep some of her powder dry. "That's why I need to interview Officer Dickerson prior to the trial, Your Honor. That's why I need to see his personnel file for more than one night before it's stolen from me. That's why I need Your Honor to grant at least one of my motions today, so I can show that the deaths that occurred that day lay at the feet of a trained law enforcement officer, not at the feet an eighteen-year-old civilian who was just waiting for his friend to cash a check."

"Are you suggesting Officer Dickerson intentionally murdered the two victims?" Cecilia practically gasped.

"Why not?" Talon returned. "You're suggesting my client did, and it wasn't his gun, or his bullets, that did the deed."

"Your Honor, this is outrageous!" Cecilia complained to the judge. "The Court can't allow this sort of allegation to go unanswered."

Gainsborough's perplexed expression remained, but he turned it from Talon to Cecilia. "I'm sure I'm not the one to answer that sort of allegation. I'm sure you will address it appropriately, at the time, to the people who matter. But right now, it's not my job to defend anyone's honor. Not the officer's. Not the defendant's. My job is to rule on the motions brought before me according to the law and to the best of my ability."

The judge tuned back to Talon. He sighed again. The sigh of a mentor, perhaps. Or a father. An old man who thought he knew more than her and was disappointed she didn't agree.

"Ms. Winter," he began what was obviously going to be a speech. "As I said, I have a job now, and it's not to help out one side or the other. But I used to have your job. I used to stand next to people accused of crimes, accused of doing the worst things human beings do to each other. I used to fight every fight and battle every battle. Sometimes I won, but most of the times I lost. Sometimes I lost because my clients were guilty and there was just too much evidence. Sometimes I lost because my clients were innocent, but the evidence seemed to show something it shouldn't have. But most of the time, I lost because juries trust the system, and they trust the prosecutors, and they trust the police. They don't want to believe they live in a society where innocent people are charged with crimes, and they put two and two together when elected prosecutors and elected judges make the decisions about what to do with high-profile cases, especially cases where the victim is one of those police officers they trust. They want to trust. They need to trust, to keep believing we live in the fair and just society they want to live in."

He gestured a loose hand at Talon, not a pointing finger exactly, but reminiscent of one. "Your best defense in this case is to convince the jury that your client didn't know what his friend was going to do. In order to do that, you're going to have to impugn the honor of the officers who took his confession. That is going to be a steep enough hill to climb. But if you add to that an accusation that the responding officer was a homicidal maniac rather than the heroic first responder Ms. Thompson is going to paint him as, then I can guarantee you will lose the jury, and they will not listen to a word you say. And your client will become another of a long list of clients who will be convicted despite what you believed were your very best efforts.

"So, I am not going to release the ballistics evidence in this case to a defense expert. I am not going to appoint a defense ballistics expert. And I am definitely not raiding the public defense coffers again for an endeavor worse than quixotic."

Talon stood motionless before the judge, her enraged expression doing the talking for her.

"You may not agree with my rulings today, Ms. Winter," Judge Gainsborough offered, "but if you follow where they lead, you may well thank me for them after the jury renders its verdict."

Talon doubted that very much. She wasn't about to take someone else's advice on how best to defend her case, and certainly not from some know-it-all judge who was trying to force her to try the case the way he would have done it, years ago, before he'd quit the game, given up the glory of being a player for the power of being a referee.

"Don't count on it," she finally said, before adding, just barely, the obligatory but definitely not heartfelt, "Your Honor."

And that was that. The hearing was over. Cecilia started packing up her stuff. Gainsborough left the bench. Talon had lost every motion. Every motion that mattered. She dropped into her chair, staring ahead blankly.

After several seconds, Luke leaned over to her. "How bad is it?"

Talon swiveled her head to him. There was no point in lying. "It couldn't be worse."

CHAPTER 32

Talon couldn't leave it like that with Luke. She couldn't send him back to his cell to sit alone, waiting for the trial date, his last image of her being a wide-eyed, dropped jaw, 'I can't believe how bad we just got screwed' expression of disbelief and horror.

She pulled her files and books together. Then she pulled herself together. Then she went back to her office and pulled Curt from his office so they could go to the jail together. She needed a witness. And, if she was honest with herself, a little support.

Talon couldn't tell if Luke looked any worse than the last time she'd seen him inside the jail. There was something about fluorescent lights and whitewashed cinderblock walls that could make anyone look sickly. But she knew he didn't look any better.

"How are you holding up?" she started, once she, Luke, and Curt were alone in the consultation room.

Luke just shrugged. "I dunno. It doesn't matter anyway. We just lost all those motions you said were important. So, I guess now the only thing left is to lose in the trial. Everybody in here was right. It doesn't matter that I'm innocent. Nobody cares."

"I care," Talon assured him.

Another shrug. "You get paid to care."

Talon half-smiled at that. "Not really. Your parents couldn't really afford my retainer. I haven't been paid even half of what this case is worth, considering how much work I have to do."

"And I haven't been paid at all," Curt pointed out.

Talon confirmed that with a nod. "I'm not gonna blow smoke up your ass, Luke," she told him. "I don't care the way you care, or the way your parents care. And yeah, I get paid to do this job. But I do it because I care about people like you. People getting railroaded because more powerful people need a conviction. If the jury says 'guilty', they will have forgotten about you before the ink dries on the headline they were chasing. But you? No, it's real for you. If they say 'guilty', then you're going away forever. That's not right. And I care about that, no matter how much I do or don't get paid."

Luke thought for a moment. "Good for you, I guess. But it doesn't seem to matter. You just lost all those motions. We're screwed, right? Maybe my parents should just save their money and let me get convicted."

"Your parents would spend every cent they have if it meant you get out of jail again," Talon said.

Luke cocked his head at that, and for the first time in a long time, Talon saw a small spark in his eye.

"Maybe that's what they should use the money for," he said. "To get me out of jail."

"They're trying," Curt put in. "That's why they hired Talon."

"No, no." Luke shook his head. "I don't mean pay a lawyer to get me off. I mean pay a bail bond company to get me out. What's my bail again?"

"Two million," Talon answered. "I'm confident your parents

don't have two million dollars."

"But they only need ten percent, right?" Luke's face lit up. "So, what's that, like twenty thousand, right?"

"Two hundred thousand," Talon corrected. "That's still a lot of money. And they don't get it back. A rich guy posts two million, he gets it all back, so long as he goes to court every day. But if a poor guy needs to borrow it from a bail bond company, he pays ten percent to them and never gets that back. The bail bond company posts the two million for him, and then they get it back when the case is over. That two hundred grand is free money for them."

"Unless I take off," Luke suggested, a smile creeping onto his face for the first time Talon could remember.

"Even then," Talon answered. "That's what bounty hunters are. They work for bail bond companies and they're authorized to hunt you down and arrest you. They turn you over to the authorities and the bond company gets their two mil back."

"Unless they can't find me," Luke persisted.

"They'll find you," Talon assured him. "Most of them are national companies. They have offices, and bounty hunters, in every state."

"What about Canada?" Luke proposed. "One of the guys in here, he said I should go to Canada."

Talon didn't have an immediate response. "Canada?"

"Yeah, Canada," Luke confirmed. "They can't extradite me from Canada, right?"

Talon laughed slightly. "If there's one country the U.S can extradite from, it's Canada. But…."

"But what?" Luke asked.

"Yeah," Curt joined in. "But what?"

Talon thought for a moment before she answered. She wanted to be careful. And she wanted to be right.

"Canada won't extradite you for felony murder," she realized. "They abolished felony murder years ago. And you can't extradite from one country to another unless both countries have the same crime."

Luke's face lit up. "So, it would work? If I can post bail, I just have to get to Canada? That's like, what, a three-hour drive?"

"Four, with traffic," Talon answered, but her mind wasn't really focused on the drive time.

"So, let's do that," Luke urged. "Tell my parents to stop paying you and figure out a way to post my bail. Then I drive to Canada and I'm free."

Talon frowned. "It's not that simple."

"Why not?" Luke asked. "Seems pretty simple to me."

Curt nodded. "It does seem pretty simple."

"They could still extradite you on the robbery," Talon explained.

"Can I get life in prison for robbery?" Luke asked.

Talon shook her head. "No. You'd be looking at eight to ten years. Maybe another five if Miguel really had a gun, but there's no evidence of that. So, yeah, eight to ten."

"And I'd get time off for good behavior, right?" Luke pressed.

Talon nodded again. "Yeah. One third. So, you'd really only serve like six or seven years. You'd be twenty-five when you got out."

Luke slapped the table. "Let's do that, then! Easy."

"Not easy," Talon said. "And not simple. It's way more complicated than that. Even if your parents could scrape up enough money to pay a bonding company."

"Why?" Luke demanded.

Talon sighed. She turned to her investigator. "Why don't

you go use the bathroom or something, Curt?"

"But I don't have to go to the bathroom," he protested.

"Irrelevant," Talon replied.

But Curt tipped his head to side. "I don't understand."

Talon rolled her eyes. "Do you want me to give you a nickel and tell you to go to the movies? Geez, just get out of the room. Tell the guard you have to pee. I don't need a witness for this."

"Oh." Curt nodded. "Got it."

He started to stand up, but Talon stopped him. "Actually, I do need a witness for this first part." She turned back to her client. "Luke, I cannot advise you to flee. Leaving the jurisdiction after posting bail is a felony and I can't advise you to commit a crime. I also can't advise you to violate the conditions of your release, which include appearing for every court date and accepting the judgment of the court, whatever that might end up being."

She turned back to Curt. "Okay, you can go now. And don't hurry."

Curt gave her a thumbs-up and a wink. "Number two. Got it."

Talon rolled her eyes again and waited while Curt exited the room and asked the guard for directions to the nearest bathroom. Once the door was closed again behind him, Talon looked across the jail table at Luke.

"I can't advise you to flee," she repeated, "but if you did, it would be smart."

"So, that's what we're gonna do?" Luke confirmed.

It was tempting. The chessboard had fallen over and all of Talon's pieces were on the floor. No, it was worse. The board was still very much in place, but Cecilia had captured all of her pieces. It was tempting to grab the board and throw it across the room.

But Talon shook her head. "No, Luke. It's not going to

happen."

"Why not?" Luke asked.

"Because your parents don't have two hundred thousand dollars," Talon answered. "And even if they did, the bonding company would want them to put up everything else they own as collateral, in case you took off. Because, Luke?"

"Yeah?"

"Everyone knows you're gonna take off, Luke," she explained. "Even the jailhouse lawyers in here are giving you that advice. That's why your bail is so high. And no bonding company is going to risk two million dollars on you. Not when you can drive to Canada in an afternoon. Everybody knows that's the smart play here. And that's why you're stuck in here."

Luke's expression dropped. "But if I can't run, what am I going to do?'

"Fight," Talon answered. "Those are two options, right? Fight or flight. And you can't flee. So, you have to fight."

Luke dropped his eyes to the floor. "But I'm gonna lose."

Talon wasn't allowed to promise a specific result. It was against the ethical rules. And it was also against reality. No one could guarantee what a jury would do. But she needed Luke on board. She needed him to have some hope, other than a pipe dream of a road trip across the northern border. And there were no witnesses.

She reached across the table and took his hand. "No. We're going to win. I promise."

CHAPTER 33

There weren't supposed to be surprises in chess. Not for the master. Not for the winner. The other side was supposed to be surprised when everything the master expected to happen unfolded. But Talon had been surprised. And she wasn't finished being surprised.

Some surprises were good, like when a new client burst through the door wanting to hire you. Some surprises were bad, like when the judge denied all of your motions to compel the discovery you needed to properly defend your client. And some surprises were just, well, surprising.

"Lieutenant Johnson from the Tacoma Police Department is here to see you."

Talon just stared at the speaker on her desk phone, unsure if she'd heard Hannah correctly.

"Lieutenant Johnson? Are you sure?"

Talon could hear Hannah ask the visitor his name again, and the response. "Yep," Hannah said. "Lieutenant Johnson. He has another delivery for you."

Talon wondered why the Lieutenant had stopped by

unannounced. And she tried to keep herself from hoping that delivery was what she hoped it was. "I'll be right there."

She stood up from her desk and made her way out to the lobby, adopting a tough, 'this had better be worth it' expression and gait. But when she reached the lobby, it was clear it was very much worth it.

Lieutenant Johnson raised up another heavy-looking box of papers. "I heard you lost the first copy," he said, his biceps straining against the weight of the box. "I brought you a replacement."

Talon was pleased. Grateful, even, But suspicious.

"Did Fassbinder send you?" She crossed her arms. "Or Thompson? Who sent you?"

Johnson lowered the box again and smiled slightly. "I sent myself, ma'am. I heard what happened. Or at least the result of it. You lost the papers I delivered to you. But my job was to make sure you got those documents. If that means I have to bring you a replacement, well, I don't mind a field trip. It's good for an old man to get out."

Johnson looked to be in his early fifties and fit. He was hardly old, and he certainly didn't seem to need the exercise.

Talon nodded at the box. "So, that's exactly what you brought me before?"

Johnson nodded. "Yes, ma'am. Page for page." He paused. "Actually, I think there might be something extra in it this time. Something the lawyers may not have known to include."

Talon narrowed her eyes. "I'm a lawyer, too, you know."

"I do know," Johnson confirmed. "And that's why it's included this time."

"What is it?" Talon asked.

But instead of answering, Lt. Johnson asked her, "Have you ever been to Birchwood?"

Talon took a moment, then shook her head. "Is that a bar?"

Johnson laughed politely. "No, ma'am. It's a town. Sleepy little place on your way up to White Pass. One gas station, two bars, and three cops."

"Sorry." Talon shrugged. "Never heard of it."

"Well, I'm not surprised," Johnson replied. "It's not really the kind of place you go to. It's more the kind of place you leave from. If you know what I mean."

Talon thought for a moment. "I don't think I do."

Johnson smiled, but more to himself than her. He set the box down on the floor. "Just so you know, Ms. Winter, not all cops like all other cops, at least not just because they're cops. One bad apple doesn't just ruin the barrel. It ruins the reputation of the barrel. And the reputation of all the other barrels too."

Talon took a beat. "Now, I definitely don't know what you mean," she said.

"I think you'll figure it out." Johnson smiled at her. "That's *your* reputation. I expect you'll live up to it.

CHAPTER 34

Talon wasn't entirely sure what her reputation really was, but she knew one thing: she wasn't a quitter. She wasn't just going to let Cecilia chase her few remaining pieces around the chessboard. Not when Johnson had given her a piece to move into play. If she could find it.

There were hundreds of pages in the replacement box, and Talon hadn't had time to study them all so that she could easily identify whatever had been added. But at the very end—and she was smart enough to check there first to see if anything had been added—she found a single piece of paper bearing the seal of The Town of Birchfield, Washington.

It was just a letter to Tacoma P.D. confirming that Dickerson had worked as a police officer in their three-officer department for approximately one year. The end date was shortly before Dickerson joined Tacoma P.D. The letter didn't include anything more than name, rank, and employment dates. It wasn't a letter of recommendation, just a verification of employment. And that was suspicious enough for Talon.

She still had a copy of the public records request she'd sent to Tacoma P.D. on her computer. The thieves hadn't deleted that. It was a small matter to change the name and address of the recipient, and the date range for the records. The ask was the same: Any and all records regarding Todd Dickerson, including but not limited to his personnel records and any investigation by internal affairs.

She gave the public records request to Hannah to file, then returned her attention to the replacement records. There wasn't much of use, but at least she had something. She might be able to bootstrap Dickerson's general zealousness into an itchy trigger finger, and his social media photos of a probable date with a white supremacist as a motive for shooting Miguel. She couldn't count on getting anything back from The Town of Birchfield prior to the commencement of trial. And if she did get a response, it was likely to be the same sort of blacked-out pages she'd received from Tacoma. She didn't let herself dare wish for better.

But when the envelope from Birchfield arrived just five business days later, and when she saw that it was a thick packet of papers, not a one-page denial of her request, she let herself feel a small glimmer of hope.

'Be careful what you wish for,' the saying went. 'You just might get it.'

I sure fucking hope so, Talon thought as she tore open the envelope.

She'd wished for another chess piece to attack with. Anything. A rook. Maybe a knight. Even a bishop.

What she got was a queen.

Across the top of the document, in all caps, were the words, 'INTERNAL AFFAIRS INVESTIGATION', followed by the summary:

Subject: Todd Dickerson
Rank: Police Officer

Allegation: Excessive Force, Racial Bias
Finding: Sustained

Talon's eyebrows shot up. Her heartbeat raced. Her mouth curled into a smile. "Sustained?" she repeated aloud, as if she herself couldn't believe it. She looked at the word again and nodded. "Sustained."

* * *

"So, what was the allegation?' Curt asked when she grabbed him from his office across the hall and dragged him into hers to tell him about the bombshell development from the sleepy little Town of Birchfield. "What did he do?'

"He beat the shit out of a Hispanic teenager," Talon smiled ear to ear despite the subject matter. "Some kid caught shoplifting at the only store in town. He was on his way over the pass to Yakima, when they stopped off for some snacks and to use the bathroom. The store owner thought he and his brother looked suspicious, so he called the cops. Well, the town is the size of my office, so the cops responded immediately. Dickerson was the only one on duty and he just went full police brutality on the kid. Put him in a choke hold, threw him to the ground, kicked him, punched him. He really fucked him up."

"Shit." Curt shook his head. "So, he's just a bad cop with a temper problem."

"No, he's a racist cop," Talon said, "with a Hispanic problem. The kid was American, but his parents were born in Guatemala. He had dark skin and was speaking Spanish with his brother. When Dickerson showed up, he just immediately put hands on the kid, then started yelling all these racial slurs. Called him a 'dirty Mexican'—which wasn't even the correct nationality. Called him a 'wetback', and told him to 'go back to Mexico and make tortillas.'"

"Tortillas?" Curt made a bemused expression.

"I know, right?" Talon agreed. "But it wasn't funny when it was punctuated with a boot to the face. The kid had to go the hospital. And then Dickerson booked him for shoplifting and resisting arrest."

"Did he get convicted?" Curt asked.

Talon shook her head. "He didn't even get charged. The store owner ratted Dickerson out. He called the chief of police and told him what really happened. I mean, even if he did try to steal a candy bar, he didn't deserve to get beat up and called racist names by a cop."

"Good for the store owner." Curt said.

"Definitely," Talon agreed. "But bad for Birchfield Police Officer Todd Dickerson. The chief made sure the kid was released with no charges filed. Then the mayor reached out to the family and offered to pay the kid's medical bills."

"That was nice of them," Curt observed.

But Talon shrugged it off. "I'm not sure about that. They just didn't want to get sued. The same way they didn't want to get sued by Dickerson. They told him to go find another job, but when Tacoma P.D. came asking about him, all they did was confirm his dates of employment. Nothing about why he'd been fired."

"Real brave," Curt huffed.

"Cops are weird," Talon said. "They're the first ones in on some of the most dangerous stuff that ever happens. Active shooters, you name it. But sometimes, when the brave thing to do is to call out a fellow officer—well, then, bravery can seem pretty scarce."

Curt thought for a moment, frowning. His expression lightened. "This is huge. Maybe the prosecutor will give you a deal now. There's no way she wants this to get out."

But Talon shook her head. "She's still not going to give me a deal. It's out of her hands. And anyway, she's convinced herself she's in the right. There's nothing more dangerous than a self-righteous prosecutor. Except maybe a know-it-all judge afraid to cross the prosecutor's office in an election year. Cecilia will just file another motion to suppress all this Birchwood stuff from the trial. And if we end up in front of Judge Gainsborough again, the motion will be granted."

"So, what are you going to do with it?" Curt asked.

"Nothing now," Talon answered with a grin. "Then everything."

CHAPTER 35

Lieutenant Johnson had given Talon a queen for her chessboard. But when it really came down to it, Talon wasn't playing chess. She wasn't playing checkers, or backgammon, or field hockey either. She was a lawyer, and she was trying as hard as she could not to play games with the life of her client.

'Trial is fast approaching' became 'Trial is tomorrow' fast enough. Faster than expected. But that's how it always was. The final days leading up to the start of the trial accelerated, each shorter than the last, with more to get done, until there was no time left for anything except that one last jail visit, the night before trial, to hold the client's hand and tell him to at least try to get some sleep. They had a big day tomorrow.

"You scared?" Talon asked Luke, her voice reverberating ever so slightly off the painted cinderblocks of the jailhouse meeting room walls. She was alone. This wasn't a conversation for Curt. This was the bond between an attorney and the person who had no choice but to put all of his faith in his attorney.

Luke hesitated, then nodded lightly. "Yeah," he admitted.

"Good," Talon said.

Luke looked incredulous. "Good that I'm scared?"

"Good that you told me the truth," Talon answered. "I already know you're scared. You'd have to be. You better be. But now I know something even more important. You're done lying to me. I know I can trust you. And that's going to be vital starting tomorrow morning."

"Oh." Luke nodded and looked down for several seconds. He looked up again at Talon. "Are you scared?" he asked her.

The truth was, Talon was scared. Scared of losing. Scared of failing him. Scared of a system driven by the whims of prosecutors, and dependent on the judgment of twelve random people who could never really understand the seriousness of the decision being put to them. Scared of not doing every last thing she could possibly do, as well as she could possibly do it, to save Luke from spending the rest of his life in prison.

Scared of losing.

But it wasn't chess. It wasn't a game.

It was a young man's life.

And it was all on her.

"No, I'm not scared," she lied. "I'm ready."

CHAPTER 36

In case Talon didn't fully understand that it wasn't all just a game, the point was made clear when she pulled out of her parking spot on South 9th Street to head down the hill from the jail to the waterfront, but instead of stopping at the red light at Tacoma Avenue, she blew right through it, her brakes failing completely.

She stomped on the brake pedal repeatedly, but only picked up speed as she barreled toward Fawcett, Market, and finally Pacific Avenue. Finally, because if she didn't figure out how to stop her car with the brake lines cut, she was going to hit the bottom of the hill and launch right into Commencement Bay.

The light at Fawcett was green, so she didn't have to worry about cross traffic, but the light at Market was definitely red, and she was definitely speeding toward it. The hill down to the waterfront wasn't quite San Francisco proportions, but it was close. Every second she wasn't slowing down was a second she was speeding up. And if she remembered her high school physics class right, her rate of acceleration was accelerating too.

The brake pedal was pressed to the floor, with no effect. The speedometer read 37 m.p.h. and increasing. And a minivan was making its way through the intersection directly ahead of her. Talon jerked at the wheel to swerve around the back of the crossing vehicle, her tires squealing and her heart in her throat.

She started honking her horn to warn the other drivers and pedestrians, but that wasn't going to slow her car down any. Ninth Street was actually a series of inclines between the flat sections of the cross streets. When she hit Broadway, literally, she was over 45 mph and bottomed out her car, slamming her against the seat and sending sparks flying. She had two blocks left before she shot across Fireman's Park and plummeted down the hill onto Dock Street and into the water below.

She reached down between the seats and pulled up as hard as she could on the emergency brake. It didn't stop the car—she was going too fast—but it slowed her down slightly, and locked her wheels, sending the back end of the car swerving. It didn't stop her, but it did give her an idea. Ninth went flat for a block between Pacific and the park, with a curve to the right onto A Street. It was her only chance.

The lights at Commerce and Pacific were green—small mercies—so she focused on getting her car to slow, even a little bit. She released the emergency brake, then pulled it up again just as she hit the flat out of Commerce. That slowed her a bit more than it had when she was headed directly downhill, but it didn't stop her. Not even close. She had one more chance.

She hit Pacific hard. The front of her car slammed into the four-lane road and she heard a pop from her front driver's-side tire. It took her a moment to regain herself enough to pull up again on the emergency brake and turn hard to the right. The car screeched into a moderately controlled spin, slowing as it tried to carry its forward momentum on tires locked sideways. As the car approached the end of Pacific and the start of the small patch of grass between her and the drop-off to the water, Talon released the emergency brake and pumped the gas pedal. Her wheels engaged and she was propelled in the direction the car was actually facing: down A Street.

'Street' was a generous label. It was much more of an alley. It was narrow and crowded, with street parking on either side, and telephone poles sticking out of the narrow sidewalk right next to the road. She pointed the car for the last telephone pole on the left, pulled the emergency brake up one more time, and braced for impact.

She hit the pole at about twenty miles an hour. Fast enough to rattle her bones and snap her head forward, but slow enough to finally stop the damned car. The front end was crumpled, but the telephone pole held.

Talon just sat there, slumped in the driver's seat, sweaty and panicked and breathless and relieved. After a minute, Talon raised her gaze and looked at the telephone pole that had saved her life. There was a sign bolted to it: '2-Hour Parking Only'.

She dropped her head again. "Tow me."

She wasn't moving her car. She was barely moving herself. But the adrenaline already in her bloodstream from the incident was joined by more, triggered by her realization that whoever had cut her brake lines could be coming up on her right then to finish the job. And she knew, whoever they were, they had a gun.

All cops had guns.

She undid her seatbelt, grabbed her briefcase, and pulled herself out of the car, a dozen questions competing for her attention.

Who did this?

Why?

When?

How did they know where I was?

It was that last one that won the competition. She looked at her car. They could have seen her car and run the plate. But cutting her brakes hadn't been a crime of opportunity. It was planned. They knew where she was and they came to her car, knowing she would be inside the jail for long enough to meet with her client—and to sabotage her car.

They knew where she was. And she knew how they knew.

She reached into her briefcase and pulled out her cell phone. She'd been doing criminal defense long enough to see the warrants cops used to be allowed to track a person's phone. With the right equipment—and they had the right equipment—they could narrow down a person's location to a particular room in a house. They weren't supposed to use the equipment without a warrant, but she felt pretty confident that anyone who was willing to cut her brake lines—and burglarize her office and trash her car—wasn't going to be worried about the niceties of the Fourth Amendment.

She tossed her phone on the floor of her car and locked the car door. She was going to have to walk, but at least they'd have to find her the old-fashioned way. Track her down on the street. Fortunately, it was getting dark and her condo was only a mile or so up the street.

The thought of calling the cops and hoping for actual help flashed momentarily through her mind, albeit uninvited. Maybe she could contact Lieutenant Johnson. He seemed like one of the good cops.

But no. She couldn't trust him.

Johnson was still a cop.

And all cops were johnsons.

CHAPTER 37

The quickest way to her condo was due north on Pacific Avenue until it turned into Ruston Way. On any other day, it would have been a beautiful walk, right along the water, with a view of the bay, Vashon Island, and the Kitsap Peninsula.

But it wasn't any other day.

It was night—almost—and Talon didn't care about having a view of anything. What she cared about was making sure no one had a view of her.

So instead of the quickest way—the predictable way—Talon walked three blocks back up the hill and turned north on St. Helens, then zigzagged her way through Tacoma's Stadium District, alternating her route between the main streets with corner stores and street lights and the side streets with tall trees and craftsman homes. Past the Landmark Theater, Stadium High School, and Annie Wright Academy, until she reached the far end of the Old Town neighborhood, where her condo was. She knew she needed to approach it from the rear. She just didn't know how she was going to get inside without going around front.

She hurried toward the back of the condo building and

confirmed what she was pretty sure she already knew. She'd never really had a reason to consider all of the entrances and exits to her building before, but examination of the exterior revealed only three options: the front door, which she was trying to avoid; a side service entrance, which she didn't have a key for; and an entrance through the underground garage, but the secure gate to the garage was down.

Talon took a moment to consider her options. She could stand near the side door and wait, hoping someone might exit through it. But she had no reason to believe that would happen, and she didn't like the idea of standing still for that long.

She could wait for someone to drive out of the garage and duck under the gate. That was more likely to happen than someone using the service door, but then she'd find herself in a poorly lit parking garage. Not exactly the definition of safe. If someone were waiting for her in the shadows, she wouldn't see them until it was too late.

That left the front door. They might be watching it, but they didn't seem to be guarding it. She peered around the corner from the far side of the building. There was no one near the door. If she moved quickly, maybe they wouldn't see her.

And if they did, well, then let them come. There was a reason she decided to go home instead of hiding out at some other, improvised location.

She hurried to the front door, her key extended. Insert, turn, pull, and she was inside. She pulled the door closed against the resistance of the slow-close mechanism attached to the top of the doorframe. When it latched, Talon felt her heart slow just a bit. She was almost safe.

The elevators were visible through the glass windows at the front door, so Talon headed for the stairs. Her unit was only on the second floor anyway. In a few moments, she pushed open the door from the stairwell and half-jogged to her door. Another quick flick of her keys and she was inside her condo. Tired, cold, alone, and scared. But armed.

She locked, bolted, and chained the door behind her, then proceeded directly to her bedroom. She pulled the gun safe out from under her bed and keyed in the combination. 9mm semiautomatic. Two full magazines. She positioned herself on the floor, seated, back against the wall, behind her bed with a view of the door. She slid one magazine into the handgun and placed the other on the floor next to her. Then she waited.

Talon wasn't convinced they would actually attack her in her own home. The brakes were proof they wanted it to look like an accident. If her car had crashed into the bay, they wouldn't have been likely to actually retrieve it, and if they had, the damage from the fall would have hidden what were likely very small punctures in her brake lines—enough to drain the brake fluid, but not as obvious as actually cutting them. An attack in her home would definitely not look like an accident.

Then again, it could look like just another unsolved murder. It depended on how desperate they were, and what their assessment of her readiness for them was.

She looked down at the pistol in her hand. She would take out at least one of them. They probably knew that. She hoped they knew that.

The next hour passed quietly enough. Silently, in fact. Save Talon's breathing in the empty, dark condo. The second hour was equally uneventful. By the time the third hour had almost passed, Talon was considering letting herself get some sleep. The adrenaline had drained away—most of it anyway—and she felt exhausted, both physically and mentally. She couldn't stay up all night. And she still had trial in the morning. They weren't going to stop her from trying the case.

She could lock her bedroom door, and sleep on the floor behind the bed, the gun within quick reach. She didn't need much sleep, but she was pretty sure she couldn't stay awake any longer either. She started to stand up. And that's when she heard it.

A noise. The only noise she'd heard for three hours.

Not the front door. The back door. The slider to her balcony. The loud click of the locking mechanism being released. Then the long, slow scuff of the slider being opened as quietly as possible.

Talon lowered herself back onto the floor. She raised the handgun, holding it with two hands, pointing it toward the bedroom door. Whoever it was would be backlit from the ambient light behind them. She'd see them before they saw her.

She listened for footsteps, bumping into unfamiliar furniture, anything that might give her an idea of where the intruder was. But there was no sound until suddenly the silhouette of a large man appeared in her hallway, heading straight for her bedroom.

Talon pulled the slide back to load a round into the chamber. At the sound of that noise, the intruder called out.

"Oh my God! Don't shoot! Talon? Is that you?"

Talon knew the voice.

"Curt?!" She lowered the gun. "Curt, is that you?"

"Yes," he confirmed in the darkness. His hands were raised over his head. "Don't shoot me."

"What are you doing here?" Talon demanded, her hands shaking from the new dump of adrenaline.

"I could ask you the same question," Curt responded.

Talon thought for a moment. "I live here."

"Right," Curt acknowledged. "I meant what are you doing

here in the dark with a gun pointed at me?"

"It's not pointed at you anymore," Talon said. She stood up, still holding the gun, but pointed down at her side. "How did you get in here? *Why* did you get in here?"

"Can I put my hands down now?" Curt asked.

"Yes, yes, of course," Talon answered impatiently. She strode over to the wall by the door and switched on the bedroom light. She squinted against the sudden brightness. "What are you doing here? How did you get inside?"

Curt squinted, too, and lowered his arms again. "I was looking for you," he explained. "You weren't answering your phone. I just wanted to check in and make sure you didn't need anything else before tomorrow morning."

"So, you broke into my house?"

"No," Curt said. Then, "Well, yeah. Obviously. But not at first. At first, I went over to the jail. I thought maybe you were still there. But you weren't. So, I headed down the hill to swing by your office. That's when I saw your car, parked all weird against that telephone pole. I stopped to check it out. One of your tires was flat and your phone was on the floor. I got worried, so I came looking for you."

Talon sighed. "That's sweet," she said, "but—"

"I brought your phone!" Curt interrupted, pulling it out of his pocket.

"But stupid," Talon adjusted her thought. "I left it there for a reason. I didn't want them tracking me."

"Tracking you?" Curt asked. "What are you talking about? Who? What's going on? Why are you hiding here in the dark with a loaded gun?" He looked at the gun still in her hand. "It is loaded, right?"

"Oh, it's loaded," Talon confirmed. "How did you get in my

condo?" she asked again.

"Well, I couldn't get in the front door," Curt explained, "so I climbed up the balcony. Those sliders are easy to crack open. That's why you should have a wooden rod in the slide-track. You don't, so I'm inside."

Talon took a moment, then a step back. "And why are you inside, Curt?"

"I told you," Curt answered. "I was worried about you. Your car was crashed. Your phone was abandoned. Your office was empty. This was the last place I could think of to look. With everything that's been happening, I just—"

"What's been happening, Curt?" Talon tightened her grip on her 9mm.

"Your car being vandalized," he said. "Your office being burglarized. Then you don't answer your phone and you leave your car damaged and abandoned? I knew something was up."

"Why didn't you just call the cops?" Talon challenged. Curt was filling up the short hallway to the front area of the condo, blocking her way to the exits.

Curt tilted his head at her. "Is that a joke? Who do you think has been doing all this? Isn't that what you asked me?"

"I did," Talon acknowledged. "Now I'm not so sure. You wanted to be a cop, didn't you, Curt?"

"A long time ago," Curt admitted. "I already told you that story. I'm glad I didn't become a cop. I like what I do. I like who I work with. I like..." But he trailed off.

"What do you like, Curt?" Talon took another small step back. She had enough room to raise the gun.

Curt grimaced and looked down. "I... I like *you*, Talon. A lot." He looked up again, locking eyes with her. "I was really scared something bad had happened to you."

Talon appraised Curt's eyes. The tinge of red at the corners, the slightly widened lids, the slight but discernable extra wetness.

She reached over and set the gun on her dresser, then reached out to put a hand on his cheek. "I like you too, Curt," she said. "But not like that. You can sleep on the couch."

Curt smiled weakly, a glint of hope still in those moist eyes. "Even though it's the night before trial?"

Talon grinned back and shook her head. "Especially because it's the night before trial."

CHAPTER 38

Three hours of restless sleep. Perfect way to start an aggravated murder in the first degree trial. Talon dragged herself out of her bed and into the shower. She washed away the previous night's craziness and that morning's sluggishness and steeled herself for the day. When she emerged from her bedroom, dressed to kill, she was actually startled to see Curt passed out on her couch. She was in trial mode and had forgotten he had spent the night.

It was sweet of him—breaking and entering notwithstanding. And she couldn't overlook that at least a portion of his motivation had been his hope, however small, to get lucky with her again. But last night was over. Trial day beckoned.

"Get up!" She kicked the couch. "I've got work to do."

Curt jerked awake, covering his eyes with his forearm against the morning sun. "Wha—? Where? Oh. Right. Wow." He squinted up at Talon. "Crazy night, huh?"

"Get up," Talon repeated. "And get out. Trial starts in an hour. I need you out of my condo before I leave."

Curt propped himself up on an elbow. "No, you need a ride." He pointed over to the large trial briefcase and two full document boxes stacked near the door. "Unless you're going to roll that all the way to the courthouse. It's uphill, remember?"

"How could I forget that hill after last night?" Talon grumbled. "Fine. I need a ride. Which means I need you up. Now. I can't be late."

Curt nodded and swung his feet off the couch. He was still in his clothes from the night before. "Can I at least shower?"

"Of course, you can shower," Talon answered. "Right after you drop me off at the courthouse."

* * *

Talon made her way to the courtroom, pulling her trial briefcase and rolling file boxes behind her. Earlier in the case, she had been hoping they might draw Gainsborough for the trial. After he shafted her on the discovery motions, she was relieved they didn't get him after all. But they got Kirshner. Talon was going to need to be at the top of her game. But that was true anyway, she supposed.

Cecilia was already in the courtroom, although Luke hadn't been transported quite yet. Talon rolled down to the defense table and started unloading her materials. She didn't much feel like greeting Cecilia, politeness and professionalism notwithstanding, but forced herself to do it anyway. Saying hello was normal and neutral—it didn't mean anything. Declining to say hello meant something, and Talon didn't want to telegraph any information at all to Cecilia.

"Morning," Talon greeted her opponent, albeit with the least possible amount of words.

"Morning, Talon," Cecilia replied. "Ready?"

Talon nodded even as she continued to unload her briefcase. "Of course." She didn't reciprocate the inquiry.

"Me too," Cecilia volunteered anyway. "I think Kirshner is a good draw."

Talon shrugged. "Good enough."

Cecilia waited a moment for something more from Talon, but nothing was forthcoming. So, she stuck out her hand. "Good luck, Talon. May the best woman win."

Talon regarded Cecilia's outstretched hand. She didn't grasp it. "You know that's not what this is about, right? This isn't a game. It's not some lawyer competition between you and me. You're trying to put an eighteen-year-old kid in prison for the rest of his life and I'm trying to stop you. It's not the fucking Olympics."

Cecilia let her hand drop. "I'm sorry you feel that way."

Talon shook her head. "That's a start. I hope you feel sorry about a lot more than that by the time this trial is done."

"You won't win, Talon," Cecilia challenged. "The law's on my side."

"Fine," Talon responded. "You take the law. I'll take justice. And we'll see who wins."

"I think we both know who'll win," Cecilia said.

"Then here's hoping we're both wrong," Talon concluded. She turned her back on Cecilia then, not least because the side door of the courtroom opened and in marched her client, in an ill-fitting suit and flanked by armed corrections officers.

"Luke," Talon greeted him as he reached the defense table. The officers undid Luke's handcuffs and leg chains. The only thing between him and the exit was the officers. But that would be enough. Luke wouldn't make it five feet before being crushed under four hundred pounds of cop. "You ready?"

"I don't know," Luke answered. "How do you get ready to sit still and let a bunch of other people decide the rest of your life?"

Talon thought for a moment. "I don't know," she admitted. "You probably don't. Just focus on today. Tomorrow focus on tomorrow. One day at a time. This is going to take weeks. I don't need you to do much, but I do need you to pay attention. And I need you to look innocent."

Luke scoffed. "How do I do that?"

"Are you innocent?" Talon asked him.

"Of course," Luke protested.

"Good," Talon answered. "Then just let yourself look how you feel inside. Innocent, and scared shitless."

Judge Kirshner made her entrance at that point. The bailiff called out the traditional demand to rise for the judge and a few moments later, Kirshner was seated above them. Blonde hair again in a bun, glasses on her nose, and an appropriately serious frown on her lips.

"Are the parties ready for trial in the matter of The State of Washington versus Lucas James Zlotnik?" she inquired to formally begin the proceedings.

"The State is ready," Cecilia answered.

"The defense is ready," Talon confirmed as well.

"Good." Judge Kirshner nodded. "Are there any preliminary motions that need to be addressed before we select the jury?"

Talon frowned. "I don't believe so, Your Honor. All of the defense motions were already denied, er...addressed at previous hearings."

Kirshner narrowed her eyes at Talon. "I'm not going to tolerate any disrespect toward the bench, Ms. Talon."

"Understood, Your Honor," Talon answered. "I'm sure we both hope there will be no reason for it."

Kirshner held her glare at Talon for a few more seconds. Talon thought she saw the faintest of smiles flicker in the corner of the judge's mouth, but she couldn't be sure. Still, Kirshner didn't engage the argument further. "Ms. Thompson," she addressed the prosecutor. "Are there any preliminary issues from the State?"

Cecilia clasped her hands in front of her. "No, Your Honor. We're ready to pick a jury."

Kirshner nodded again. "All right then. Let's pick a jury. Bailiff, call for the panel."

* * *

Jury selection was a misnomer. The jurors weren't selected, exactly. Instead, a panel of potential jurors were questioned by the judge and the attorneys, and then each side could deselect potential jurors. The first twelve who were left became the jury.

Talon and Cecilia alternated twenty-minute questioning sessions. Cecilia went first, of course. Like everything else in trial work, part of it was performance. And part of the performance was introducing the jurors to some of the themes in the case. The judge informed the jurors of the charge—"Murder in the First Degree with Aggravating Circumstances"—but otherwise the attorneys weren't allowed to get into the specifics of the case. They had to tiptoe around it. Cecilia asked about being responsible for someone else's actions. Talon asked about saying things that weren't true. And the jurors answered the questions put to them. The ones who talked the most were the ones most likely to be stricken by one side or the other.

Potential Juror Number 13 had been falsely accused (he claimed) of sexual assault by a step-niece. He'd fought it and won at trial. He thought prosecutors only cared about winning and cops would definitely lie on the stand. A great juror for Talon. So, of course, Cecilia used one of her six strikes against him.

Potential Juror Number 7 had only ever had good experiences with the police. She'd even worked as a volunteer with them. When they put on that badge, they took an oath to be perfectly upstanding and ethical, and it would take a lot to convince her otherwise. Talon struck her.

Potential Juror Number 24 kept raising his hand to answer questions, but his responses were off topic and somewhat incoherent. He didn't trust cops, but he thought people charged with a crime were probably guilty. Cecilia struck him, but only because she beat Talon to it.

When they were all done with the questioning, and both attorneys had used all of their strikes, they were left with a jury of twelve people who were not only too dumb to get out of jury duty, but too dull to have any interesting opinions on anything of import to the case.

Those twelve took their spots in the jury box and Judge Kirshner swore them in, having them stand and raise their right hands to "swear or affirm you will well and truly try the case, and render a true verdict, according to the law and based on the evidence given to you at trial."

After receiving a dozen "I do"s, Judge Kirshner invited the jurors to be seated, then instructed them to, "Please give your attention to Ms. Thompson who will deliver the opening statement on behalf of the State of Washington."

CHAPTER 39

Cecilia stood and nodded up to the judge. She began with the formalistic opening flourish only a prosecutor could get away with. "Thank you, Your Honor. Ladies and gentlemen of the jury, counsel, may it please the Court, my name is Cecilia Thompson, and I represent the people of the State of Washington."

She stepped over and took a position in front of the jury box, the jurors facing her in two rows. Cecilia centered herself exactly between jurors three and four, the exact right distance from them to be heard without being too close. She paused, clasped her hands in front of her, then launched.

"This is a case about choices," she said. "This is a case about consequences. It's a case about the law, and collective responsibility, and community safety. It's a case about protecting those who put their lives on the line to protect the rest of us."

She paused for effect. The jury didn't know anything about the case yet, except the charge. They were dying to know. And Cecilia was the one who got to tell them first. She used that advantage to pull them into the story she was going to tell. If she did it well enough, they wouldn't want to leave her story to even consider Talon's counter narrative. And Talon could see already, Cecilia was likely to do it very well indeed.

"The judge told you," Cecilia continued, "the defendant is charged with murder. Murder in the first degree. Murder in the first degree with aggravating circumstances."

Say 'murder' again, Talon thought to herself, but she kept her expression blank as she pretended to take notes.

"I'm about to tell you a story," Cecilia said. "A story about what happened that day. About what the evidence will show. But..."

She raised a cautionary finger

"—I will not tell you that the defendant actually killed anyone."

Now she really had the jurors' attention. *'Murder? But he didn't kill anyone? How can that be?!'*

"And the reason I won't tell you that," Cecilia went on, "is because he didn't kill anyone himself. He didn't shoot anyone. He didn't stab anyone. He didn't strangle anyone. He didn't bash anyone over the head with a candlestick in the library. But he still committed a murder. A murder in the first degree, with aggravating circumstances."

There we go, Talon thought. *Two more 'murder's. Well done.*

"So, you may wonder," Cecilia continued, "when I finish my opening statement, 'Why is the defendant charged with murder if he didn't actually kill anyone?' You may wonder, 'Did I miss something?' 'Did she leave something out?' The answer to that will be, no, you didn't miss anything."

Cecilia finally unclasped her hands and took a few slow steps to her right. Pacing was a common mistake of nervous trial attorneys, but a calm, thoughtful stroll from one side of the jury box to the other would allow the jury to see more of her body language and would communicate a quiet calm to reinforce her confident words.

"But I can't explain it all to you right now," Cecilia told them. "Not because I couldn't, but because I'm not allowed to. Only the judge can tell you what the law is, and she will do that, but not until the end of the trial. She will explain to you how someone can be guilty of murder even if they themselves didn't kill anyone. But, again, she won't do that until the very end."

Cecilia had reached the end of the jury box, so she turned back and continued her confident gait, hands extended slightly to emphasize her points.

"So, don't judge my opening statement now based on whether it meets what you thought murder was when you walked in here this morning. Judge it later based on what the judge tells you murder actually is, under the law. But I will tell you this: the law can hold you responsible for things you may not have intended but still knew might happen. And in this case, the defendant, Lucas Zlotnik, knew someone could end up dead when he agreed to be the getaway driver for an armed robbery."

And there it was. 'Getaway driver.' That label. Talon knew it was coming, but it still hurt when Cecilia finally whipped it out and plastered it on her client. It was pre-formed, one-size-fits-all, ready-to-go. It was the entire case. And if the label stuck, Luke was going to die in prison.

"The story starts on an average afternoon, right here in Tacoma," Cecilia finally launched into the facts of the case. Well, her facts, anyway. "The defendant, Lucas Zlotnik, was at his home, where he still lives with his parents. He got a text from his friend, Miguel Maldonado. They had plans that day. Plans they were smart enough not to put into detail in their texts. Miguel simply texted his buddy, Luke, to see if he was ready to go. And his buddy Luke texted back. Absolutely. He was ready."

By then, Cecilia had made her way back to the center of the jury box. She wouldn't move from it again.

"The defendant drove over to Miguel's house," she said. "Miguel lived at home with his parents too."

Talon wondered if the repeated digs at Luke and Miguel for living at home with their parents might be a bit too much, but a glance at the jury didn't reveal any obviously disapproving expressions. Talon returned her gaze to the legal pad in front of her.

"The defendant picked up his friend, Miguel," Cecilia continued, "and they drove directly to the Cash-Town U.S.A. store on South Thirty-Eighth Street, right by the Tacoma Mall. Cash-Town U.S.A. is one of those payday loan stores. You write them a check for eight hundred dollars, postdated to your next payday, and they give you seven hundred dollars in cash right now. A hundred dollars pure profit for them, so long as your check clears. And they have ways of going after you if it doesn't."

Cecilia raised a hand at the jurors. "Now, how Cash-Town U.S.A. conducts their business doesn't matter when it comes to the crime of robbery. You can't rob a payday loan store just because they charge really high interest on short-term loans. But it does matter when you're planning a robbery. Infamous bank robber Willie Sutton was once asked why he robbed banks, and his answer was, 'Because that's where the money is.'"

Cecilia nodded at the old story. "But not anymore. Banks are all digital now. Our paychecks and bank accounts and mortgage payments are all just zeroes and ones in some big bank computer somewhere. No, where the money is, where the cash is, is places like Cash-Town U.S.A. If you spend the day handing out seven hundred dollars in cash to customer after customer, you're going to have a lot of hundred dollar bills in your cash drawers. So, why did the defendant and Miguel choose to rob the Cash-Town U.S.A. on South Thirty-Eighth Street by the Tacoma Mall? Because that's where the money was."

Talon noticed that Cecilia had skipped over the part where Luke was supposed to know Miguel planned a robbery. But Talon also knew it was coming. And she knew it was going to hurt.

"So, the defendant drove his friend, Miguel, to the Cash-Town U.S.A. and waited outside in the car, engine running, while Miguel went inside to rob the place."

Cecilia paused and put a finger to her lips. "But how do we know all this? If they were smart enough not to put it in their texts, then how do we know what their plans were? How do we know that the defendant knew his friend planned on robbing the place, rather than maybe just going inside to get a payday loan?

"How?" Cecilia repeated. "I'll tell you how."

Cecilia turned around and pointed right at Luke. "He confessed."

Yep, that hurt.

Cecilia turned back to the jurors. "That's right. The defendant gave a full confession to the detectives after he was arrested. He admitted to going to the Cash-Town U.S.A. to rob it. He admitted knowing what Miguel was going to do inside. And he admitted to waiting outside to drive Miguel away when he came running out of the Cash-Town with thousands of dollars in untraceable cash in his hands."

Then, just in case they didn't get it, "The defendant confessed to all that. He confessed to being an accomplice to robbery. He confessed to being the getaway driver."

That label again. It was looking pretty sticky.

"That's how we know." Cecilia pointed at Luke again. "Because he told us."

Cecilia paused again. She seemed to be gathering herself up. Very dramatic. Very effective, Talon knew.

"But he waited outside," Cecilia said. "He didn't know what happened inside. But you will. By the end of this trial, you'll know what happened inside. And then you'll know why the defendant is guilty of murder."

Another pause, then she launched into it. "When the tellers at the Cash-Town U.S.A. realized they were being robbed, one of them immediately called 911. Tacoma Police dispatch put out a priority one callout, which means all hands on deck. Anyone close drops whatever they're doing and gets to that Cash-Town U.S.A. as fast as they can. The two closest officers were Officer Todd Dickerson and Officer Christopher McCarthy. They arrived separately, but entered the Cash-Town together, guns drawn, ready to stop the robbery in progress."

Cecilia pointed a finger at the jury again. "Now, how do we know what happened inside, if the defendant was outside? Well, you're going to hear from Officer Dickerson. He's going to tell you exactly what happened when he and Officer McCarthy went inside. But you're not going to hear from Officer McCarthy."

Cecilia stopped and looked back at Luke again, the disdain clear on her face—intentionally so, Talon knew.

"You're not going to hear from Officer McCarthy," she finally turned back to the jury, "because he's dead. He died in the shootout that happened when the police responded to the robbery the defendant was the getaway driver for."

Cecilia hardened her expression. "In fact, Officer McCarthy isn't the only person who died inside that Cash-Town U.S.A. that day. Miguel, the defendant's friend, died too. Also from gunshots. It was a crazy, volatile, violent situation. Exactly the sort of thing you would expect if you try to rob a store. You know the police are going to respond. You know they're going to try to stop you. And you know they have guns.

"When the defendant drove his friend to the Cash-Town U.S.A. that afternoon, he knew what could happen. He didn't want it to happen. He wanted Miguel to get away with it. He wanted Miguel to be faster than the cops. That's why he was there, waiting outside, engine running. So Miguel could run out and they could drive away before the police arrived. That was the plan. That was the *defendant's* plan."

Cecilia shook her head. "But you don't get to decide what part of the plan you own and what part you don't. The police did their job. They responded to a robbery and they stopped the bad guys. But the bad guys stopped one of them. Forever."

Cecilia clasped her hands again in front of her, that gesture of sincerity, then she raised those clasped hands to her chest to emphasize her concluding remarks—part argument, part entreaty.

"If you plan to rob a bank and your buddy goes inside and gets himself killed, that's not murder," she said, "because he signed up for it too. But if someone who was not a participant in the crime dies, then that death is a murder. And if that someone is a police officer, doing his duty, putting his life on the line to protect all of us, then that's also an aggravating circumstance.

"And so, ladies and gentlemen of the jury," Cecilia concluded, "when this trial is over, and after you've heard all of the evidence, I am going to stand before you again and ask you to return a verdict of guilty to the crime of murder in the first degree with aggravating circumstances. Thank you."

With that, Cecilia unclasped her hands and walked briskly back to her seat at the prosecution table.

It was finally the cop-killing getaway driver's turn to talk. Well, his lawyer's turn.

"Now, ladies and gentlemen," Judge Kirshner said, even as Talon stood up, "please give your attention to Ms. Winter, who will give the opening statement on behalf of the defendant."

CHAPTER 40

Talon stepped out from behind the defense table. She didn't bother with the whole 'May it please the Court' routine. That was formality. Formality and propriety and polite deference to the powers that be—those were the things that would get her client convicted. The law said her client was guilty. She needed the jury to say 'Not Guilty' anyway.

She walked directly up to the jury box, right where Cecilia had started her remarks. Then she took one step closer.

"Getaway driver," Talon boomed, her voice a little too loud for her proximity to her listeners. Then she said it again, but quieter. "Getaway driver."

She took that step back and nodded. "That's kind of all you need to know, isn't it? I mean, if he was the getaway driver, he was in on the robbery. And I mean, really in on it. Getaway driver, that's not just a small part. That's central. Vital, even. Not just anybody gets to be the getaway driver. I mean, anybody can go inside and hold a gun and stand behind the main robber like some kind of super villain henchman. But the getaway driver? Oh, no, that person needs to be one of your top people. Dependable. Ready to go. Know every possible escape route. Somebody the inside robbers can really trust."

She took a step to the side and gestured toward the prosecution table. "The getaway driver. We all know what that means. And that's why the prosecutor wants to stick that label on Luke. Because if it really does stick, then you don't have to think anymore. Getaway driver equals robber. Robbery plus death equals murder. Murder plus police officer equals murder in the first degree with aggravating circumstances. All very easy, see? You won't even need to think about the actual case. Just remember that label, vote guilty, and you'll be home in time for dinner."

Talon knew when to pause too. She nodded her head to herself a few times, then raised a finger. "But if we're going to label someone, if we're going to label a criminal defendant who is supposed to be presumed innocent, if we're going to label a real, living, breathing person, my client, eighteen-year-old Lucas James Zlotnik," she pointed at him, "then let's get the label right."

She centered herself again in front of the jurors and raised her hands, open palmed toward them. Another gesture of sincerity. "The label we should use isn't 'getaway driver'. The label we should use," the slightest of pauses, "is 'fall guy'."

Talon moved quickly to explain, lest the jurors dismiss it out of hand. "Luke is the fall guy because he didn't kill anyone, and his friend, Miguel, didn't kill anyone. The only person who killed anyone was Officer Todd Dickerson. The shots that killed Officer McCarthy were fired by the same gun that killed Miguel. The gun of Officer Todd Dickerson."

The jurors looked appropriately surprised. Cecilia had left that little detail out.

"There was no shootout. Miguel didn't have a gun. Officer Dickerson is the one who killed those two young men that day. But rather than hold a police officer responsible, or even just throw our hands up at the senseless tragedy of it all, they wanted a scapegoat. They wanted someone to blame. A police officer was dead. They needed someone to blame. But they weren't going to blame the other police officer, and Miguel was dead. That left Luke. Poor stupid, naïve Luke, sitting in his car out in the parking lot, waiting for Miguel to cash a check so they could go hang out that afternoon, completely unaware of what his friend had planned."

Talon shook her head. "No, that's not a getaway driver. That's a scapegoat. That's someone for the cops and the prosecutors to throw their rage at. And it's someone they want you to throw your rage at too. 'A police officer is dead,' they say. 'Someone has to pay for it,' they say. 'And that someone,' they say, 'is Luke Zlotnik'."

Talon took a moment to look again at her client. He was looking back at her—what else would he be doing? He looked young and pitiful in his overly large suit.

"Luke is eighteen years old," Talon said. "Technically, he's an adult, but in a lot of ways he's still just a kid. A kid who was in the wrong place at the wrong time with the wrong friend."

And that was really the thrust of her case. Fall guy. Scapegoat. Wrong place at the wrong time. Wrong friend.

But there was one small problem with that case theory. And as much as Talon would have liked to ignore it, she knew she had to address it.

"I mention Luke's age," Talon said, with another quick glance at her client, "not because it would ever excuse an actual murder."

'Actual murder'. See, what I did there, Cecilia?

"But it does explain what happened after the killing," Talon said. "After Officer Dickerson shot and killed both his friend,

Miguel, and Officer McCarthy. It explains why Luke would misjudge just how deep of trouble he was in and say whatever he thought he needed to say to get out of it."

Talon took another moment and raised clasped fingers to her lips. "Ladies and gentlemen, take a moment and consider the situation Luke found himself in when the rest of those police cars pulled into that tiny parking lot at South Thirty-Eighth Street. Consider what it must have been like for him to see the parking lot fill up with lights and sirens, to see officers rush into the Cash-Town U.S.A., weapons drawn. Consider what it was like when he heard the gunshots—again, from Officer Dickerson's gun—knowing his friend was inside. Then consider what must have been going through his mind when he was yanked from his car by uniformed police officers with their own guns drawn, pointed at his head. Consider all of that."

A brief pause, then, "And now consider all that, and Luke really didn't know what Miguel was going to do. Consider all that, and Luke really thought his friend was just going to cash a check so they could hang out and party a little bit that afternoon. Consider all that, and Luke had no idea what was going on other than his friend went into the Cash-Town store, shots were fired, and he was suddenly under arrest for murder."

Talon took a moment to scan the jurors, meeting each of their gazes. "Consider what that must have been like for eighteen-year-old Luke Zlotnik. And then you'll understand why he told the cops whatever they wanted to hear. And they definitely had something they wanted to hear. They wanted answers. They wanted someone to blame. They wanted a fall guy."

She stepped back and threw her hands up. "But don't take my word for it. I'm just his lawyer. What I say isn't actually evidence. Oh, and by the way, what she says," Talon pointed at

Cecilia, "that isn't evidence either. Evidence is what the witnesses say. And the defense is going to call an expert witness who is going to talk to you about false confessions."

Talon scanned the jury again for any sign of eye-rolling or suppressed groans. But there were none. They were listening. She couldn't ask for anything more at that point.

"You're going to hear from Dr. Natalie Ross," Talon continued, "one of the foremost experts on false confessions. She's going to explain to you why a person might confess to something they didn't do. And specifically, she's going to explain to you why Luke confessed to something he didn't do.

"She'll do a better job of explaining it than I will right now," Talon went on, "but it basically comes down to power, and saying whatever you think you need to in order to get out of a bad situation. You're going to hear Luke's confession. I'm sure Ms. Thompson is going to play it for you—the part the cops bothered to record anyway. And when you do hear it, listen for one thing in particular: does Luke ever confess to murder? Or does he confess to something less, in order to get out of trouble? Well, he thought he was going to get out of trouble."

Talon opened those hands again to the jury. "When Ms. Thompson plays that taped statement for you, remember what I'm telling you now, and keep an open mind until you hear from Dr. Ross later in the trial."

Not a 'confession' anymore. Just a taped statement. A subtle change, but a very intentional one.

"Also keep in mind what this was like for Luke," she entreated the jurors. "Luke is only eighteen years old. He's just driving his friend, Miguel, to the nearest Cash-Town U.S.A. so Miguel can get some cash. Miguel goes inside and Luke is just sitting in the car, waiting, listening to the radio. All of a sudden, a bunch of cop cars show up. Cops rush into the store where his friend is, guns at the ready. Shots are fired. More cops show up and drag him out of his car. They drive him downtown and tell him he's under arrest for murder. Unless..."

A pause, a raised finger, a knowing sideways glance.

"Unless he cooperates. Unless maybe he helps them figure it all out. And won't he be more believable if he admits to knowing something about what was going on? Not the murder. Oh no, no, no. But the robbery? Yeah, maybe the robbery. After all, who knew you could get charged with murder if you admitted to a robbery?"

Talon stopped again and pointed at the jurors. "You all didn't know that until a few minutes ago when Ms. Thompson stood up and told you. And Luke sure as heck didn't know it either. But the cops did.

"So, when you hear that taped statement, when you hear what Luke did say, also listen for what he didn't say. And remember that you're going to hear from an expert witness who's going to tell you the confession is false, and you shouldn't rely on it."

Talon paused again. She took a moment to catch her breath and collect her thoughts. Make sure she'd said everything she wanted to say. She had. There was just one more thing to address. But she needed to be careful. If she put it all the way out, Cecilia would cut it off, root and stem—or Judge Kirshner would, on Cecilia's motion. So instead of a root or a stem, she planted a seed.

"The other evidence the State is going to put forward is the testimony of Officer Todd Dickerson," she said. "He is the only witness to what actually happened inside that Cash-Town U.S.A. The prosecutor didn't mention it in her opening statement, but there's no video. The security cameras were pointed down at the teller stations to catch employee theft, not toward the lobby to record police officers shooting and killing people."

Several of the jurors frowned at that, but Talon couldn't know if they were frowning at the thought of a police officer killing people, or at Talon's repeatedly referencing it.

"No one wants to believe cops do the wrong thing," Talon said, "whether intentionally or accidentally. No one wants to live in a country where cops sometimes shoot and kill unarmed civilians. But they do. *We* do. It's easier to believe the bad guys deserve it. But they don't. At least, Miguel Maldonado didn't. He didn't deserve to die. Christopher McCarthy didn't deserve to die. And Luke Zlotnik doesn't deserve to be punished for it all. He's not a murderer. He's just a fall guy."

Talon took a deep breath and stepped back over to the defense table. She put a hand on Luke's shoulder and concluded her remarks.

"At the end of this trial, I'm also going to stand before you. I'm not going to ask you whether Officer McCarthy or Miguel Maldonado deserved to die. Of course they didn't. And I'm not going to ask you whether Officer Dickerson should be held responsible for it. That's not for you to decide. I'm just going to ask you one question: Should Luke Zlotnik be convicted of murder for something he didn't know about and didn't do? And based on the evidence, there is only going to be one answer. The answer will be 'No' and I will ask you to return a verdict of 'Not Guilty.' Thank you."

Talon stepped over and took her seat next to Luke.

"Thanks," he whispered. "That was pretty good."

Talon had to suppress a frown, lest the jurors see it. *Only 'pretty good'?*

"What happens next?" Luke asked.

Talon looked over at Cecilia, standing up, ready to start her case-in-chief. "Now they try to convict you."

"The State may call its first witness," Judge Kirshner told Cecilia.

"Thank you, Your Honor," Cecilia replied. "The State calls Emily McCarthy."

CHAPTER 41

It was pretty standard in a murder case to start with the widow. It packed an emotional punch and let the prosecutor talk about what a great guy the victim was. But it didn't really do much to advance the case. It wasn't like Talon was arguing that Officer McCarthy wasn't dead. So, Cecilia put the grieving Emily McCarthy on the stand. Mrs. McCarthy talked about her fallen hero of a husband. They put up a nice photo of him on the projector screen. And when the direct examination was done, Talon stood up and said, "No questions, Your Honor."

You don't cross examine the widow.

Talon was expecting a similar situation with the State's second witness, Janice Henderschott, the teller Miguel tried to rob. Again, Talon wasn't contesting that Miguel intended to rob the Cash-Town U.S.A. She was just arguing that Luke didn't know about it. She anticipated standing up again to announce she had no questions. But Janice Henderschott was not a good witness. And a shark can't just ignore it when a drop of blood hits the water.

"Could you please state your name for the record?" Cecilia started, once Judge Kirshner had sworn in the witness.

"Janice Henderschott," she answered. She was just an average looking woman, average height and weight, with average length brown hair, and dressed in a forgettable outfit. The only thing that was remarkable was the look of wide-eyed fear in her eyes.

Talon and Cecilia were used to being in court. The cops and medical examiners were regularly in court testifying. Even Emily McCarthy lived her life adjacent to her husband's career in the criminal justice system. But Janice Henderschott was just a teller at a check cashing store. She'd probably gotten the job for no more reason than they were hiring when she was looking. And now everyone was looking at her.

"And how are you employed, ma'am?" Cecilia continued.

But Henderschott just stared at her.

"Where do you work?" Cecilia tried.

"Oh," Henderschott said. "Um. At Cash-Town U.S.A."

Cecilia waited for a bit more explanation from her witness. Maybe a branch location, or a description of the services she offered. But no. Janice Henderschott just stared at her, hands shaking, waiting for the next question like it was a school exam.

"Is that one of those places where people can get payday loans?" Cecilia prompted.

Henderschott nodded. "Yes," she almost whispered.

And so it went. Cecilia pulling teeth, and Talon actually finding herself drawn in by the awkwardness of it. By the time Cecilia finally got to Miguel approaching her teller window, everyone in the courtroom was torn between curiosity to hear what happened next and an overwhelming desire to hear it from anyone but Janice Henderschott.

"Okay," Cecilia exhaled after extracting the fact that a man had approached Henderschott's window. A young man. A young man who looked like he might have been Hispanic, or Native American, or even Filipino. Just not Swedish or Irish. But he definitely did walk up to her window.

"Can you describe his demeanor?" Cecilia asked.

Henderschott just stared at her, shaking her head slightly.

"How was he acting?" Cecilia tried.

A shrug.

"Was he nervous?" Cecilia tried.

"Objection." Talon stood up. "Leading question."

Cecilia sighed, but didn't argue.

"Objection sustained," Judge Kirshner ruled. "Rephrase the question."

Instead, Cecilia pressed forward. "Did he say anything to you?"

Henderschott nodded.

"You need to answer out loud," Cecilia reminded her.

"Yes," Henderschott managed to answer.

"And what did he say?"

Henderschott thought for a moment. "I don't remember exactly."

Cecilia exhaled audibly, losing the battle to hide her exasperation. Talon, on the other hand, was trying to manage her growing excitement.

"Did he say anything alarming?" Cecilia prompted.

"Objection again, Your Honor." Talon stood up again. "Leading."

Kirshner thought for a moment, then had to agree. "Sustained. Rephrase, Ms. Thompson."

Cecilia thought for a moment. "To the best of your recollection, please tell us what the young man said when he came to your window."

Henderschott took several moments to answer, her hands wringing and her eyes darting around the courtroom. "He said something about giving him the money in the cash drawer."

"Okay." Cecilia visibly relaxed. "And did he say what would happen if you didn't do as he asked?"

Henderschott shook her head and shrugged. "I, I'm not sure. I think so."

"What did he say?" Cecilia prompted. "About what would happen if you didn't give him the money?"

Another shrug. "Something bad."

"Is that what he said?" Cecilia attempted to clarify. "Give me the money or something bad will happen?"

Henderschott frowned. "I'm not sure exactly. It was kind of a long time ago. It was very scary. I just remember being scared, and thinking something bad would happen if I didn't give him the money."

Cecilia's shoulders dropped. "And that feeling, that something bad would happen, was that because of whatever he said?"

"Objection," Talon stood for a third time. "Still leading."

Talon was right, but Kirshner didn't want to look like she was playing favorites, so she threw Cecilia a bone. "I'm going to overrule that objection. The witness may answer, if she's able."

"Go ahead and answer the question," Cecilia instructed.

But Henderschott shook her head. "I don't remember the question."

Cecilia blinked hard at her witness, but refrained from any other reaction. She simply repeated the question for her. "Your feeling that something bad would happen, was that because of whatever the man said to you?"

Henderschott thought for a moment, then nodded. "Yes."

Cecilia visibly relaxed. It wasn't perfect—far from it—but it was at least some evidence that Miguel had tried to rob the place by demanding money and threatening the teller.

But Talon was happy too. She loved the smell of blood in the water.

"So, what did you do next?" Cecilia moved on.

"I pressed the panic button under the counter," Henderschott answered.

"And then what?"

"I ran out the back door," Henderschott finally had some animation to her response. "I was so scared."

"I'm sure you were," Cecilia empathized. But she was done trying to extract information from this witness. "No further questions, Your Honor."

Cecilia spun around and hurried back to her seat. Talon stood up slowly as the judge invited her, "Any cross examination, Ms. Winter?"

Talon smiled. "Oh, yes, Your Honor."

The easy play was to rip Janice Henderschott to shreds. Go after her poor memory and confused demeanor. Leave her even more of a quivering pile of jelly than she already was.

But that wasn't the smart play.

For one thing, the jury wouldn't like it. Jurors would give a defense attorney some slack in being aggressive, even obnoxious, with a cop or a victim, depending on the crime, but Janice Henderschott was just pathetic. Talon didn't need to turn that into *sym*pathetic.

More importantly, though, Talon didn't want to give her a chance to improve her answers. She had already testified, a couple of times, that she didn't remember exactly what Miguel said. If Talon asked her a third time, well, she might just remember, and chances were, it wasn't going to help Luke any. Talon understood the value of the testimony Henderschott had given her, and knew not to get greedy.

No, the smart play was to ask Janice Henderschott the questions Talon was also going to ask Officer Todd Dickerson.

"So, Ms. Henderschott," Talon started, almost casually as she approached the witness stand—slowly, like one might approach a small animal about to run away. "The person who approached your window, he was a man, correct?"

Henderschott cocked her head at the obvious question. "Uh, yes."

"A young man?" Talon followed up.

Henderschott nodded cautiously. "Yes."

"A young man with darker skin?" Talon expounded.

"Yes," Henderschott confirmed.

"And you already testified," Talon reminded her, "that was pretty scary, wasn't it?"

Henderschott nodded. "Yes. I was scared."

Talon smiled. "Thank you, Ms. Henderschott. No further questions."

Cecilia shot to her feet. She knew what Talon was trying to imply. But she hesitated when Judge Kirshner asked her, "Any re-direct examination, based on those answers?"

Cecilia looked at her witness for a long moment and thought better of it. "No, Your Honor."

She knew she should get the civilian off the stand. It was time for the cops anyway.

CHAPTER 42

The next slew of witnesses were all cops. There were a lot of
them, but most of them had little of value to say. It was almost as if
Cecilia was trying to bury Dickerson right in the middle of her case.
Maybe the jury would even be bored of cops by the time Dickerson
took the stand. Especially if Talon went after every one of them for
being a gun-toting, badge-wearing proto-fascist bent on caging and
killing anyone with darker skin tone than Crayola's 'peach'. Talon's
schtick would be worn out before she got a chance to use it against
the one cop she really needed to wound on the stand.

That was Cecilia's plan. It wasn't Talon's.

Talon didn't need to cross examine the cop who set up the
perimeter crime scene tape any more than she needed to cross
examine the widow. Effective cross examination was not death by a
thousand cuts. It was a few, well-placed, fatally deep slashes.

But you couldn't just stand up and say, 'No questions,' again
and again, cop after cop. Declining to cross examine the widow
looked classy. Declining to cross examine the cops looked cowardly.
Which made Luke look guilty. So instead of no questions, Talon
asked the same question to every single cop Cecilia padded her case

with: "You didn't see my client do anything, did you?"

She would have liked to have added, 'And you never heard him confess to anything, did you?' but even if the regular line cops who didn't interact with Luke at all would have answered, 'No,' it only would have lent additional importance to the confession when the jury finally heard it. And Talon knew the jury was going to hear it.

Talon didn't know the exact order of Cecilia's witnesses. The prosecutor didn't have to tell her. But Talon could see what Cecilia was trying to do. She wanted to bury Dickerson in the middle of her case-in-chief, after the beat cops, but before the experts. His testimony would still be important, but Talon's cross would start to be forgotten as Cecilia propelled the case forward to autopsy and the confession. It was smart. It was exactly what Talon would have done.

So, the first cop was the officer who maintained the crime scene log. He literally stood at the edge of the taped-off crime scene, holding a clipboard for all the other officers to sign in and out of the scene. Next was one of the perimeter security guys. Then the 'stayed outside waiting for back up' guy. Then the 'first guy inside after the gunshots' guy. And so on. And Talon asked every one of them the same question.

"You never saw my client commit any crime, did you?"

And they all gave slightly different versions of the same answer: "No, ma'am."

Then Cecilia called a SWAT sergeant who wasn't actually at the crime scene. Ever. Although that wasn't obvious at first.

"Could you please state your name for the record?" Cecilia began her direct examination.

"Bobby Jones," he answered. He was a strong looking man, with thick forearms and a military style haircut.

"What's your current rank and assignment?" Cecilia asked next. There was no need to ask where he worked; he was decked out in full SWAT combat gear.

"I'm a sergeant with our Special Weapons and Tactics team," Sgt. Jones answered. "SWAT."

Cecilia nodded. "Do you have any experience with active shooter situations like the one involved in this case?"

"Yes, ma'am," Sgt. Jones said. "That is one of the main reasons for a SWAT callout."

"Can you explain, what are some of the general steps police would take in a situation like the one in this case?"

"Certainly," Sergeant Jones said. He turned then to the jury to explain the history and role of SWAT teams. It was a bit rambling of an answer, but it was interesting, and the jury seemed engaged. They also seemed to appreciate that he was talking directly to them, instead of them eavesdropping on a conversation between the witness and the lawyer. That was no accident; they trained the cops at the police academy to testify that way.

"Is there a difference in the response," Cecilia asked, "if you know the suspect is armed as opposed to only thinking he *might* be armed?"

"You have to assume the suspect is armed, ma'am," Sgt. Jones explained. "Officer safety always comes first."

"Of course," Cecilia agreed. Then a sort of strange question, "Are you familiar with the incident in this case?"

Talon looked up from her notetaking. *That's a strange way to ask what he did at the scene,* she thought.

"I wasn't there, ma'am," the sergeant answered, "but I read the reports."

Wait. What? Oh, hell, no. Talon jumped to her feet. "Objection, Your Honor. I need to be heard outside the presence of the jury."

Kirshner frowned, but Cecilia didn't protest, so the judge acquiesced. The bailiff escorted the jurors into the jury room.

"Do you want the witness excused as well?" Kirshner asked. The question itself showed Kirshner knew what Talon's answer would be and she was prepared to grant the request.

"Yes, Your Honor," Talon said, and Judge Kirshner instructed Sgt. Jones to wait in the hallway.

Once the officer was out of the courtroom, Talon addressed the judge. "I'm confused, Your Honor. If this witness wasn't there that day, why is he testifying? Is the prosecutor trying to use him as some sort of expert on tactics or something? If so, I wasn't given any notice they intended to call him as an expert, and I'm entitled to that under the court rules."

Judge Kirshner looked over to Cecilia. "Ms. Thompson, do you intend to endorse this witness as an expert on police tactics?"

Cecilia shifted her weight from one foot to the other and back. "Not exactly, Your Honor. He happens to have experience in these sorts of situations, and I thought it would be helpful to the jury if they could see how these sorts of situations play out."

"So, an expert," Kirshner translated. "And you're objecting, Ms. Winter?"

"Absolutely I'm objecting," Talon confirmed. "He's not an expert. He's just a cop who's going to say another cop was justified in killing an unarmed man."

"That's not what he was going to say," Cecilia claimed, but not very convincingly.

"Did you give notice to Ms. Winter of this expert?" Kirshner cut to the chase.

Cecilia shook her head. "No, Your Honor. I guess I didn't really think of him as an expert in the classic sense."

Talon looked sideways at Cecilia. That was even less convincing.

"But that's fine, Your Honor," Cecilia offered. "I don't need to ask him any more questions."

"Of course not," Talon complained. "He already said it was okay to assume every suspect is armed. What more did you really need him to say? The damage is done."

Talon had the option of moving for a mistrial, but there were two problems with that. First, mistrials were rarely granted in murder trials, except for the most egregious errors. Second, a mistrial meant a new trial, and a new trial meant Janice Henderschott would get another chance to remember what Miguel actually said to her.

"I'm not going to ask for a mistrial," Talon let everyone know. "But I would ask the Court to strike the officer's testimony in total and instruct the jury to disregard it completely."

The jurors couldn't actually do that. They heard what he said; they couldn't just un-remember it. But it would be embarrassing for Cecilia and would telegraph to the jury that the judge didn't like at least part of the prosecution's case.

Which is why Cecilia objected to the proposal. "I don't think that's necessary, Your Honor. We barely got past name, rank, and serial number. I won't ask any more questions, Ms. Winter can cross examine or not based on what he's already said, and then we can move on to the next witness."

"So, I can cross examine him," Talon mocked, "and give him a chance to say everything all over again? Maybe open up new avenues to showcase his expertise in murdering civilians?"

"Ok, that's enough, Ms. Winter." Judge Kirshner took back control. "That sort of language is unnecessary." She paused to collect her thoughts, then gave her ruling. "I'm not going to strike the officer's testimony. It's too much to strike. One question-and-answer is strikable, maybe two, but not that much testimony. Ms. Thompson, you may not ask any more questions of this witness. Ms. Winter, you can cross examine, if you wish. When you're finished, we will move on to the next witness."

So, the judge was splitting the baby. That heralded tradition of judges refusing to make hard decisions. The wisest judges were even referred to as 'Solomonic'. Talon thought that was a load of crap. A judge's only job is to make decisions. Solomon avoided that and took a cheap cop out. And judges had been doing it ever since.

"Thank you, Your Honor," Cecilia said.

Talon didn't say anything.

Judge Kirshner ordered the witness and the jury back into the courtroom.

Once everyone was assembled, Cecilia stood up and announced, "No further questions."

That was a nice telegraph to the jury that whatever Cecilia had been trying to do, whatever Talon had objected to when they were out of the room. Talon had won. But that wasn't enough for Talon.

"Any cross examination, Ms. Winter?" the judge asked.

"Oh, yes," Talon answered as she stood up.

She walked up to the witness stand, one step too close, just inside the sergeant's personal space. "So," she asked, "you're okay with a police officer killing unarmed civilians?"

Sgt. Jones was taken aback. "What? Uh, well, I mean... You see, every situation is different, and—"

"It's a yes or no question," Talon interrupted. "Are you okay with police officers killing unarmed civilians? Yes or no?"

Jones hesitated, but then answered, "Under certain circumstances, the shooting of an unarmed suspect can be justified."

"Is that a 'Yes'?" Talon pressed.

Jones nodded. "That's a 'Yes'."

"Wow," Talon said back to him. "No further questions."

Judge Kirshner didn't give Cecilia an opportunity to do any re-direct examination. Instead, she excused Jones and asked Cecilia if she was ready to call her next witness. Talon knew the answer. Jones was meant to set the table. But the next witness was the main course.

"Yes, Your Honor," Cecilia rose to answer the judge. "The State calls Officer Todd Dickerson."

CHAPTER 43

All eyes went to the courtroom door as in walked the State's star witness—and double murderer—Officer Todd Dickerson.

He was shorter than Talon expected, even after seeing his Facebook pictures. His racist girlfriend must have been short too. He seemed to be trying to make up for his stature through bodybuilding, but his thick arms and neck just made him look even shorter. His walk to the front of the courtroom was more of a strut. He knew everyone was looking at him and he seemed to like it. There was no hint of any humility at having taken two lives, no matter the circumstances.

The judge swore him in, his posture impossibly rigid, and he took a seat on the witness stand. Cecilia came out from behind her table, but conducted her examination standing directly in front of it. About as far away from Dickerson as possible. Talon wondered whether it was intentional or subconscious.

"Please state your name for the record," Cecilia began.

"Officer Todd Dickerson," he replied. Talon noted that 'officer' wasn't actually part of his name, but found it interesting he thought his job was such an integral part of his identity. Again,

Talon wondered if it was intentional or subconscious.

"How are you employed, sir?" Cecilia continued.

"I am a police officer," was the answer. Again, more a statement of identity than occupation.

"How long have you been a police officer?"

"Fourteen years," Dickerson answered. "All of it as a patrol officer. I have never sought promotion or advancement."

Talon already didn't like Dickerson. She hoped the jurors were starting to feel the same way.

"Officer Dickerson," Cecilia moved ahead, "were you involved in an incident that took place at the Cash-Town U.S.A. store on South Thirty-Eighth Street in Tacoma?"

"Yes, I was."

"How did you come to be involved in that incident?" Cecilia asked.

"A priority one call came out over dispatch," Dickerson explained. He didn't turn to deliver his answers to the jury like he would have been trained to do at the academy. Instead, he kept an almost disconcerting focus on Cecilia as he answered her questions. "That means every officer is supposed to stop whatever he's doing and respond to the call address. I was about to pull some guy over for speeding, but I had to let him go. His lucky day, I guess."

Dickerson actually laughed at his little joke. Talon wondered if maybe no one had told him he'd killed two people.

"How long did it take you to get to the incident address?" Cecilia continued.

"Two minutes, maybe three," Dickerson answered. "I drove top speed and was the first officer to arrive."

"Did any other officers arrive right after you?"

"Yeah, Officer McCarthy pulled into the parking lot behind me," Dickerson said. "He and I were the first two on scene."

"Did you wait for additional officers to arrive before taking any further action?"

"No, ma'am," Dickerson seemed proud to answer.

"Why not?"

"Time was of the essence," Dickerson said. "It was a priority one call. That meant lives were at risk. Two officers were enough. We needed to move before the subject barricaded himself inside or started taking hostages."

"So, what did you do?" Cecilia asked next.

"Officer McCarthy and I took up positions on opposite sides of the main entrance. If we'd had more officers, some of them would have gone around to secure the back entrance, but there was no time. Officer McCarthy and I burst into the store, weapons at the ready."

"Weapon," Cecilia repeated. "That means firearm, right?"

"Yes," Dickerson confirmed. "I held my weapon at the low ready before entering the store. When we entered, I immediately located the suspect and trained my weapon at his chest."

"Where was the suspect standing?"

"He was approximately halfway to the rear entrance," Dickerson said, "so I ordered McCarthy to go around behind him and cut off that escape route."

"Ordered?" Cecilia questioned.

"Told," Dickerson corrected himself with a slight roll of the eyes. "It was a rapidly evolving situation. Anything could have happened. Someone needed to take charge."

"And that was you?" Cecilia ventured.

"Yes," Dickerson was obviously pleased to say. "You can't let the suspect be in charge. They already have several advantages. They started it, they could bunker down, they could take hostages, and they're desperate. They don't play by the rules. You have to establish dominance immediately."

"And did that work?" Cecilia asked. "Establishing dominance?"

Dickerson took a moment before answering. "I would say no."

"Why not?"

"I ordered the suspect to get on the ground, but he refused to follow my commands," Dickerson explained. "I ordered him to show me his hands, but he also refused that command. That became an issue."

"How so?" Cecilia asked.

"If he had just shown us his hands and put them over his head as commanded, we would have been able to confirm he wasn't a threat," Dickerson answered. "But he refused, so we had to assume he was still a threat."

"So, what happened next?" Cecilia continued.

"Officer McCarthy was circling around behind the suspect," Dickerson said, "and I continued to give commands to the suspect to show his hands and get on the ground. But the suspect continued to ignore my commands."

"Did you believe the suspect was armed with a firearm?" Cecilia asked.

"We had to assume he was," Dickerson said. "The report was armed robbery. He wouldn't show us his hands. So, yes, ma'am, we had every reason to believe he was armed."

"What happened next?"

"It all happened very fast," Dickerson answered. "I had my weapon trained on the suspect. Officer McCarthy was taking up a position behind him to cut off a possible escape route out the back door. The suspect suddenly raised his hands, pushing them out and toward me. Officer McCarthy called out, 'Gun! Gun!' So, I returned fire. The suspect must have flinched because my first volley missed, but I succeeded in striking the subject with a second volley. Unfortunately, because the suspect moved when Officer McCarthy yelled, 'Gun!', my first shots missed the suspect and struck Officer McCarthy."

Dickerson showed absolutely no remorse for killing McCarthy. Talon knew he wouldn't care about killing Miguel, but she expected some regret at downing a fellow officer.

"Did the suspect actually have a gun?" Cecilia asked.

"I believe he did, yes," Dickerson answered. "But after shots were fired, I held position until other officers arrived. When they did, I exited the building and didn't interact again with the body of the suspect."

And that was it. *'Hi, I'm Officer Todd and I kill people,'* Talon thought ruefully.

"Thank you, Officer Dickerson," Cecilia concluded her examination. "No further questions."

"Cross examination?" Judge Kirshner invited.

Talon nodded and stood up. Of course she was going to cross examine the person who actually committed the acts her client was charged with. But she took her time before starting. She wanted to size him up for a few moments longer. It was her first time questioning him, despite her best efforts. After just enough time for it to get awkward, she was ready.

"Returned fire?" she began. "But he never fired at you."

"I don't know that," Dickerson responded quickly.

"You don't know," Talon's eyebrows shot up, "whether he fired a gun at you?"

"No, ma'am," Dickerson answered confidently. "I don't remember him firing at me, but in moments of high stress, it's possible not to notice everything that happens. You can get tunnel vision and only be able to focus on the one life-or-death thing you're doing. In that moment, one hundred percent of my attention was focused on firing my own weapon."

"So focused you missed and shot your partner," Talon pointed out.

"The suspect moved before I could fire," Dickerson responded.

"I thought your gun was trained on his chest?" Talon questioned.

"It was."

"How did you miss?"

"People miss all the time, ma'am," Dickerson said. "It's not a stationary target like at a firing range. Also, I don't even know for sure it was my shots that killed Officer McCarthy. I don't know for sure that the suspect didn't shoot first. Maybe at Officer McCarthy. Maybe that's why he yelled, 'Gun!'"

Talon took a moment to just stare at Dickerson. "Really?"

"I don't know, ma'am," Dickerson repeated. "I'm not a ballistics matching expert. I know the suspect presented a fatal threat and I know I neutralized that threat."

Talon thought for a moment. "Well, I mean, if the suspect— if Miguel actually had a gun and he actually fired shots at you or Officer McCarthy, those bullets would have been recovered later by the forensics officers, right? Maybe dig a bullet out of a wall or something?"

Before Dickerson could say 'I don't know, ma'am' again, Cecilia stood up. "Objection. Calls for speculation."

Talon spun and glared at Cecilia. *Are you fucking kidding me?*

"I'm going to sustain the objection," Judge Kirshner ruled without asking for Talon's input. "If this witness didn't participate in evidence collection, then you should end this line of questioning."

Talon offered a tight smile and an even tighter nod. "That's fine, Your Honor. I definitely have another line of questioning."

Talon took a moment to gather herself, then stepped closer to Dickerson. "You've been a police officer for fourteen years, is that right?"

"That's right," Dickerson confirmed.

"And the last thirteen years have been with Tacoma P.D., right?"

"Correct."

"Your prior job was with the Birchwood Police Department, up in the foothills near Mount Rainier, correct?"

Dickerson's expression tightened. "That's correct, ma'am."

"And the reason you had to leave the Birchwood Police Department," Talon grinned as she struck, "was because of a sustained finding of excessive force against another young, unarmed, Hispanic male, isn't that true?"

Dickerson responded with a forceful "No!" at the exact same time that Cecilia yelled, "Objection!" and Judge Kirshner called out, "Ms. Winter!"

Talon couldn't quite wipe the smile off her face. But Kirshner was anything but smiling.

"Ladies and gentlemen of the jury," she said, "the bailiff is going to escort you to the jury room while I discuss a matter with the attorneys."

"I'd like the witness to be excused as well," Talon requested.

Kirshner frowned, but then nodded at Dickerson. "Please wait in the hallway, Officer."

Dickerson complied and, in a few moments, both the jury and the witness were out of earshot.

"What do you think you're doing, Ms. Winter?" Judge

Kirshner demanded.

"Um, my job, Your Honor," Talon answered. "This witness has a history of excessive violence against young Hispanic men. The jury is entitled to know that. In addition, he just committed perjury. He said there was no sustained finding of excessive force, but," Talon pulled a set of papers out of her briefcase, "I have the internal affairs investigation right here. There was most definitely a sustained finding of excessive force."

"He said that wasn't the reason he left," Cecilia pointed out. "Your question was whether that was the reason he left, and he said no. He didn't say there was no finding."

Talon's smile finally faded a bit. Cecilia was right. "Well," Talon said, "I can explore that more fully."

"Don't get ahead of yourself, Ms. Winter," Judge Kirshner warned. "I'll decide whether you get to ask any more questions in this area. Ms. Thompson, I take it from your reaction that you were surprised by this information?"

"Yes, Your Honor," Cecilia confirmed. "This is the first I've heard of it."

"Ms. Winter," Kirshner demanded, "did you provide this information to Ms. Winter in advance, as required by the court rules?"

"I did not, Your Honor," Talon admitted. "The court rules only require the defense to hand over information we actually intend to use at trial. I didn't know for sure whether I was going to use this information until after Ms. Thompson finished her direct examination of Officer Dickerson. If he had admitted that his use of force was excessive and unreasonable and he was the one who caused Miguel Maldonado's and Officer McCarthy's deaths, then I would not have brought up the business at Birchwood P.D."

Kirshner stared at Talon for several moments. "Did you

really think there was any possibility at all that Officer Dickerson would say any of that during his direct examination?"

Talon shrugged. "A girl can hope."

"Your Honor, this is a huge discovery violation," Cecilia complained. "I had no idea about any of this."

Talon shrugged at her. "It's not my fault you didn't look into the background of your star witness. Maybe you shouldn't have tried so hard to keep me from finding things out about him. If you'd worked with me, we both could have known in advance."

"This isn't Ms. Thompson's fault," Judge Kirshner interjected. "It's yours. You should have disclosed this information prior to the witness taking the stand."

"Again, Your Honor, I didn't know if I was going to use the information until after he took the stand," Talon responded. "In case Your Honor has forgotten, you denied my motion to get a copy of Officer Dickerson's personnel file. If you had granted it back then, we wouldn't be where we are now."

It was never a good idea to piss off the judge. It was even worse when you were kind of right.

"We are where we are now," Judge Kirshner growled, "because you violated the discovery rules, Ms. Winter. You were the one who decided not to disclose this. You were the one who opted for the cheap theatrical moment rather than follow proper procedure. Even if I accept your argument that you didn't know you were going to use it until after Officer Dickerson's direct examination, you could have asked for a recess after the direct, and then provided the information to Ms. Thompson. I would have given her time to review it and we could have addressed any objections in advance."

"Objections you would have sustained," Talon said, "thereby prohibiting me from asking about it at all."

"Don't presume to know how I would have ruled, Ms. Winter," Judge Kirshner warned. "But if I had ruled that way, it would have been for good reason and I would have expected you to abide by my ruling."

Talon opened her mouth to respond again, but Kirshner wasn't having any more.

"Just like you will abide by my ruling now," the judge said. "You are prohibited from asking any more questions about this topic. Not one more question. I am suppressing the evidence on the basis of your failure to provide the information to Ms. Thompson before raising it in front of the jury."

Talon wasn't completely surprised. She knew Kirshner was likely to suppress the information. That was why she hadn't told anyone about it beforehand. But there was one little problem with how it had all played out.

"I would ask for permission to clarify the last question and answer, Your Honor," Talon requested. "I understood Officer Dickerson's response to mean that there was no sustained finding of excessive force. Ms. Thompson understood it to mean there may have been such a finding but that wasn't why he left Birchwood. I'd like to just clarify that and then I'll be done with my cross examination."

"Ms. Winter," Judge Kirchner drew the name out as she breathed it down at its owner, "I'm not sure whether to be impressed by your advocacy or offended that you think I would actually grant that request. Not only am I not going to allow you to ask any further questions on this topic, I am going to strike your question and answer and instruct the jury to disregard it completely."

Talon nodded. She wasn't surprised by that either. But, as they say, you can't unring a bell. "Understood, Your Honor."

Judge Kirchner looked to her bailiff. "Bring in the jury. Ms. Thompson, fetch your witness. Let's get back on the record.

Once the jury was in the box and Dickerson was on the stand, Judge Kirchner formally struck the last question and answer from the record and instructed the jury to disregard it. Which, Talon hoped, was kind of like highlighting it, underlining it, and drawing a big red circle around it.

"Any further questions for this witness, Ms. Winter?" Judge Kirshner's voice made clear what answer she wanted.'

"No, Your Honor." Talon threw a disgusted look at Officer Dickerson. "I'm finished with this witness."

Cecilia was smart enough to not ask any more questions either, lest she inadvertently open the door to that prior excessive force allegation after all.

Thus ended Dickerson's testimony. Talon had drawn blood, but the judge had stepped in to wipe it off.

Talon didn't know what the jury would do with all that.

CHAPTER 44

After Dickerson, it was all downhill for Cecilia. Not brakes-cut, hurtling-toward-a-watery-death downhill, but downhill just the same. Talon returned to her limited, surgical questioning. She knew it was the most effective method, but she still worried the jury would think she just didn't have that much to say.

The next witness was the medical examiner. Nothing earthshaking. Both victims died of gunshot wounds. Miguel took a bullet to the heart. McCarthy took one to the carotid artery in his neck. Neither was survivable. None of that was really at issue. Talon just confirmed that all of the bullets removed from both Miguel and McCarthy were collected and sealed in evidence bags. But the medical examiner couldn't say they were all from the same gun.

That was for the ballistics expert to say. Which he did when he testified right after the medical examiner. That is, he confirmed the bullets were all fired from the same gun. But he couldn't say exactly which gun. Which gave Talon a little something more to talk about on her cross examination.

After Cecilia announced, "No further questions," Talon

stood up and approached the witness for her cross exam.

"You say all of the bullets were fired from the same gun?" Talon began.

"Yes, that's right," the ballistics expert answered. He was a short, squat man, dressed in a jacket that wasn't quite tweed but still had elbow pads. His name was Ernest Pfleger, and he'd worked for the State Patrol Crime Lab for over thirty years, almost all of it squinting into a microscope to compare markings left on bullets as they traveled down gun barrels.

"And how can you tell that again?" Talon asked, even if only to remind the jurors before Talon got to her real point.

"Well, as I mentioned earlier," Pfleger said, "bullets are softer than the barrel of the gun. Gun barrels have grooves cut into them which twist as they go down the barrel. Those grooves are called rifling and that's what gives the bullet its spin, which allows it to cut through the air like a football. In order for that to work, the raised part of the twist, called the lands, presses against the bullet as it travels down the barrel, forcing it to twist and spin. Those lands aren't perfectly smooth though. There are microscopic irregularities—bumps, if you will—that scratch the bullet as it travels down the barrel. These irregularities are just a byproduct of the manufacturing process and are unique to each firearm. That means the pattern of scratches left on the side of a bullet by a particular firearm will be the same for every other bullet fired from that firearm, but different from any bullet fired from a different firearm."

"So, it's essentially a fingerprint, but for a firearm?" Talon translated.

"Exactly."

"Even if you can't identify a specific firearm as the source of the bullets," Talon continued, "can you narrow it down at all based on general characteristics?"

Pfleger nodded. "Yes. Different manufacturers produce their barrels in different ways. Some have four grooves; some have five or even six. Some twist to the left, some twist to the right. So, at a minimum, I can say that a given bullet was fired from, say, a barrel with four lands and grooves with a left twist. Then there are certain models of firearms that have four lands and grooves with a left twist. Those are possible sources of the bullet. Any model with more or less grooves, or the opposite twist can be excluded."

"Okay," Talon nodded along. "So, how would you positively identify that a particular firearm fired a particular bullet?"

"I would need to test fire the firearm myself," Pfleger explained to the jury. "Then I could compare the bullets that I know I fired from the firearm with the bullets provided to me for examination. If they match, I know it's the same firearm. It's kind of like taking the fingerprints of a burglary suspect. You may be able to get fingerprints off the window, but you need to compare them to a known person's fingerprints to make a match."

"Can you do that in every case?" Talon followed up.

"No." Pfleger shook his head.

"Why not?" Talon asked.

"The firearm isn't always recovered," Pfleger explained.

"Oh, okay," Talon said. "Like, the suspect threw it in the river or something?"

"Right."

"Were you able to identify a specific firearm as the source of the fired bullets in this case?" Talon asked. She knew the answer, but she wanted the jurors to know it too.

"Uh, no," Pfleger admitted.

"Why not?

"No firearm was ever submitted to me for test firing," Pfleger explained.

"No one asked you to do it?" Talon confirmed.

"Correct."

"And who would ask you to test fire a known firearm to see if it was the source of fired bullets?"

"Usually the lead detective," Pfleger answered. "Or the prosecutor."

"But no one ever asked you to do that in this case?"

"No."

Talon took a moment to let that all sink in.

"You said earlier," she circled back, "that even without a specific firearm to test fire, you could still narrow down the list of possible firearms based on the number of lands and grooves and the direction of the twist. Is that right?"

"Yes, that's right."

"The list of firearms which could have fired the bullets in this case," Talon said, "does it include the .40 caliber Smith and Wesson Model 22?"

Pfleger nodded. "Yes, it does."

"And the Smith and Wesson 22 is one of the standard-issue firearms for officers in the Tacoma Police Department, isn't it?"

Pfleger nodded again. "Yes, it is."

Talon nodded as well. "Thank you. No further questions."

Talon turned and headed back to her seat. She had basically just accused Cecilia of hiding evidence. It was difficult for a prosecutor to prosecute a defendant when she had to defend herself.

But Cecilia was too smart to take the bait. When Judge Kirshner asked her if she wanted to conduct any re-direct examination, Cecilia stood up calmly and informed the Court, "No,

Your Honor. No further questions for this witness."

And that left just one more witness for the State's case-in-chief. The cop who took Luke's alleged 'confession.'

CHAPTER 45

"The State calls Detective Danny Wolcott to the stand."

Cecilia announced her last witness with that second wind that comes from knowing you're almost done with a huge, complicated, weeks-long task. Her smile seemed to extend the entire length of her body.

Talon was hoping Wolcott would look the part she needed for her counter narrative, namely the Bad Cop. The kind of cop who would beat a confession out of a suspect in a darkened room with a single light bulb hanging from the ceiling. But that wasn't what actually happened. Luke's confession wasn't beaten out of him; it was tricked out of him, by someone he thought he could trust.

Wolcott was short, bald, and overweight, with a thick mustache and a disarming smile, even as he made his way up to the judge to be sworn in. He looked like a favorite teacher or a funny uncle. If he had any rubber hoses, it was to make balloon animals with them.

Wolcott took the witness stand and Cecilia began her direct examination.

"Could you please state your name for the record?"

"Daniel Wolcott," Uncle Teacher answered.

"And how are you employed, sir?'

"I am a detective with the Tacoma Police Department," he answered. Then, anticipating Cecilia's next question, he added, "I've been a detective for twenty-one years and was a patrol officer for six years before that."

"Thank you," Cecilia replied. "Detective Wolcott, were you involved in the case we're discussing here today?"

Wolcott nodded. "Yes, I was."

"And how were you involved?"

"I interviewed the suspect." Wolcott nodded toward the defense table. "Lucas Zlotnik. The defendant."

"Did you also go to the scene?" Cecilia asked.

Wolcott shook his head. "No, I went directly to headquarters, met the transport officers there, and took custody of Mr. Zlotnik."

"Did you speak with him alone?" Cecilia asked.

"Yes," Wolcott answered. "Sometimes I'll bring a junior detective with me, kind of for training, but it was pretty busy that night. Everybody was out in the field."

"Do you sometimes bring another detective," Cecilia followed up, "so you can play good cop/bad cop?"

Wolcott laughed. "No. That doesn't actually work. We do good cop/good cop. I'm a police officer. My job is to help people. That includes suspects of crimes. I can't expect them to help me if I'm not willing to be kind to them."

Talon could see why Wolcott was such a successful interrogator. He just seemed like the kind of guy you could trust. No wonder Luke confessed.

"Okay, then," Cecilia moved on. "So, prior to speaking with the defendant, did you advise him of his constitutional rights?"

"Absolutely," Wolcott assured. "I never start an interview until after I've read the person their rights, even if they're just a witness."

"Great," Cecilia acknowledged. "And did the defendant agree to speak with you?"

"Yes, he did."

"Did you make an audio-recording of his statement?" Cecilia asked.

"Yes, I did."

Cecilia took a moment to walk over to the section of the bar directly in front of the bailiff, where all of the exhibits were laid out. She selected a CD in a paper sleeve and handed it to Wolcott.

"I'm handing you what has previously been marked as Exhibit One," she said for the record. "Please examine the marking on that disc, Detective Wolcott, and tell me whether it appears to be related to this case."

Wolcott extracted the CD from its envelope and took a moment to look at the face of the disc. "Yes," he said. "It appears to be an audio-recording of the interview I conducted with Mr. Zlotnik."

"How do you know that?" Cecilia asked.

Wolcott pointed to the writing on the disc. "It has the case number, the suspect's name, my name, and the date. And at the bottom it says, 'Suspect Interview'."

Cecilia looked up to Judge Kirshner. "Your Honor, the State moves to admit Exhibit One."

"No objection," Talon offered. Any objection would have been overruled anyway.

"The State moves to publish the exhibit," Cecilia followed up.

"You want to play it for the jury?" Kirshner translated.

"Yes, Your Honor," Cecilia said.

"Any objection, Ms. Winter?" the judge asked.

"No objection, Your Honor," Talon responded. After all, why should she be afraid of the so-called confession? She'd already told the jury it was a lie. And her expert would say the same thing. The jury might as well hear it, if only so they can choose to disregard it.

Cecilia walked over to a small laptop computer on her counsel table, connected to a set of speakers. She pressed the side of the computer and a disc tray popped out. She dropped in Exhibit One, and pressed the tray back in. A few mouse-clicks later, the audio-recording started and everyone in the courtroom leaned forward to listen:

Danny Wolcott (DW): Alright. This is Detective Danny Wolcott of the Tacoma Police Department and I am taking the statement of Lucas Zlotnik. Did I say that right? Zlotnik?

Lucas Zlotnik (LZ): Yeah, that's right.

DW: Okay, great. Okay. So, this is the statement of Lucas Zlotnik. The time is approximately 1724 hours. And Lucas, do I have your permission to record this?

LZ: Yeah.

DW: Okay, thanks, Lucas. Is it Lucas or Luke?

LZ: Uh, Luke, I guess.

DW: Okay, great. Luke. Alright then, Luke. We've been talking a little bit about what happened today at the Cash-Town U.S.A. Do you remember that?

LZ: Yeah, sure. I remember.

DW: Okay, great. So, why don't we just kind of start from the top? You know Miguel Maldonado, right?

LZ: Uh, yeah.

DW: And how do you know him?

LZ: I dunno. He's a friend, I guess.

DW: A friend. Right. Great. Okay. Is he like your best friend, would you say?

LZ: I dunno. I mean, I don't really have— Sure, yeah, he's my best friend.

DW: Okay, great. And so, today you and Miguel drove over to the Cash-Town U.S.A. on Thirty-Eighth, over by the mall, right?

LZ: Yeah.

DW: And who was driving?

LZ: Uh, I was driving. We took my car. I picked him up.

DW: Okay, great, great. And whose idea was it to go to the Cash-Town U.S.A. again? I think you said it was Miguel's idea, right?

LZ: Yeah, sure. It was Miguel's idea.

DW: Okay, and what was the plan?

LZ: Uh, I'm not really sure what you mean.

DW: Why did you go to the Cash-Town store? What was your plan for going there?

LZ: Oh. Uh, yeah, well, it wasn't really my plan.

DW: But you knew about it, right?

LZ: Uh...

DW: Right? You knew what the plan was, right?

LZ: Uh, yeah. I mean, sure, I guess so. Like I said, it was more Miguel's plan.

DW: Okay, but you knew about it. So, what was the plan then? Was it just to cash a check or was it something different?

LZ: Uh, something different, I guess.

DW: Something different, you guess. Alright. And that something different, that was to rob the place, right?

LZ: Uh. Um. Yeah.

DW: And like you said, it was all Miguel's idea, right? Not yours?

LZ: Yeah, it wasn't my idea.

DW: In fact, he just wanted you to wait in the car, right? Not go in with him, just wait outside in the car until he came out again.

LZ: Uh, yeah. I waited in the car.

DW: While Miguel went inside, right?

LZ: Right.

DW: And he said something to you when he got out of the car, didn't he?

LZ: Uh, yeah.

DW: What did he say again?

LZ: He, uh, he just said something like, 'I'm going to make a withdrawal' and then patted his coat pocket.

DW: And you assumed that meant he had a gun, right? In his coat pocket?

LZ: I, uh, I never saw any gun.

DW: Right. No, of course not. But he patted his coat pocket like he had a gun there, right?

LZ: Sure.

DW: And he could have a gun there, right? I mean it was a big enough pocket or whatever, right?

LZ: I, uh, I guess so.

DW: So, I mean, you kind of knew he had a gun then, right?

LZ: I never saw any gun.

DW: Sure, sure. But the plan was to rob the place, and you were supposed to wait in the car, and he made a joke about making a withdrawal and then patted his coat pocket where he could have had a gun, right? So, I mean, you kind of knew he had a gun, right?

LZ: If you say so.

DW: It doesn't really count if I say so, Luke. You have to say so. You knew he had a gun, right?

LZ: Sure. I knew he had a gun. But I never saw any gun.

DW: Okay, sure. Great. You're doing great, Luke. We're almost done.

LZ: Okay. Good.

DW: Right, right. And so it's clear for the recording, you didn't know Miguel was going to shoot anybody, right?

LZ: Right.

DW: And you didn't know anyone was going to die, right?

LZ: Right. Totally.

DW: Right. And you certainly didn't want anyone to get shot or die, right?

LZ: No, of course not.

DW: You just knew Miguel was gonna rob the place and you were supposed to wait outside in the car. Right?

LZ: Uh…

DW: Right?

LZ: Yeah, sure. Right.

DW: Okay, great, Luke. Really great. Thank you.

Cecilia stopped the recording. "Thank you, Detective Wolcott." She ejected the disc from the laptop. "No further questions."

But Talon had some questions. She stood up and approached the witness.

"Let's back up a little from what we just heard, okay, Detective?" she began. "That recording, it's only a part of the entire conversation you had with my client, isn't that correct?"

Wolcott nodded. "Yes. We talked briefly before turning on

the recorder."

"Briefly," Talon repeated. "Oh, okay. But you didn't record any of that allegedly brief conversation, did you?"

"No, ma'am," Wolcott admitted.

"You could have, though, right?" Talon asked. "I mean, you had the recorder with you, right? You could have just turned it on as soon as you started talking to him, correct?"

"Well, you see—" Wolcott started.

"No," Talon cut him off. "It's a yes or no question. You could have recorded the entire conversation, but you didn't, isn't that correct?"

Wolcott nodded. "That is correct."

"And the reason you didn't record it," Talon asserted, "was so no one would hear you feeding him details of the event so his confession would seem more credible."

It was quite the accusation, but Wolcott had an answer ready. "No, ma'am. Sometimes suspects don't actually talk to me. Or they tell me some crazy story that's obviously made up. I don't turn the recorder on until I know the suspect has something useful to say."

"Useful?" Talon repeated that word too. "Useful in obtaining a conviction?"

"Useful in holding someone responsible," Wolcott spun it a little differently.

"And it's especially useful," Talon pressed him, "if the suspect says exactly what you told him to say before you turned on the recorder, right?"

"I'm not sure what you mean," Wolcott hedged.

"I mean," Talon explained—to him and to the jury, "that Luke said what you told him to say and that's why it was useful. Isn't that right?"

"No, ma'am. I did not tell him what to say," Wolcott insisted.

"Well, you told him some things about the case, right?" Talon asked.

"I'm not sure," Wolcott answered. He was starting to look uncomfortable. Still the favorite teacher, but the principal found something on his computer.

"You told him someone was shot to death inside the Cash-Town U.S.A., right?"

"Uh, I think I probably did tell him that," Wolcott admitted.

"Sure, you did," Talon said. "Because you told him he was a suspect in a murder, didn't you?"

"I'm not sure if I told him that exactly," Wolcott answered.

"In fact," Talon continued, "you told him he was a suspect in a murder investigation, and he could go home if he just admitted he knew it was going to be a robbery, but he didn't know Miguel was going to kill anyone. Isn't that right?"

"I don't believe I said that," Wolcott responded.

"Well, why don't we just listen to the recording?" Talon suggested sarcastically. "Oh, that's right! You don't record the parts where you pressure the suspect to give the confession. You don't record the promises you make or the lies you tell. You just get everything all wrapped up with a nice little bow, then turn on the recorder to make it seem like the suspect just confessed of his own free will."

"No one forced your client to say what he said," Wolcott defended.

"No, but they tricked him, didn't they?" Talon shot back. "Didn't *you*?

"The conversation we had before I turned on the recorder was very brief," Wolcott insisted. "Just long enough for me to confirm your client was willing to talk to me and had information useful to the investigation."

"Really quick, huh?" Talon asked.

"Yes," Wolcott said. "Very brief."

"No details about the event?" Talon asked. "Just confirmation that he's willing to talk to you and that he has information worth listening to?"

"Exactly," Wolcott relaxed a little bit. He had a few beads of sweat on top of his bald head.

"How did you know about the joke Miguel made?" Talon asked.

"Pardon?"

"If you didn't talk about the details of the event, how did you know Miguel made a joke about making a withdrawal?"

"Uh," Wolcott looked around for an explanation. "I think he's the one who mentioned that on the recording."

Talon shook her head. "No. It was you. You brought it up. You described the joke. Luke just agreed with you."

Wolcott didn't say anything.

"Do you want me to cue it up so we can listen to it again?" Talon challenged.

"No, that's not necessary," Wolcott assured. "If you say I said it first, then I'm sure that's correct. I guess we must have talked about some of the details before I turned on the recorder."

"I guess so," Talon sneered. "No further questions."

Cecilia stood up to conduct a brief re-direct examination. "Detective Wolcott, did you make any promises to the defendant regarding what charges he might face for his conduct that evening?"

"No," Wolcott said. "I just asked him to tell me the truth."

"And you recorded that truth on the recording we just

listened to?"

"Yes, ma'am."

"No further questions." And Cecilia sat down again.

"Any re-cross examination based on that, Ms. Winter?" the judge asked.

"Yes, Your Honor," Talon answered.

She marched right up to Wolcott. "That 'truth' you recorded," she used her fingers to make air quotes around the word 'truth', "you spoon-fed that to him before you went on tape so he would confess to the robbery and you could arrest him for murder."

Wolcott narrowed his eyes at Talon. "Is that a question?"

Talon scoffed. "No, I guess it's not. Nothing further."

That concluded Wolcott's testimony, and with it, the State's case-in-chief. Cecilia made it official by standing up and announcing, "The State rests."

Judge Kirshner looked down at Talon. "Does the defense intend to call any witnesses?"

Talon stood to address the judge. "Yes, Your Honor," she said. "But first, I have a motion."

CHAPTER 46

There was a standard practice in criminal cases. After the State rested, the defense made what was known as a 'halftime motion.' The motion itself was simple. Ask the Court to dismiss the case because the prosecution had failed to put on sufficient evidence to allow the case to proceed to the jury. The legal jargon for that level of sufficient evidence was *'prima facie* case.' Basically, it just meant any jury could possibly find the defendant guilty. In a drug case, if no witness ever testified that the white powder found on the defendant was actually chemically tested and found to be cocaine, then the judge should throw the case out—to prevent the jury from convicting in error. And it was all predicated on the knowledge, usually left unspoken, that juries can't be trusted to do the right thing in that sort of circumstance, because they almost always just rubber-stamp whatever the prosecution told them in opening statement.

That was all well and good for a drug case, or maybe a charge of felon in possession of a firearm where the evidence room lost the firearm and the State can't actually say for sure it was really a gun and not a fancy cigarette lighter. But in a murder case, it was pretty much impossible to win the motion. Especially when the prosecution introduced a confession.

Still, it was almost malpractice not to make the motion because failure to do so would preclude the appellate attorney from making similar arguments on appeal.

So, everyone in the courtroom knew what Talon was about to do. And everyone knew what the judge was going to do. It was almost boring.

"What's your motion, Ms. Winter?" Judge Kirshner practically yawned once the jury was safely out of hearing in the jury room.

"It's a halftime motion, Your Honor," Talon practically admitted. But she had a surprise too. She hated being bored too. "Combined with a motion to dismiss for prosecutorial misconduct."

Now, that was not boring. And not at all expected.

"What?" Cecilia shot to her feet, incredulous. "Misconduct? What misconduct?"

"Knowingly putting on false evidence," Talon explained.

"Wha, what false evidence?" Cecilia stammered.

"That so-called confession," Talon answered. "It was analyzed by an expert and found to be false. I gave you a copy of her report. I believe you may have also received a copy through other means. In any event, you didn't have anyone else analyze the confession, so the only independent evidence is that my client's alleged confession was false. But you admitted it into evidence anyway. That's misconduct."

Judge Kirshner interrupted with a clearing of her throat. "Really, Ms. Talon? That's your motion?"

"That's my motion, Your Honor," Talon confirmed. "And

I'm sticking to it."

"Making your record," Kirshner observed.

"Yes, Your Honor," Talon answered.

"Fine," Kirshner harrumphed. "Your record is made. And your motion is denied."

That was fine with Talon. She knew she wouldn't win. She just wanted to poke Cecilia in the eye.

"Can I be heard, Your Honor?" Cecilia complained.

Kirshner raised an eyebrow at her. "You want to be heard on a motion where I've already ruled for you?"

"I just want to make a record," Cecilia said.

"She doesn't get to just make a record, Your Honor," Talon interjected. "If I win, there's no appeal. She doesn't need to make a record."

Kirshner nodded down at Cecilia. "Ms. Winter is right. If you just want to complain about someone calling you unethical, I would save it until you get back to your office."

"But, Your Honor," Cecilia insisted.

Kirshner sighed. "She's just taunting you, Ms. Thompson."

Cecilia took a moment, then looked over at Talon.

Talon smiled at her. "Not 'just'."

Cecilia took another moment, then exhaled sharply and stood up straight. "Fine. Thank you, Your Honor. I have nothing to add to this motion."

"Good," Kirshner replied.

"But I expect to have my own motion regarding Ms. Winter's conduct," Cecilia went on. "It will be ready in the morning. I'd like to do a little bit of research before presenting it to the Court."

Kirshner looked at Cecilia for a long moment, then sighed and turned to Talon. "Any objection to starting in the morning, Ms.

Winter?"

"None, Your Honor," Talon answered cheerfully. "It will give me extra time to prepare before starting my case-in-chief."

Cecilia looked over at Talon. "That was your plan all along."

Talon just smiled. "See you in the morning."

CHAPTER 47

The extra few hours her game with Cecilia had afforded Talon weren't actually all that necessary. It was never bad to have extra time to prepare, especially in the middle of a trial, but Talon's first witness was Dr. Natalie Ross. Talon didn't really need extra time to prepare for her testimony. Ross was a professional who had testified dozens, even hundreds of times. Talon just needed to remember to get out of the good doctor's way.

The next morning found Talon and Luke at the defense table, Dr. Ross seated in the front row of the gallery, the corrections officers guarding the exit, and the bailiff and court reporter at their respective stations—all waiting for Cecilia Thompson to arrive.

"Where's the prosecutor?" Luke whispered to Talon. He was wearing the blue suit again. "Wasn't she going to go after you for something since you went after her?"

Talon chuckled slightly. "Yeah, something like that. But if she did her research—the right research—she'll just ask the judge to move on."

Cecilia burst through the courtroom doors at that point. She looked uncharacteristically disheveled. She had a file folder and some books barely trapped against her body with one arm and while her other arm was pulling a rolling briefcase, that got hit by the closing courtroom door. She was still dressed perfectly, and her hair and makeup were flawless, but there was an unsettledness about her which Talon didn't recognize.

"Sorry, I'm late," Cecilia panted to the bailiff when she reached her table. Then she glanced up at the clock. "Oh, it's only 8:59. I guess I'm not late after all. Whew."

Talon took a moment to appraise her opponent. She could see the calm returning to her even as she set her books down and became acclimated to her familiar surroundings.

"Are you still bringing some sort of motion to get back at me?" Talon asked.

"What?" Cecilia answered, then laughed. "Oh, that? Oh, no. Of course not. That was just a ploy to buy time."

Talon cocked her head at her.

Cecilia tipped her own head at Dr. Ross. "You aren't the only one who wanted some extra time to prepare for your expert witness's testimony," she whispered.

And before Talon could think of a reply, Judge Kirshner entered the courtroom to the formal cry of her bailiff.

"Are we ready to proceed with witnesses?" Kirshner asked as soon as she sat down. That was code for, 'We're not doing your stupid motion, are we, Ms. Thompson?'

"The State is ready, Your Honor," Cecilia answered simply. Then, she went ahead and addressed the real question. "I will not be bringing any motions after all. At least," a quick side glance at Talon, "not at this time."

Talon suppressed the urge to shake her head. Mind games? From Cecilia Thompson? Prosecutors weren't supposed to do that. Maybe she should make another motion.

"Anything from the defense, Ms. Winter?" Judge Kirshner asked.

Talon shook herself from her thoughts. "Uh, no, Your Honor. Thank you, Your Honor. The defense is prepared to call its first witness, Dr. Natalie Ross."

"Excellent," Judge Kirshner said. "Bring in the jury."

CHAPTER 48

Dr. Natalie Ross strode into the courtroom, all presence and confidence. She spent a good portion of her time flying around the country, attending conferences, delivering speeches, signing books, and—fortunately for Talon, and Luke—testifying in court. She was used to travelling, so even though she arrived on a late flight and spent the night in the nearest 3-star hotel to the courthouse, she looked every bit the prepared, intelligent, trustworthy professional she was touted to be.

At least she looked that way to Talon, as she watched Ross step forward and get sworn in by the judge. Talon would just have to hope the jury thought so too.

"Good morning," Talon greeted her witness as she took her seat on the witness stand. "Could you please state your name for the record?"

"My name is Natalie Ross." Ross turned to the jurors to answer Talon's question. Cops weren't the only professional witnesses who got training on how to testify. And there was a reason the best witnesses delivered their answers to the decision-makers, not the question-askers. The jurors loved it.

"How are you employed, Ms. Ross?" Talon continued.

Again, a turn to the jurors. "I am a professor of psychology. I am also an author and professional speaker. My books and speeches are also on the subject of psychology."

"And do you also testify in court cases, Dr. Ross?" Talon asked the obvious question.

Ross smiled at the jury. "It would appear so," she said. A few of the jurors chuckled.

Nice, thought Talon. *They like her already.*

"But seriously," Ross continued. "Yes, I do occasionally testify in cases when asked and when I feel it's appropriate."

"Do you have any special education or degrees related to your current occupations?" Talon asked. She felt stupid asking such basic questions, especially ones she so obviously already knew the answers to, but the evidence rules required her to ask open-ended questions of her own witnesses. And anyway, it gave the jury a chance to hear how awesome Dr. Ross was.

"Yes," Ross told the jurors. "I have a bachelor of science in psychology and biology and a Ph.D. in psychology. I also attend continuing education courses and specialized seminars in my area of concentration."

Talon appreciated the setup for her next question. "And what is your area of concentration, Dr. Ross?"

Dr. Ross smiled again and turned to the jurors. "My area of specialization is behavioral and cognitive psychology, and within that, my concentration is on the psychology of risk and reward."

"Risk and reward in behavioral and cognitive psychology," Talon repeated back, in part to make sure the jury got it all. "Does that have any application in the area of criminal law?"

"Yes," Ross answered. "Absolutely."

Talon nodded. She knew that. "Please explain."

It wasn't actually a question, and it called for an objectionably narrative answer, but Cecilia seemed to be willing to let it slide. Not least, Talon suspected, because Ross was an engaging witness and the topic was actually somewhat interesting. Better than laying the evidentiary foundation for the admission of business records.

Ross turned again to the jurors. "Well, you see, most crimes have few, if any, witnesses. That's not always true, of course. Crimes that are committed in the heat of the moment, perhaps due to an emotional outburst or mental illness, those may have many witnesses. But generally speaking, when a person commits a crime, they take efforts to avoid detection. They will wait until a business is closed for the night; they will wear gloves to prevent leaving fingerprints; they may craft an alibi in advance; and if there are multiple actors, they will work to 'get their story straight.' And another of these ways to reduce the risk of detection is the well-known and ominous threat of 'no witnesses.'"

Talon took a moment to watch the jurors. They were loving it, nodding along at all the right moments. *Good.*

"So, how does all of that relate to behavioral and cognitive psychology?" Talon asked.

"In behavioral and cognitive psychology, we're interested in why people behave in the ways that they do," Ross explained. "Regarding risk and reward, we focus on why people risk negative consequences in search of positive rewards. In the context of criminal behavior, people are far more likely to commit a crime if they think they can get away with it. In fact, there are several rather disturbing studies where people self-report that they would be willing to commit crimes—even serious and violent crimes—if there were a guarantee they would never be caught."

"So, people who commit crimes try not to get caught," Talon

said. "That doesn't seem difficult to believe."

Ross laughed. "Oh no, of course not. That's just the backdrop. The part that's really interesting is why so many people who have spent so much time planning to get away with a crime would nevertheless confess to the authorities when caught. The confession rate is astonishingly high if one assumes almost everyone who confesses had made at least some preparation not to get caught in the first place."

Talon nodded. "That does seem surprising, I suppose. Does psychology provide an answer to that question?"

Ross smiled and shrugged. "It tries. We're always learning, of course, but we learn because we ask. And this was an area I decided to start asking about."

"So, what did you learn?" Talon asked.

"Like all the best answers," Ross said, "this one is simple. When faced with a decision, people assess their options and choose the one they think will lead to the greatest reward. The difference between the criminal who is preparing not to be caught and the criminal who has been caught is very basic: he's been caught. The situation has changed significantly, and so the calculus of what leads to the greatest reward changes as well."

"How does that relate to confessions?" Talon asked. "Or perhaps I should say *alleged* confessions."

"Let's call them incriminating statements," Ross suggested. "Confession is a weighted word. It assumes that the statement is true, that the person making the statement really did the things they say they did, and that they are confessing to some sort of wrongdoing. An incriminating statement is merely that: a statement made by a person which incriminates them in some specific criminal activity, whether it's true or not."

"Okay," Talon agreed. "Incriminating statement. "So, why

would so many people who want to avoid detection suddenly provide incriminating statements after being detected?"

"There is really only one reason," Ross told the jurors. "The person calculates that making the incriminating statement will provide them with greater benefits than not making it."

Talon nodded. That seemed almost too obvious to be helpful. "Could you explain further?" she prompted.

"The most familiar example," Ross answered, "is probably the idea of throwing oneself on the mercy of the court. By admitting to the offense one can beg for mercy, which may or may not come. But mercy is less likely to be given to someone who insists they didn't commit the crime. It really revolves around power dynamics and the person's perception of their personal power in the system. Most individuals are pretty powerless when faced with the might of the police and the rest of the criminal justice system, which is probably why they went to so much trouble to avoid detection in the first place. So, once caught, it's actually a very rational decision to seek favor from the power structure in the hopes of a less severe penalty."

Talon took a moment before asking her next question. Up until now, it had been general theory. She was about to apply it to Luke's specific case, but she needed to make sure the jury understood the full implication of what Ross was saying.

"So, to be clear," Talon went ahead and led her witness a bit, "you're saying that when a person makes a decision about whether to make an incriminating statement to law enforcement, they're not doing it to help the police, or unburden their souls, or anything like that. They're doing it because they've made a calculation that, of whatever limited choices they perceive to be available to them, providing an incriminating statement is the one they believe will have the greatest benefit to them. Do I have that right?"

"Yes," Ross confirmed. "The person who makes no statement, the person who makes a true incriminating statement, and the person who makes an incriminating statement that isn't true—all of them have decided that will be the course of action that has the greatest reward for them personally."

"Okay. Now, you mentioned incriminating statements that aren't true," Talon said. "Are those sometimes called false confessions?"

Dr. Ross nodded to the jury. "That's it exactly. The media usually calls them that. I'm actually comfortable with that term in this context. They are doubly false. First because they aren't true, and second because they aren't actually confessions then."

"Okay, good," Talon said. "That will be easier than saying 'incriminating statements that aren't true.'"

"Definitely," Ross agreed with a smile to the jurors. Most of them smiled back.

"Are there any special dangers when it comes to false confessions?" Talon asked the good doctor.

"Oh, yes," Ross agreed. "Socially, we give a lot of weight to confessions. Parents insist on confessions from their children, spouses from one another, employers and voters and you name it. We expect people to confess, and when they do, we believe them. This is especially true in the criminal justice system.

"In fact," Ross took on an even more professorial tone, "in some parts of Europe during the Middle Ages, a confession was required for a conviction. Unfortunately, this led to a small industry in confession extraction. Torture, that is. Suspects would be tortured until they confessed, then the confession would be used against them to obtain the conviction. There's actually a museum in Germany called the 'Criminal Justice Museum' but it's really just a museum of medieval torture instruments. Very interesting."

"I'm sure," Talon reluctantly agreed. "But how does that all relate to false confessions?"

"Ah, yes." Ross nodded and turned again to the jury. "Well, you see, because we give so much weight to confessions, because we have so much faith in them, it's hard for us to imagine a situation where someone would confess to something if they didn't actually do it. We think we would never do that ourselves, but that just shows a lack of imagination. There is always a situation where a person will confess to something they didn't do, so long as they see a benefit to it greater than not giving the false confession. But we don't see that internal decision-making process. We just see the confession. And in our society, a confession always equals guilt."

"But we don't torture confessions out of people anymore," Talon pointed out.

"Torture? No," Ross agreed. "Coerce, compel, trick? Absolutely. All that I just explained to you is very common knowledge. It's not secret. The police know it too. And they receive training to exploit that decision-making process to obtain inculpatory statements from suspects. Many are true. But some are not."

"Can't the police tell when someone is making a false confession?" Talon challenged.

"Sometimes." Ross shrugged. "If they want to see it. But a lot of times, the confession is what they need to close the case. There simply isn't always the incentive to look critically at a suspect's statement to determine why the suspect would have made the statement in the first place."

Talon took a moment to nod thoughtfully, even raising a pensive hand to her chin. She looked like she was starting to understand. She was mirroring what she hoped the jury was feeling too.

"Did you yourself have a chance," Talon asked Ross, "to look critically at the incriminating statement Luke Zlotnik made in this case?"

Ross nodded. "Yes."

"And did you formulate an opinion as to whether that incriminating statement contained true or false information?"

Another nod. "Yes, I did."

"What was your opinion based on?" Talon asked. These were the three requisite questions for admissibility of an expert's opinion testimony. Did you have an opinion? What was it based on? And what was the opinion?

"My opinion was based on the particular facts of this case and my broad expertise in the area of false confessions," Ross told the jury. "Specifically, I examined the language Mr. Zlotnik used, the language he avoided, how long he hesitated before answering, his knowledge or lack of knowledge regarding the legal impact of his statements, and whether there existed any perceived benefits of providing a false confession. I also considered the interrogation technique, especially the fact that the detective spoke with him at length about the details of the case before turning on the recording device."

Time for the payoff question. "And what is your opinion as to whether Mr. Zlotnik's incriminating statement to the police was true or false?"

Ross nodded and turned again to the jurors to deliver her own mini-verdict. "It is my expert opinion that the incriminating statement provided by Mr. Zlotnik was untrue. That is, he was lying when he said he knew his friend was going to commit a robbery inside the business."

And boom, there it was. The expert just told the jury to disregard the prosecution's biggest piece of evidence. Talon could sit down. But it never hurt to make sure they really, truly understood.

"So, you're saying Luke didn't know his friend was going to rob the store," Talon repeated. It was worth repeating. "But then, why did he say that?"

Ross nodded and turned again to her lecture class of twelve. "Mr. Zlotnik is not a sophisticated person. He is relatively young and has no special training in the law. He was unaware that confessing to knowing about the robbery was tantamount to confessing to the murder. He knew he was a suspect for murder, so to avoid being held responsible for that, he admitted—falsely—to something lesser, namely being an accomplice to a robbery. But, again, he doesn't know the law. He didn't know being an accomplice was the same under the law as acting as a principal, and he didn't know being a principal or accomplice to a robbery where a non-participant dies was defined under the law as murder. Had he known that, then he would not have made the false confession."

"And you're sure it's false?' Talon wanted it nailed down hard. "Luke didn't know."

Ross shifted her weight slightly, but put on a professional smile. "It is my expert opinion, based on my personal examination of the reports in this case and my years of study and training in behavioral and cognitive psychology that Mr. Zlotnik was not telling the truth when he said he knew his friend planned to commit the robbery."

Good enough. "Thank you, Dr. Ross," said Talon. "No further questions."

Talon returned to her seat next to Luke.

"That went really good," he whispered to her. "Right?"

But Talon just frowned slightly. "Ask me again after the cross examination."

Cecilia Thompson stood up and circled out from behind the prosecution table. She moved smoothly, like a snake on the water, a predator assessing its prey.

"So," she started, "you're an expert on false confessions, is that right, Dr. Ross?"

"I would say so," Ross agreed.

"But doesn't that sort of assume the result?" Cecilia challenged. "If you're an expert on false confessions, does that mean every confession you examine turns out to be false?"

"On the contrary," Ross assured her. "I'm an expert on incriminating statements generally, not just the false ones."

"Actually, you're just a psychologist," Cecilia challenged. "The American Psychiatric Association doesn't recognize any sort of specialization in false confessions, does it?"

"The A.P.A. recognizes a specialization in behavioral and cognitive psychology," Ross explained, "and that is my specialization. Within that specialization, I have concentrated my studies on the psychology of incriminating statements."

"So, it's a hobby," Cecilia translated. "You think it's interesting."

"It is interesting," Ross agreed, "but it's far more than a hobby. Woodworking is a hobby. This is my career field."

Cecilia frowned. The snake was having trouble finding an opening. "Your opinion is based solely on the transcript of the defendant's confession, isn't that correct?"

"I also reviewed the police reports," Ross told the jurors. "I needed to know what other information the investigation turned up, and when it was discovered, in order to evaluate what information Mr. Zlotnik had at the time he decided to provide an incriminating statement."

"Confession," Cecilia tried to correct Ross.

"False confession." Ross wasn't one to be corrected.

"Agree to disagree," Cecilia quipped. It wasn't a good look, though. Prosecutors weren't supposed to be smarmy. The jury wouldn't like that. *Good*, thought Talon. Ross was winning the battle so far.

"But you didn't interview Detective Wolcott, did you?" Cecilia accused. "You say he tricked the defendant into confessing, made him think he'd be in less trouble if he lied about the robbery, but you didn't give Detective Wolcott an opportunity to explain his methods, did you?"

"No," Ross agreed. "I did not. That wouldn't have been appropriate or helpful."

"It wouldn't have been helpful to talk to the detective who took the confession?" Cecilia practically gasped.

"No," Ross answered calmly. "Because he either would have admitted it, or he would have lied and said he didn't coerce the confession. Either way, it wouldn't have changed my opinion."

Cecilia actually took a small step backward, as if she'd been punched. "You think the detective would lie?"

Ross nodded. "Yes. He lied to Mr. Zlotnik. I see no reason why he wouldn't lie to me. In fact, applying the principals I explained earlier, the most likely outcome would have been for the detective to lie to me. He would have seen the risk of helping the defense expert as a possible acquittal, which was a very adverse outcome for him, especially if it came about in part because of his own statements to me. On the other hand, if he lied and insisted he didn't feed Mr. Zlotnik any details of the crime, that he didn't suggest to Mr. Zlotnik that he was facing the real possibility of murder charges if he didn't cooperate, or that he actually explained to Mr. Zlotnik how Washington's felony murder rule worked, well, then , that would not have added anything to my analysis. I assumed that would be his position, and I came to my opinion anyway."

"So, you're saying a twenty-year veteran of the police force would lie?" Cecilia challenged.

"No," Ross responded calmly. "I'm saying the eighteen-year-old defendant *did* lie. He did not know his friend was going to rob the check-cashing business. He only said that because he thought he would be arrested for murder if he didn't say it."

And the snake lost the battle. Dr. Ross was a mongoose.

Cecilia hesitated. She probably should have just announced, 'No further questions.' No further questions meant no further damage to her case. But she couldn't end on that. So, she fell back on the old standby for expert witnesses. Old and tired.

"You got paid to come here and testify the defendant's confession was false, didn't you?" she accused.

"I was paid for my time," Ross corrected. She turned to the jurors. "I charge the same rate to testify as I do for any other service I provide, including speaking at conferences. But I do not get paid to give a particular opinion. My opinion wouldn't be worth very much if it could be purchased."

Cecilia nodded and sneered slightly at the doctor. "Well, that's one thing we can agree on."

She spun on her heel and marched back to her counsel table, announcing, "No further questions," over her shoulder as she went.

Judge Kirshner raised an eyebrow at Talon. "Any re-direct examination, Ms. Winter?"

Of course not, Talon thought. *My witness killed it.* "No, Your Honor," she stood up to say. "Thank you."

"The witness is excused," Judge Kirshner declared. She looked again at Talon. "Does the defense intend to call any further witnesses?"

Talon was still standing, having anticipated the need to answer that very question. But she couldn't. Not yet. And not in front of the jury. "Could we take a brief recess, Your Honor?"

CHAPTER 49

All the lawyers knew what Talon meant when she asked for a recess. The only possible remaining defense witness was the defendant himself. But a defendant had the right not to testify, and if he chose not to testify, no part of that could be used against him. That was so important that it was considered reversible error for a judge to ask a defendant if he wanted to testify in front of the jury. It would force a non-testifying defendant to say, 'No'. Instead, everyone would just pretend like the defendant was never going to testify anyway and everything was fine. Nothing to see here. Move along.

So, Judge Kirshner excused the jury to the jury room and waited for the bailiff to close the door behind them. Once it clicked shut, she looked down at Talon. "Is your client going to testify?"

"I'm not sure," Talon answered. "I need a few minutes to discuss it with him." She looked around the courtroom full of prosecutors and jail guards. "In private."

Kirshner frowned. She was going to give Talon the time she needed—within reason—but there were security issues with an in-custody defendant. She couldn't just let them talk in the hall.

"Judge Parsons's courtroom is next door, but they're on recess this week," Judge Kirshner said. "You can use that courtroom."

Talon looked at the corrections officers. "Will we get any privacy?"

Kirshner nodded. "Of course. Officers, you are to wait outside Judge Parsons's jury room...after you handcuff Mr. Zlotnik to the table."

Talon stopped herself from shaking her head. She understood the judge's concern—Luke was charged with murder and Canada was only three hours away—but she also understood why Luke would want to run away from a system where poor people were held in jail before they were convicted. "Thank you, Your Honor," she said.

The guards actually handcuffed Luke first, then marched him next door, then uncuffed him long enough to recuff him to the leg of the large conference table in the jury room. The table legs were recessed, so Luke was forced to slump over the table, one arm pulled underneath. When the door to the jury room closed, Talon started the discussion.

"We need to decide whether you're going to take the stand and testify on your own behalf," she said. "I can give you my opinion and advice, but it's your decision to make. I can't force you to take the stand and I can't keep you off it either."

"Okay." Luke nodded, an awkward motion given his one arm extending under the table. "What do you think I should do?"

Talon hesitated. She knew he would do whatever she said. So, she knew she'd better be right. It was always a tough call. But when faced with a difficult decision, her gut usually told her what to do. And her gut was unequivocal. "Don't testify."

Luke frowned. "Shouldn't I tell them I didn't do it? Shouldn't I tell them I didn't know what Miguel was going to do?"

Talon shrugged. "Dr. Ross just told them that. I told them that in opening statement too. If you get on the stand and say it again, so what? You're the defendant. You'll say anything to get out of trouble. Hell, Dr. Ross just said as much."

"If I testify," Luke asked, "does the prosecutor get to ask me questions, too, or just you?"

"The prosecutor gets to ask you questions, too," Talon confirmed. "That's the danger. If I could have you just tell your side of the story and sit down again, it would be a no-brainer. We'd do that in a heartbeat. But that's not how it works. If you answer my questions, you have to answer hers."

Luke frowned. "She seems like a pretty good lawyer."

Talon nodded. "She's a very good lawyer. Dr. Ross was able to handle her, but she's a professional witness. She testifies all the time, all over the country. But you? You're not ready for her. She's good, and she's prepared, and she will take you apart brick by brick. It could undo everything we just gained with Dr. Ross."

"Can I just plead the Fifth or something if she goes too far?" Luke hoped.

But Talon shook her head. "Nope. The Fifth Amendment is all or nothing. Either you take the stand and answer everybody's questions, or you remain silent and the jury doesn't hear from you at all. If you tried to invoke the Fifth halfway through cross, the judge would strike all of your testimony, even the stuff you told me. And you'll look guilty as hell."

"Shit," Luke opined.

"Yeah," Talon agreed. "You have to answer every single one

of her questions. Like, if the plan wasn't to rob the check-mart, then what was your plan? If you say you were gonna buy drugs, or Miguel was gonna cash a check he stole from his mom, the prosecutor will be allowed to argue that those are also felonies and since Officer McCarthy died in the process of those felonies, you're still guilty of murder, even if you didn't know about any robbery."

"Really? They can just change the charges?" Luke asked.

"Yep," Talon confirmed. "They can amend the charges right up until the jury begins deliberating."

"That's messed up," Luke observed.

"It sure is," Talon agreed, "but it's the law."

She saw the thoughts swirling behind Luke's eyes. "I also can't put you on the stand if I know you're going to lie," she said. "That's suborning perjury, which is also a felony. And I'd lose my bar license. So, that's not an option either."

"Sure, sure," Luke nodded, obviously disappointed.

"So, the bottom line is this," Talon said. "There are huge risks in you testifying, and only limited benefits."

"Okay," Luke non-committed.

"More importantly," Talon went on, "I think the trial has gone pretty well for us. The teller couldn't remember what Miguel actually said. Dickerson wouldn't admit he was the only one with a gun, so he's obviously a liar. And Dr. Ross just told the jury your confession was a lie and you're innocent. Honestly, I don't think we need you to testify."

Luke sat up taller—as tall as he could handcuffed to the underside of a conference table. "You think we're going to win?'

Talon raised her palms at him. "I just think the trial has gone better for us than it could have. Putting you on the stand risks all of that."

Luke sighed. "Okay, good. I don't want to testify. I want to tell them I didn't do it, but I'm scared of the prosecutor, and I'm scared of what I might say, and I'm scared they won't believe me. I'm... I'm just scared."

Talon hesitated, but then put a hand on Luke's shoulder. "I know."

CHAPTER 50

Five minutes later, everyone—except the jury—was reassembled in Judge Kirshner's courtroom.

"Have you made a decision about the defendant testifying?" the judge asked Talon.

"Yes, Your Honor, "Talon answered. "Mr. Zlotnik will not be testifying. The defense rests."

Kirshner nodded and exhaled audibly. It was always a bit of a respite to reach the conclusion of evidence in a trial. It was all downhill from there. Just closing arguments and jury deliberations.

Talon was tempted to argue for another night to prepare her closing argument. Cecilia was likely to agree, because she'd get that extra night of preparation, too. But it also meant another night with Curt on her couch.

The mechanic had identified a hole in the brake lines where the fluid had leaked out, but he couldn't say it was intentional sabotage. Maybe she drove over a sewing needle or something. They hadn't come for her again, and maybe it was all just a coincidence—a terrifying, life-threatening coincidence—but Talon wasn't about to put her chips on that square. It was time to end the case.

"I'll be ready this afternoon," Talon confirmed. She had to be.

That meant a morning of honing her already half-prepared remarks. A light lunch, enough to sate her hunger but not so much to make her sleepy or risk her already half-anxious stomach reacting badly at the worst possible time. And a quick check-in with her already half-terrified client.

"We're almost done," Talon encouraged him. Fortunately, the jail was connected to the courthouse. She didn't waste too much time walking next door to meet with him. But she still made sure to finish her closing first. He might need some words of encouragement, but he needed the words in her closing argument even more. "How are you holding up?"

Luke shrugged. It was almost his default reaction. But spending 24 hours a day with someone else in control of your body and your fate could have that effect on a person. "I'm glad we're almost done. But I'm kinda scared too."

"Because sometimes the end can be bad," Talon knew. "But I've done everything I could to avoid that outcome."

"Sure," Luke acknowledged. "But it might not matter. Right?"

Talon frowned. She wanted to tell him everything would be alright. That the jury would see the truth. That justice would prevail. But she knew the truth. "Right."

* * *

Everyone assembled in Judge Kirshner's courtroom at 1:00 p.m. The gallery was completely full. All the witnesses who had been prohibited by court rule from watching other witnesses testify were allowed to return for the closing arguments. Officer McCarthy's widow was in the front row, right behind Cecilia's table—and next to Officer Dickerson. Luke's parents were in the front row on Talon's side, along with everyone who had spilled into her office that morning so long ago. The Maldonados sat behind them, next to their lawyer, Greg Olsen. Curt was on the other side of Olsen. Further in the back was Craig Donaldson, Cecilia's boss, along with a cadre of junior prosecutors and newbie defense attorneys, taking a break from their busy day to watch a couple of heavy hitters slug it out in the last round. And a single 'pool' news camera in the back for the dozen reporters covering the case. It was a cop-killer case, after all.

"Shit," Luke breathed as he sat down next to Talon and surveyed the room. "It's packed."

Talon just nodded. She was nervous enough about doing the best possible job. She didn't need a reminder of the hundred eyes watching her. She couldn't exactly ignore it either. Especially when Luke turned around and waved at his parents.

"Eyes front," barked the corrections officer still standing directly behind him. With that kind of crowd, the guards were going to stay within arm's reach of the defendant, even if it kind of gave away that whole 'held in custody pending the outcome of the trial' thing.

Luke faced forward again and sighed. "I really don't want to spend the rest of my life not being allowed to say hi to my own parents."

Talon nodded and placed her hand on his, but didn't say anything.

A glance to the side confirmed Cecilia was already in her own zone. She had all of her notes and materials placed out in front of her, in perfectly aligned stacks, each an inch apart, and a blank legal pad in front of her, pen laying atop it at the ready.

The prosecutor always went first. So, while Talon's closing

needed to have enough flexibility to respond to any of Cecilia's arguments she hadn't already anticipated, Cecilia's closing argument was more of a prepared speech. She got to write on the blank slate first.

Well, second actually. Judge Kirshner got to talk first. She drew the boundaries of the slate.

Everyone knew to stand up when the judge entered the room, even without the bailiff's command to do so. Kirshner took her seat on the bench and instructed everyone to sit down. This was it, the end, and with it came the increased formality of any ritual. Judge Kirshner confirmed both sides were ready—they were—then had the bailiff bring the jury into the room. Once they were seated, she began her portion of the closing argument ceremony.

The prosecutor would argue the evidence presented in court proved beyond a reasonable doubt the defendant violated the law. The defense attorney would argue the evidence was insufficient to prove a violation of the law. But first, the judge had to tell the jury what the law was.

"Ladies and gentlemen of the jury," Judge Kirshner began, as her bailiff began handing out paper packets to the jurors. "In a moment, you will hear the closing arguments of the lawyers, but before that, I will instruct you on the law."

The jury instructions were over thirty pages long. And Kirshner was going to read every word of them out loud in open court. In the old days, the jurors didn't get copies, so they really had to pay attention—or they were supposed to. Until someone figured out, they really didn't—or couldn't. So now they get copies, and the attorneys could refer to them in their arguments.

It would take Kirshner at least twenty minutes to read them all out. Talon and Cecilia both already knew what was in each instruction. They were standardized forms, approved by the State

Supreme Court, upon recommendation from a committee of prosecutors and defense attorneys. In theory, a judge could give an instruction outside of the approved ones, but it usually meant a reversal on appeal. The standard forms were appeal-proof, so they were the ones always used. Talon knew them by heart. She only half listened, as she went over her planned remarks one more time, but a few of the more salient instructions interrupted her concentration.

"It is your duty to decide the facts in this case based upon the evidence presented to you during this trial. It is also your duty to accept the law from my instructions, regardless of what you personally believe the law is or what you personally think it should be. You must apply the law from my instructions to the facts that you decide have been proved, and in this way decide the case."

"A defendant is presumed innocent. This presumption continues throughout the entire trial unless during your deliberations you find it has been overcome by the evidence beyond a reasonable doubt."

"A person commits the crime of murder in the first degree when he or she or an accomplice commits or attempts to commit the crime of robbery and in the course of or in furtherance of such crime or in immediate flight from such crime he or she or another participant in the crime causes the death of a person other than one of the participants."

"It is an aggravating circumstance that the crime was committed against a law enforcement officer who was performing his or her official duties at the time of the crime."

"If you find from the evidence that each of the elements of the crime has been proved beyond a reasonable doubt, then it will be your duty to return a verdict of guilty. On the other hand, if after weighing all of the evidence you have a reasonable doubt as to any one of these elements, then it will be your duty to return a verdict of not guilty."

"As jurors, you have a duty to discuss the case with one another and to deliberate in an effort to reach a unanimous verdict."

The instructions always ended with the same few sentences, and when Judge Kirshner finally got to the words that both Talon and Cecilia knew signaled the end of the reading of the instructions, Talon looked up from her notes. It was 'go' time.

"Because this is a criminal case," Kirshner concluded, "each of you must agree for you to return a verdict. When all of you have so agreed, fill in the verdict form to express your decision. The presiding juror must sign the verdict form and notify the bailiff. The bailiff will bring you into court to declare your verdict."

She set the packet aside and looked directly at the jurors again. "Now, ladies and gentlemen of the jury, please give your attention to Ms. Thompson who will deliver the closing argument on behalf of the State."

CHAPTER 51

Cecilia stood up slowly and stepped out from behind the prosecution table. She didn't repeat the formal 'May it please the Court' or thank all of the participants. Instead she walked directly to the jury box, and Talon realized she'd only done that archaic introduction for her opening statement so it would be that much more powerful when she didn't do it for her closing. They were both playing chess.

"When a person shows you who they really are," she began with the increasingly well-known saying, "believe them."

She turned and pointed at Luke.

"When a person tells you what they did," she said, "believe them."

Again facing the jury. "And when, in the hours immediately after the death of Officer Christopher McCarthy, the defendant gave a full confession to Detective Wolcott detailing that he knew his friend, Miguel, was going to rob the Cash-Town U.S.A. and he was going to wait outside as the getaway driver... believe him."

She stepped to the prosecution table and picked up her own copy of the jury instructions. "And when you believe him, then you convict him. Convict him of murder in the first degree. Murder in the first degree of an on-duty police officer. Because, ladies and gentlemen, that is exactly what he did, that's what he said he did, and that's what he's guilty of."

She didn't look at Luke again, but rather ignored him as she finally called him by name. "Luke Zlotnik is guilty of murder in the first degree with aggravating circumstances."

Talon nodded slightly to herself. She knew that would be the thrust of Cecilia's presentation. Believe the confession. And why shouldn't it be? If they did, Luke was done.

"Now, I expect," Cecilia said, "Ms. Winter will stand up after me and ask you to ignore the confession. She'll talk about what their professional hired-gun witness claimed. She'll say it was coerced and unreliable and her poor little client just didn't know how much trouble he would be in when he confessed to being an accomplice to an armed robbery."

Talon could feel the jurors looking at her, but she kept her eyes focused on her notepad, pretending to be taking notes, calm and confident as anything. Like she didn't even really need to listen to the prosecutor. But, of course, she did.

"So," Cecilia continued, "it's important to look at all of the evidence together. This isn't just a case where the defendant confessed to the crime—although we have that too. In addition, we have all of the other investigation and all of the other evidence which shows beyond any reasonable doubt that the defendant is guilty of murder."

Cecilia began a slow pace as she counted off the evidence on her fingers. "To begin with, we have the evidence that this was, in fact, an armed robbery. A very dangerous situation where anything can happen and people can get hurt, even killed. You know that now. And Miguel Maldonado and Luke Zlotnik should have known that, too, before they put the lives of every Cash-Town U.S.A. employee, every responding officer, and yes, even of themselves, in very deal danger. So real, in fact, that two people lost their lives that day."

Cecilia nodded to Emily McCarthy, a tight frown pulled across her mouth. But she didn't give a nod to the Maldonados, seated right behind the Zlotniks on the other side of the gallery.

"It's worth mentioning at this point," Cecilia stopped walking and gestured to the jury with an open, thoughtful hand, "that this is why you can be convicted of murder for something unplanned that happens during the crime you did plan. You can be, and should be, held responsible for the foreseeable consequences of your acts. The legislature agrees and that's why it's a crime if someone dies while you're committing a felony. It only makes sense."

To cops and prosecutors, maybe, Talon thought. *But not to average citizens whose children were facing life in prison for things other people did.* And, Talon hoped, not to the jurors either. Or at least to some of them. She scanned their faces to see if anyone wore a skeptical expression, but they all just seemed interested, attentive, engaged. *Damn.*

Cecilia returned to her thoughtful, finger-ticking stroll. "Next, we have the absolutely incontrovertible fact that someone did die. Two people died, in fact. But, while the death of anyone is a tragedy, and Luke Zlotnik will spend the rest of his life knowing he contributed to the death of his friend, the death of Miguel Maldonado is not murder. Not legally anyway. Because the law doesn't just define crimes. It's also designed to protect the public. If a person, like Miguel Maldonado, attempts to commit armed robbery and is shot and killed by officers during that attempt, that isn't murder. That's just the risk that comes with attempting something so inherently dangerous. That's why the law excludes the deaths of other participants in the crime. Miguel was a participant in the crime. His death was not murder.

"But," Cecilia stopped walking and pointed a finger at the sky, "the death of a law enforcement officer responding to that inherently dangerous armed robbery? The death of Tacoma Police Officer Christopher McCarthy? That is a crime. That is murder."

Another respectful nod to Emily McCarthy—just in case anyone could possibly have forgotten her, seated in the front row, dressed all in black.

"And it doesn't matter one bit who pulled the trigger," Cecilia asserted.

She threw a quick glance at Talon. "The defense attorney may spend some time talking about who 'really' shot Officer McCarthy. She may go on and on about how it was Officer Dickerson who actually pulled the trigger. And that's fine. Let her. It doesn't matter. It doesn't matter one whit."

One whit? Talon frowned at the word. *Who still says 'whit'?* An uptight prosecutor defending one cop from shooting another cop, she supposed.

"Again, the reason this is a crime," Cecilia continued, "the reason this is murder, is that the defendant created the situation which enabled the death to happen. The defendant planned and assisted an armed robbery. If it had been successful, you can be sure he would have wanted his share of the money. But it wasn't successful, and he deserves his share of the blame. His share of the consequences."

Cecilia had made her way back to the center of the jury box. She stopped and squared her shoulders at them again.

"So, now let's talk about the defendant's confession," she said. "It is important evidence. It might even be the most important single piece of evidence in the case. But," another finger to the sky, "it's not that important. It's not necessary. This case stands on its own even without it."

Talon couldn't stop from frowning. This was a good road for Cecilia to go down, Talon knew. And Talon might not be able to bring all of the jurors back up it.

Then again, Talon only needed one of the jurors to refuse to convict, and she'd at least get a hung jury—and a new trial. Cecilia needed all twelve to be unanimous. Talon could afford a stray juror stuck down at the end of Confession Doesn't Matter Road.

"Imagine this case without the confession," Cecilia invited the jurors. "The defendant drives his friend to the Cash-Town U.S.A. His texts show they planned it in advance. The defendant parks a couple of stores down. His friend goes inside, probably armed. The defendant waits outside, engine running. Police respond and block his car in. His friend makes a sudden furtive movement and officers are forced to fire. His friend dies. The police find the defendant still sitting in his car, still waiting for his friend who just died trying to commit an armed robbery. That, ladies and gentlemen, is murder."

The raised hand came down and joined its partner in an earnest front-of-the-body clasp. "Now," Cecilia said, "add the confession. Add the defendant's own words confirming everything I just said. Add the details that the defendant provided, like his friend cracking a joke about making a withdrawal while patting his coat pocket. Add all that, and the case is closed. Done. Proved beyond any and all reasonable doubt."

Cecilia turned one last time and took a long look at Luke Zlotnik. Doing so invited the jurors to follow suit. And the judge. And the gallery. Everyone in the room took a moment to look at the defendant. It was deafening.

Cecilia nodded to herself and turned back to the jury. "This is a terrible case, ladies and gentlemen. Tragic isn't a strong enough word. Two people are dead—a young man at the beginning of his life and a police officer who died defending the community he swore to serve and protect. And now, another life hangs in the balance. Young Luke Zlotnik sits there accused of murder, facing all of the consequences that will come from that. But he doesn't sit there by accident. He sits there because of his own decisions. The exact gunshot may have been someone else's action, but it was his decision to carry out the crime he and Miguel planned that day. The judge told you in her instructions, 'You must reach your decision based on the facts proved to you and on the law given to you, not on sympathy, prejudice, or personal preference.'

"I'm not sure Luke Zlotnik deserves any sympathy for his role in the death of Officer Christopher McCarthy," Cecilia said, "but if one of you thinks he might, if you look at that young man over there and wonder whether it solves anything to throw his life away too, well, then I say to you—no, *the judge* said to you—that doesn't matter. You cannot base your verdict on sympathy. You base your verdict on the law and the facts."

One last look at Emily McCarthy.

"And the fact of the matter," Cecilia concluded, "is that Luke Zlotnik is guilty under the law of the murder of Officer Christopher McCarthy. That is the fact of this case. That is the law of this case. And that is the only proper verdict in this case. Thank you."

Cecilia gave a quick bow to the jurors and walked briskly back to the prosecution table. No matter what else, she was done. It was Talon's turn.

"Now, ladies and gentlemen of the jury," Judge Kirshner said, "please give your attention to Ms. Winter who will give the closing argument on behalf of the defendant."

CHAPTER 52

Talon rose to her feet. She took a moment to look down at Luke and put a hand on his shoulder. It was partly performance— everything in trial work was partly performance—but it was also partly heartfelt. No matter what, this was the last thing she could do for him. She desperately hoped it would be enough.

She walked out from behind her own table and walked up to the jurors again, for the last time. She, too, eschewed any sort of formal opening. She, too, was aware of the courtroom full of people, all staring at her, waiting to see what magic words she would employ to try to pull victory from the jaws of defeat.

But there was no such thing as magic words. Except the two she hoped she'd hear when the jurors finished their deliberations.

"Not guilty," she said. "That is the fact of this case. That is the law of this case. And that is truly the only proper verdict in this case. Not guilty."

Talon needed to neutralize Cecilia's arguments, so she figured she might as well start where Cecilia left off. But it wouldn't be enough just to mimic Cecilia's closing and add the word 'not' in front of every guilty. It wouldn't be enough to explain why Cecilia hadn't proven the case. Talon needed to convince the jury not just that Luke was 'not guilty'—she needed to convince them he was actually innocent.

"This case," Talon continued, "this entire case," she gestured to the gallery, and specifically to Emily McCarthy, whose expression made clear she was not happy being used as a prop by the defense attorney too," is a tragedy. An absolute tragedy."

It was also good to acknowledge where Cecilia was right. Even if only to twist it back on her.

"But don't make the tragedy worse."

Talon opened up her stance to look back at Luke. "I don't agree with everything Ms. Thompson just said, of course. But we can both agree this case presents a danger that you will render your verdict based, not on the facts and the law, but on sympathy. We just disagree as to what the biggest danger is for that misplaced sympathy.

"Ms. Thompson asked you not to have any sympathy for my client. But I don't think that's where the biggest danger is." She turned again to the gallery. Again to Widow McCarthy. "I think the biggest danger for misplaced sympathy is with the people who lost their lives that day. And the danger is that you will do what everyone else in this case has done since Officer Dickerson fired the shots that killed Christopher McCarthy and Miguel Maldonado. Your sympathy for the victims will drive a desire to hold someone responsible for their tragedy. It will drive a desire to convict someone for their murders. It will result in my client being found guilty even though, in fact and in law, he didn't commit the crime."

Talon could do the pace and count thing, too, but she could tell she had the jurors' attention. The entire courtroom was silent, save her voice. Luke and Miguel's family rooting for her; McCarthy and Dickerson and Donaldson rooting against her. But everyone was listening to her. That's what mattered.

"The jury instruction Ms. Thompson read to you, the one about sympathy," Talon pointed out, "doesn't limit itself to sympathy for the defendant. It says you can't let your verdict be influenced by sympathy at all. And that includes sympathy for the victims and their families. And why is that? Because it's normal to have sympathy for victims. It's normal to have sympathy for victims' families. In fact, I would submit to you, it's not very normal to have sympathy for defendants. We don't have sympathy for defendants. We have anger at them. Hatred for them. Disdain, scorn, and contempt for them. You would never feel sympathy for someone who is actually guilty of murder. If you think they didn't do it, you might have sympathy because they were wrongly charged with the crime. But you're not going to think someone is guilty of murder, then acquit them anyway because you feel sorry for them."

Talon shook her head. "No, that doesn't happen. That's not what that instruction is talking about. It's talking about sympathy for the victims. It's talking about wanting to give them something for the loss. It's about finding someone guilty of a crime because it's easy, or convenient, or what everyone seems to want you to do. It's about convicting someone of murder because you feel sympathy for the victim's family.

"And ladies and gentlemen, that is exactly what you may not do."

Now it was time to pace, or at least take a step to the side to make sure the jurors could see Luke. She may have just told them the law didn't mean sympathy for Luke, but she sure as hell wanted them to have it anyway.

"Everyone involved in the prosecution of this case," Talon continued, "has felt sympathy for Officer McCarthy. Most have also felt at least some sympathy for Miguel Maldonado. But it has been that very sympathy that has led us here today, on the precipice, about to convict an innocent man of a murder he did not commit.

"Because it's a tragedy.

"And tragedies should be fixed. Righted. Avenged."

Talon shook her head again.

"But that's the whole point of a tragedy. It can't be fixed. It can't be righted. And, ladies and gentlemen, don't let yourself be tricked into trying to avenge it. That's not your role. And it wouldn't work anyway. Because vengeance is for the guilty and Luke Zlotnik is innocent."

Talon began the thoughtful pace in earnest, in part to cue the jury that she was being thoughtful. Intelligent. Analytical. Not just an advocate for one side, but an advocate for the truth. At least, she hoped it looked that way.

"The truth of the matter," she began her lecture on the weakness of the State's case, "is that the prosecution has failed to prove several important parts of their case. It might be hard to see that at first, because Ms. Thompson jumped all the way to the end of the story in her closing argument. But if you back up, if you slow down, if you pay close attention and do the job you took an oath to do, then you will see that this entire case is the result of tragic decisions and a rush to judgment. If you back up, slow down, and pay attention, you'll realize, this entire tragedy happened because a few well-meaning people were scared by a young, brown, teenage boy."

That sent a shock wave of discomfort and recrimination through the courtroom. Several of the jurors crossed their arms. Phrases like "Oh, my God" and "How dare she?" popped out of the angry murmurs that exploded from the prosecution side of the gallery. But not all the jurors crossed their arms. And Talon could back up her allegation.

"Think back to the testimony of Janice Henderschott," Talon prompted. "She never once testified that Miguel actually said he was robbing the place. He never said, 'This is a robbery.' He never showed her a gun. She just got scared. She thought it was a robbery. But that doesn't mean it was. It means a young, brown, teenage boy said something to her that scared her. Something she can't even remember now. And because she was scared, she pressed the robbery alarm. That's how this case began."

It was always risky to attack civilian witnesses. Jurors could have sympathy for witnesses too. Janice Henderschott didn't ask to be involved in this. But she was. And Talon couldn't fail to point out the role she played in it. Especially if Talon could spin that role to her client's advantage.

"So, when the police were called out," Talon continued, "they were already thinking, 'This is a robbery.'" Not, 'This is a trouble unknown' call where they might arrive looking for indications of what was actually going on. No, they were told by dispatch: this is an armed robbery. That's how they treated it. And that's what they saw when they arrived—even if what they saw wasn't actually a robbery."

Talon could look out at the gallery too. She let her gaze linger on the Maldonados. The jurors might not have been told who the Hispanic family in the gallery was, but Talon guessed at least a few of them could figure it out.

"They burst into the Cash-Town U.S.A., pistols drawn and ready to take down the armed robber," Talon said. She could also point a finger to the sky. "The only problem is, Miguel wasn't armed. He was just standing there. Officer Dickerson told you that. He was just standing there, and Officer McCarthy was able to circle around behind him without Miguel doing or saying anything to try to stop him. That doesn't sound like an actual robber."

Talon took a moment to assess her audience. Not the gallery, the jurors. They were all listening to her. At least one of the arm-crossers had uncrossed her arms again. For the most part, they looked interested in what she had to say, but not particularly moved by it.

"Then, Officer Dickerson killed Miguel," Talon declared. "Shot him dead where he stood. Three shots, center mass. He never stood a chance. It was practically an execution. Except executions don't usually take out members of the audience. But Officer Dickerson was so eager to stop the young, brown, teenage boy—he was so threatened by the young, brown, teenage boy, he was so scared by the young, brown, teenage boy, that he opened fire even though his partner, another officer, was directly behind Miguel, directly in the line of fire.

"Every bullet fired in that store was fired by Officer Todd Dickerson. Every bullet that tore through someone's body and killed them was fired by Officer Todd Dickerson."

Talon hesitated, but only for a moment. She couldn't argue facts not in evidence, and Cecilia and Kirshner had done a pretty good job of keeping her facts about Dickerson out of evidence. But Talon had slipped in just enough before Cecilia's objection to say, "Officer Dickerson, who had to leave his old department and start over with Tacoma P.D."

That, of course, led to another objection. Cecilia sprang to her feet. "Objection, Your Honor!"

"Sustained," Judge Kirshner barked without giving Talon any opportunity to respond. "The jury is to disregard the last statement by defense counsel. Move on, Ms. Winter, or we send the jury out to address your conduct."

Talon knew Cecilia would object. And she knew Judge

Kirshner would sustain the objection. She was also pretty sure the judge would be pissed and say something roughly along the lines of what she'd just said. All of which underscored Talon 's main point to the jury.

"This case is a tragedy, fueled by people in power assuming the worst and desperate to find someone to blame."

Talon could feel Judge Kirshner's scowl on the back of her neck, but she pressed on.

"Janice Henderschott thought Miguel was a robber because he said something that scared her. The police who responded thought Miguel was a robber because that's what Janice Henderschott reported. Officer Dickerson thought Miguel had a gun in his hand because that's what Officer McCarthy called out. And Officer McCarthy and Miguel both died as a result of those ill-informed, unsupported assumptions. An absolute tragedy."

Talon shook her head, lowered her eyes, and allowed the echo of the word 'tragedy' to hold the room for a few moments.

"Then it was time to find someone to blame." Talon raised her gaze again to the jurors. "Two people were dead. A police officer was dead. You don't just let a police officer die. Not in the line of duty. Not without consequences. But Officer Dickerson had simply made a mistake, and anyway, he was on the same team. And Miguel was already dead. That was unsatisfying. Surely there was someone who could take the blame. Surely there was someone who could bear the brunt of the anger and recrimination that comes from the death of an officer in the line of duty.

"Surely," Talon called back to her opening statement, "there was a scapegoat."

That got the reaction she wanted from the jurors. Even the ones whose arms were still crossed at her would remember that word from her opening. She'd had a plan for the trial, and she'd brought it full circle.

She pointed again to her client. "Luke Zlotnik was that scapegoat. He still is that scapegoat. At least until you conclude your deliberations and return that verdict of 'not guilty.'"

That would have been a nice way to end her closing. Circling back to the beginning of her comments, ending again on the most important part: vote not guilty. But there was the small matter of the confession still to address.

"That just leaves the so-called confession," Talon said. "It's no coincidence that Ms. Thompson started her closing argument with that. And it's no coincidence she didn't want to talk about all the leaps of faith everyone took, all the conclusions they jumped to, to get us to the point where she could stand up and ask you to convict someone of murder in the first degree with aggravating circumstances just because he was too scared, too ignorant of the law, to tell the nice, friendly, helpful detective to go pound sand."

'Pound sand' was in-court talk for 'fuck himself.' Talon was pretty sure everyone in the courtroom knew that too.

"You heard what Dr. Ross had to say," Talon continued. "She told you: that confession was false. Luke didn't really confess, because what he said wasn't true. He didn't know what Miguel had planned. In fact, after Janice Henderschott's testimony, I'm not sure any of us know what Miguel actually had planned. But we do know one thing: Luke didn't know."

Too many 'know's, Talon knew. She pressed on.

"So, why would he say that he knew about the robbery, if he didn't?" Talon asked. It was really the central question of the entire case. Good thing she had an answer for it. Or an explanation anyway. "The answer is pretty simple. Just like all of you before you were picked as jurors for this case, Luke didn't know he could be charged with murder if someone died during a robbery that he admitted to helping plan. He knew he'd been arrested for murder. He knew his friend was dead, and he knew a police officer was dead. He knew he was a suspect in a murder, because the cops told him that. And they told him that to scare him.

"It worked."

Again, a turn and look at Luke Zlotnik. Again, everyone else looked at him too. And Talon was glad he was wearing that borrowed suit that was definitely too big on him. The one he'd worn every other day of the trial, like a freshman wearing his dad's suit to homecoming. He looked young. He looked naïve. And he looked scared. Talon decided to go ahead and label it.

"He was young," she said. "He was naïve. And he was scared. It's not hard to imagine. And it wasn't hard for Detective Wolcott to exploit."

She turned back to the jury and gave them what she hoped was a sincere, disarming, 'let's just be real' type of shrug. "Look," she said, "I understand we all have jobs to do. Ms. Thompson has a job to do. I have a job to do. Judge Kirshner has a job to do. You all have a job to do. But so did Detective Wolcott. And his job was to get a confession out of the only surviving suspect so they could charge someone with Officer McCarthy's murder. That would let them wrap up the case, and it would have the side benefit of drawing attention away from the fact that the one who really shot and killed Officer McCarthy was one of their own."

Talon allowed a half-smile. "Can you imagine what it would have been like for Detective Wolcott if he hadn't gotten the confession out of Luke? If he couldn't crack some eighteen-year-old kid? He would have had to go back to all of his fellow officers and tell them he'd failed. That some kid had punked him. That they were left with Janice Henderschott's paranoia and Officer Dickerson's itchy trigger finger.

"No, that wasn't going to happen." Talon shook a knowing head. "No, he was going to get that confession. The bad news was, Luke wasn't guilty. The good news was, Luke didn't know the law."

Talon stepped over to her counsel table and picked up her copy of the jury instructions. "When the judge read you the jury instructions, she told you it was your duty to accept the law in her instruction, 'regardless of what you personally believe the law is or what you personally think it should be.' The reason she had to say that is none of you probably knew you could be convicted of murder for what someone else did during a robbery. But I know that. Ms. Thompson knows that. The judge knows that. If you work in criminal justice, you know that.

"Detective Wolcott works in criminal justice. He knew that. And he knew Luke didn't."

Talon held up the packet of jury instructions. "Detective Wolcott didn't need to get Luke to confess to murder. There was no way that was going to happen. Even people who are guilty rarely confess to murder. But people confess to lesser crimes all the time. Hell, some people commit lesser crimes because they want to be caught, like homeless people in the winter in places like Chicago and Detroit.

"Detective Wolcott knew he couldn't get Luke to confess to murder," Talon explained, "but he used that to get Luke to confess to something less, but would still be murder under the law. He got him to confess to being the getaway driver to an armed robbery where someone died. Even though the main reason Luke agreed to say he did that was to avoid being charged with murder."

Talon frowned. "Well, surprise. You're getting charged with murder anyway. Detective Wolcott is the hero, and Officer Dickerson is no longer the one responsible for the death of Officer

McCarthy. Time for arrests and press conferences and jury trials and sending a young man off to prison for something he didn't do. Case closed."

Talon paused. She was almost done. And the worst part of being almost done was that once she was done, she couldn't do any more to help Luke.

"There's one more jury instruction I'd like to point out to you," Talon began her wrap-up. "There were a lot of instructions, so you probably can't remember them all without looking, but toward the end there, right after she told you not to let sympathy affect your verdict, Judge Kirshner told you something else." Talon opened the packet to the specific instruction. "She told you, 'You have nothing whatever to do with any punishment that may be imposed in case of a violation of the law. You may not consider the fact that punishment may follow conviction except insofar as it may tend to make you careful.'"

Talon looked again at her client, inviting the jurors to do the same with an openhanded gesture toward the eighteen-year-old, Luke Zlotnik, wide-eyed and scared to death.

"Please, ladies and gentlemen," Talon implored them. "Be careful."

With that, she let her shoulders drop and walked back to take her seat at the defense table, finished. She put another hand on Luke's shoulder—heartfelt, but still performance.

"I did everything I could," she whispered to him.

"I know," Luke whispered back. "Will it matter?"

Talon frowned. "We'll know soon enough."

CHAPTER 53

Of course, soon enough never was. Although Talon would have been willing to wait a very long time for the right verdict.

By the time Kirshner, Cecilia, and Talon had all finished talking, the afternoon was almost over. The jury had less than an hour to pick a foreperson and begin to process of deciding how they were going to begin their process. Juries were rarely sequestered any more, so at 5:00 p.m. the jurors each got to go home to family and friends, after being admonished by the judge not to talk about the case to anyone, except their fellow jurors when they all returned the next morning to resume their deliberations.

Talon went home too, via a couple of bars, and she and Curt stayed up late watching an old *Pink Panther* movie on TV. The 60s were weird. The next morning, Talon went into the office and sat at her desk, pretending she was able to do anything other than stare at her phone waiting for it to ring.

Actually, she didn't really want it to ring. Not yet. Quick verdicts were usually prosecution verdicts. It was the long, drawn out, 'what could they be talking about' deliberations that were better for defendants. Bonus points if the bailiff reported hearing arguing through the jury room door. The best thing Talon could do was focus on something else to take her mind off the wait. That was also the last thing she could possibly do.

So, by midmorning, she decided to take a break from the work she hadn't been doing and head into the break room to see if there was anyone she could talk to who'd take her mind off the interminable wait. Luckily, Olsen was refilling the coffee pot. He was always refilling the coffee pot.

"Greg!" Talon called out a little too loudly. "How's it going? What did you think of the closings?"

Olsen nearly dropped the coffee pot at Talon's bellow. "Oh, uh, right." He regained himself. "Uh, I thought they were good. Very good. Hers was very good, I thought. But yours was better. Yeah, yours was definitely better."

Talon crossed her arms and frowned at the rambling answer. "Sounds like you're trying to convince yourself."

Olsen laughed a little. "No, it's not that. I'm just not sure it's going to matter. You had good arguments. You had an expert. But they still have a dead cop."

Talon nodded. "Yeah, I know. There must be a better way of deciding something this important. Twelve people who, by requirement, know nothing about the law get to decide whether somebody broke a law so complicated and arcane it takes the judge two pages to explain."

Olsen scooped coffee grounds into the coffee maker. "The only other way would be to let the judges decide. But you don't seem like the type of person who would trust a government employee to make that kind of decision."

"And an elected employee at that," Talon scoffed. "Yeah, you're right. This is the best we can do, but it's still not good enough. I mean, you know how lawyers will say, 'If you tried this case ten times, the prosecutor would win seven of those' or whatever?"

"In civil, we say the plaintiff," Olsen reminded her. "But yeah. It's a way to explain the strength of a case."

"But really, it only explains how crazy the system is," Talon replied. "If the result of the case depends, not on the evidence or the lawyers, but on which twelve people get to vote, that's crazy. It should be, 'If we tried this case ten times, the prosecution would win ten times.' Anything less than that shouldn't be charged. If there's a chance even one jury out of ten would acquit, then we shouldn't let the other nine convict."

"Spoken like a true defense attorney," Olsen raised his empty mug to her. The coffee was still brewing, and loudly. "Maybe you can get a rule change so that every criminal defendant gets ten trials."

"And have to wait on ten verdicts?" Talon laughed. "No way. Waiting on one is bad enough."

Olsen looked at his watch. He was old enough that he still wore a watch. "How long do you think they'll be out?"

"Maybe until tomorrow?" Talon guessed. "There was actually a lot of evidence and I gave them a lot to talk about. They will probably go back and look at what the teller actually said. They'll need to work through the felony murder instruction to make sure they know exactly what the State has to prove. Plus, there's all the stuff Dr. Ross told them, so they'll need to go back through his so-called confession again with her testimony in mind. Also—"

"Hey, there you are." Hannah half-ran into the break room. She pointed at Talon. "I called your office, but you didn't answer."

"What is it?" Talon asked, but the floor was already dropping out of her gut.

"The court called," Hannah said. "You have a verdict."

CHAPTER 54

Schrödinger's Verdict.

So long as the jury hadn't reached its verdict, there was still a possibility Luke was innocent. A chance he would beat the charges. A reason to fight.

But when the lid was lifted and the verdict read aloud in open court, Luke would either be guilty or he would be innocent. Nothing in between.

Talon had actually let herself believe she might win the case. The cop-killer case with the confession. But the trial had gone better than she'd expected. The State's witnesses were weak. Her witness was beyond strong. When she sat down after her closing argument, she really, actually thought there might be a chance she would win.

But the verdict was too fast. There was too much evidence, too many issues, for them to discuss everything they should have discussed in only a few hours. That meant they didn't discuss everything. That meant they jumped to their conclusion. Just like everyone else had.

But still, even as Talon walked into the courtroom, her stomach in a knot and the blood pounding in her ears, there was still a chance that cat was still alive. A chance Luke would be found not guilty. A chance he wouldn't die in prison.

Talon walked past the same crowd of people who'd assembled for the closing arguments the previous day. At least it seemed to be the same people. She didn't really look closely. There was only one person she was looking at. Her client. Eighteen-year-old Luke Zlotnik, seated in that same damn suit, hunched over the table, crushed under the same weight of anticipatory dread that made it hard for Talon to put one foot in front of the other.

She dropped herself into the seat next to Luke and tried to sound brave. Not that it mattered anymore. "You ready?" she asked.

Luke didn't look at her. His eyes were glued to the tabletop. He shook his head slightly. "No."

Talon nodded. She put that hand on his shoulder again, maybe for the last time. "Yeah. Me neither."

Cecilia was already at her table. She managed to look coolly detached despite the good (for her) omen of the quick verdict. The guards were closer than usual, in case Luke reacted badly to the verdict. The bailiff stood up to announce the entrance of Judge Kirshner. Talon stood up, too, but barely heard the bailiff's invocation. She sat down again as soon as the judge reached the bench.

"The jury has reached a verdict," Judge Kirshner informed everyone, rather unnecessarily. Everyone already knew that. That's why they were there. "Bring in the jury," she instructed.

There was an old trick for guessing what a jury's verdict was. If, when they filed into the courtroom to deliver the verdict, they looked at the defendant, then it was a not guilty verdict. But if they avoided looking over at the defense table, then it was a conviction.

The jurors filed into the courtroom. They didn't look over at the defense table.

"Would the presiding juror please rise," Kirchner instructed.

Juror No. 4 stood up. A middle-aged white man. Not just a rule follower, a rule enforcer. Not good.

"Has the jury reached a verdict?" Kirshner asked.

There was so much formality in the reading of a verdict in a criminal trial. The stakes couldn't be higher, and everyone in the courtroom just wanted to know what the result was. The jurors should simply walk in and give a thumbs up or thumbs down. The ceremony just added to the agony.

"Yes, Your Honor," Juror No. 4 answered. He had a piece of paper in his hand. The verdict form.

"Please hand the verdict form to the bailiff," Kirshner instructed.

The juror did as directed, and the bailiff took possession of the verdict form. Talon was sure the bailiff snuck a peek at what word, or words, were written in the blank, but she didn't see him do it. Still, that meant thirteen people knew the result, but she and Luke still didn't.

The bailiff handed the form to the judge who took a moment to read it. Now fourteen people knew. Kirshner looked up from the paper and over at the defense table. "The defendant will stand for the verdict," she declared.

Luke looked at Talon. His eyes were wide and red-rimmed. She could see his heartbeat in the hollow of his throat. He didn't look like he had the strength to stand, so Talon stood up first and pulled him to his feet.

"I didn't do it," he whispered to her, his voice cracking. "I'm innocent."

Talon squeezed his arm. "I know, Luke. I know."

"In the matter of the State of Washington versus Lucas James Zlotnik," Kirchner read the verdict form aloud, "We the jury, find the defendant... *guilty* of the crime of murder in the first degree."

Luke collapsed into his seat, pulling Talon halfway down with him. The gallery exploded into a cacophony of cheers and sobs. There was a special verdict form too. The one for the aggravating circumstance of the victim being a police officer. Kirchner started reading that finding, too, but her voice could hardly be heard over the sounds of celebration and despair. But Talon knew the result. McCarthy was a cop. That was never in question. If the jury found Luke guilty of murder, they were going to find the aggravator too.

It was over. All over.

Talon looked down at Luke. He was slumped onto the table, his head in his hands, his back wracked with the sobs Talon could see more than hear. She knew his family was crying, too, but she couldn't bring herself to look. Instead, she looked up at the indifferent judge who had denied her motions and suppressed her evidence. She looked over at the prosecutor who had secured herself a promotion on the convulsing back of an innocent man. And she looked at the jury, still too cowardly to look Luke in the eye as they took his life away for something he didn't do.

Luke was innocent. Talon knew it.

But it didn't matter.

An innocent eighteen-year-old man was going to spend the rest of his life in prison.

Talon had done everything she could to try to stop it.

But she didn't stop it.

And that was the worst part of being a criminal defense attorney.

END

THE TALON WINTER LEGAL THRILLERS
Winter's Law
Winter's Chance
Winter's Reason
Winter's Justice
Winter's Duty

THE DAVID BRUNELLE LEGAL THRILLERS
Presumption of Innocence
Tribal Court
By Reason of Insanity
A Prosecutor for the Defense
Substantial Risk
Corpus Delicti
Accomplice Liability
A Lack of Motive
Missing Witness
Diminished Capacity
Devil's Plea Bargain
Homicide in Berlin
Premeditated Intent

ALSO BY STEPHEN PENNER
Scottish Rite
Blood Rite
Last Rite
Mars Station Alpha
The Godling Club

ABOUT THE AUTHOR

Stephen Penner is an attorney, author, and artist from Seattle.

In addition to writing the *Talon Winter Legal Thrillers*, he is also the author of the *David Brunelle Legal Thriller Series*, starring Seattle homicide prosecutor David Brunelle; the *Maggie Devereaux Paranormal Mysteries*, recounting the exploits of an American graduate student in the magical Highlands of Scotland; and several stand-alone works.

For more information, please visit *www.stephenpenner.com*.